• BOOK 2 •

SKYBORN

CALL OF THE CROW

Aeries Mountains
Cloudston
Linden
Thelantis
Thraille
The Thornmoors
Crane Clan
The Clandoms
Finch Clan
Quail Cla

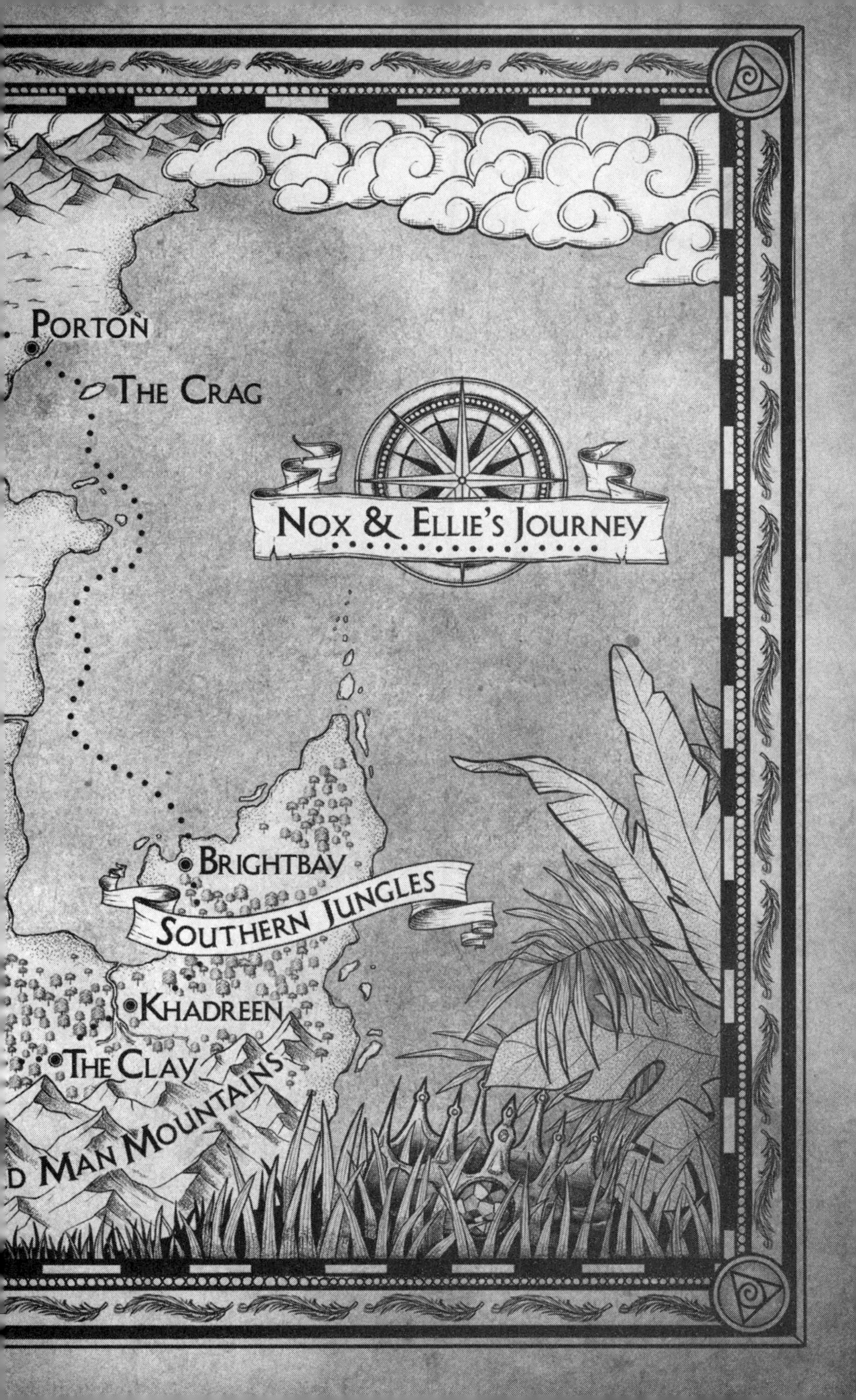
Porton
The Crag
Nox & Ellie's Journey
Brightbay
Southern Jungles
Khadreen
The Clay
d Man Mountains

• BOOK 2 •

SKYBORN

CALL OF THE CROW

JESSICA KHOURY

Scholastic Press / New York

Library of Congress Cataloging-in-Publication Data available

ISBN 978-1-338-65242-0

10 9 8 7 6 5 4 3 2 1 22 23 24 25 26
Printed in Italy 183

First edition, February 2022

Book design by Maeve Norton

FOR NANCY,
BELOVED GRANDMOTHER AND
FELLOW BIRD NERD

CHAPTER ONE
· CORION ·

As crown prince of the Clandoms, Corion was used to keeping odd hours.

He never knew when his father, King Garion, might summon him before dawn in order to critique the changing of the guard. Sometimes he didn't make it to bed till well after three in the morning because his father wanted to drill him on the names of every Eagle ancestor who'd ever sat on the Aerie Throne. Being the royal heir meant being prepared for all sorts of strange tests, drills, and assignments.

But he certainly *wasn't* used to being woken in the middle of the night by a blade pressed against his throat.

Eyes wide, Corion lay very still, letting his eyes adjust to the darkness. His gaze flicked to the door, then all around his grand room, but he saw no sign of his guards. There was only the lean shadow of the man bending over him, his eyes hidden behind a mask of silk. The dark outlines of his wings blocked what moonlight might have trickled through the window; they were spread to their full length, stretching even wider than Corion's four-poster bed.

"Good evening, sweet princely pie," hissed the shadow. Corion saw the pale gleam of his teeth as his lips parted in a savage grin. "What a plump and perfect little pet you are! What must it be like, to be so pampered you can't tie your own boots?"

Every muscle in Corion's body drew taut as he muttered, "Actually, I *can* tie my own boots."

Was the man an assassin? A kidnapper? If so, he was a fool. Even if he cut Corion's throat this moment, he'd never escape the palace before a dozen Goldwing knights had buried their swords in his belly.

Still. How *had* the man gotten in here? How had he slipped past the twenty guards between Corion's room and the nearest palace entrance?

"What do you want?" Corion whispered. "Money? Remove your blade, and we can talk."

The shadow only chuckled.

Then, from the doorway, a deep voice said, "He is here to see me, Corion."

The prince swallowed, his throat touching the edge of the blade as he did. "Father."

"Put down the knife, Hunter," ordered King Garion, stepping into the room. He held a slim candle, its light barely strong enough to illuminate his regal features. "You've made your point."

"Have I?" said the shadow. "I once told you I could cut any throat in the kingdom, Your *Majesty*, and yet you have forgotten poor Hunter, let me languish in boredom for years. I want *work*."

"Why else do you think I've summoned you from your web, spider?" The king's voice simmered with disdain. "Back away from my son or be crushed beneath my heel as you should have been years ago."

With a hiss, the stranger withdrew the dagger. Corion let out a long, shaky breath and sat up.

"What's going on?" the prince demanded, eyeing the tall man who still loomed over his bed. Who was this creature who dared speak to the king of the Clandoms as if he were beneath him? Usually, Garion punished such insolence with a week in the stocks—or worse.

But now his father only walked closer, setting the candle on an iron table. Its light seemed to shrink, revealing nothing of the stranger's features.

"This man is called the Hunter," said King Garion, speaking to

Corion but never taking his eyes off the intruder. "And he is here because I summoned him. But there was no need for these theatrics."

"What's the job?" said the Hunter. "A throat to be sliced? A hand to be diced? It's been so long, *too* long, oh King. You promised work, as much as I could want. But I'm *bored*. You've neglected your Hunter. My blades thirst."

"Yes, yes." Garion waved a hand dismissively. "You disgusting creature, you'll have your hunt."

"He's the assassin," whispered Corion, looking with new interest at the Hunter. "Is this him, Father? The secret assassin you always said you kept in your back pocket, for the hour of most desperate need?"

"I am in nobody's *pocket*!" protested the Hunter.

"Wrong," snapped Garion. "You are mine completely. Or have you forgotten what you swore to me the day I spared your life?" The king turned to Corion, the dark gold feathers of his wings shining in the light of the candle; they must have been freshly oiled to gleam like that. "Nearly a decade ago this beast set a building on fire—just to watch everyone inside burn. He's no man, but a killer, who feeds on death as a bee feeds upon flowers."

"You didn't execute him for it?" gasped Corion.

The Hunter snickered.

"As far as the public knows, I *did*." Garion gave him a smug grin. "Here is a lesson for you, son: Never let a bad dog go to waste. Leash it, train it to heel when you call, and the day will come when it will serve you well. My dog here is a secret weapon, capable of jobs even my Goldwings cannot carry out—or should not be *seen* to."

"Enough chatter!" howled the Hunter. "What's the job? Is it a duke? Is it a whole garrison of rebels?"

"A boy," said Garion. "It's a boy I want, by the name of Nox Hatcher, though he was once called Tannox Corvain. So far my knights have failed to bring him to me. We suspect he's fled to the mountains."

Corion withheld a sigh.

This again.

It'd been weeks since the Race of Ascension, which had started out in celebration and feasting, and had ended with his father burning down an entire neighborhood in an attempt to capture some low-life thief of a Crow clanner. Since then, his father had become obsessed. Every day he called for a report from his knights, and every day they brought the same news. Not so much as a feather had been found of the one called Nox Hatcher, nor of the three kids he'd been spotted with when he fled Thelantis: a piebald, with one brown wing and one white; a Falcon girl; and a Sparrow.

Corion recalled the Sparrow, for he'd seen her with his own eyes. *Ellie Meadows.* Now, there was a girl worth remembering. She'd won the Race of Ascension, something no low clanner had ever attempted, much less accomplished. Then she'd turned out to be a thief too, having burglarized a fortress and attacked the king's own soldiers. Now she was on the run with the Crow and two other criminals, with the entire force of Goldwing knights hunting them.

And, apparently, this Hunter too.

Corion shuddered. He'd only known the man a few minutes, but he was the most terrifying person the prince had ever met. Rubbing his throat, he eyed the dagger and hoped his father's so-called *leash* was as tight as he claimed. Even if the king did have the assassin under control, Corion wouldn't sleep easy for a while after this.

"A *boy*," sneered the Hunter. "Here I stand, more hearts stilled beneath my hands than all your paltry knights combined, and you send me after a *child*?"

"That's exactly what I'm doing," retorted the king. "Dispose of his cohorts and bring him to me alive, preferably, but if you can't manage it . . . Well, the important thing is, I want him out of the way. For good."

The Hunter cocked his head, as if considering the job—actually *considering*, not snapping to attention with a crisp "Yes, Your Majesty!" as any sane citizen would have done.

In the end, though, he nodded. "Very well. I'll consent to this child's play if only to stretch my wings a bit. But after this, oh high and mighty King, I want *real* work."

"You'll take what I give and be grateful," growled Garion. "Now get out of my palace. Your stench is fouling the air."

With a hiss, the Hunter flicked his wings and backed away. At first, Corion was confused—the door was on the other side of the room.

But then the man shrank into the tiny barred window, folding himself through the iron rods as lithely as if his bones were made of paper, and then he dropped away into the night. A moment later, he lifted away on broad, silent wings. *Vulture clan*, thought Corion, identifying the man's feathers at last.

"How . . . ?" Corion stared at the window. It was built to *prevent* intruders, its narrow slats barely large enough for a cat, much less a full-grown man.

"I believe he was a circus contortionist before he turned to murder," commented the king, scratching his stubbly chin.

"He put a *knife* to my throat!" cried Corion, slinging himself to his feet and facing his father. His hands were still shaking. "And you acted like it was nothing!"

"Bah." Garion flipped his hand. "He wouldn't dare harm you in truth. He knows I'm in control. With a word from me, he'd be due straight back to the gallows."

Corion was not soothed.

"At any rate," said Garion, "that's my little problem settled. The Crow boy will be mine within the week."

But as the king took his candle and left the room, Corion couldn't help thinking that his father had said much the same words back when he'd first dispatched the knights to find the Crow boy and his friends.

He'll be mine within the week!

That had been nearly a month ago.

Whoever the Crow really was, he was proving to be anything but ordinary. Corion couldn't remember the last time a criminal had evaded the Goldwings for this long.

But then, remembering the fire in that Sparrow girl's eyes, he wasn't surprised.

If *she* was involved, he'd bet the Hunter was in for the chase of his life.

CHAPTER TWO
· ELLIE ·

Thwack!

"Ow!" yowled Ellie, stumbling back and falling hard on her rear. She clapped a hand to her forehead, already feeling the knot that would swell there. "You cheated!"

Across a courtyard of stone, a tall boy in a blue tunic laughed and twirled his staff. Like Ellie's, it had a large hook on one end, with a smaller one protruding opposite. The boy's hair was dark and long, tied in a ponytail, while his wings were the glossy white of the Swan clan. "No, *you* were overthinking your defense again. Every time you do that, you get slower."

With a huff, Ellie took the hand he offered and bounced back to her feet. She shook out her reddish-brown wings, shedding dust and leaves.

"Again," she said.

"We've been sparring all morning," sighed the boy. "Don't you ever *rest*?"

From atop a carved bear statue, a small, freckled kid let out a snorting laugh. His wings—one brown, one white—spread to steady himself. From the collar of his shirt peeped a tiny furred face with two white horns between its ears. "Rest? Ellie Meadows? She's never even heard of the word!"

"Nobody asked you, Twig!" shouted Ellie. She blew a flop of hair out of her eyes and dropped into a defensive stance, her lockstave lowered like a sword. "C'mon, Charlo. Let's go again. I'll be ready this time."

"Well, *I'm* tired," said Charlo. "And hungry."

With that, he plopped down and snagged a nearby satchel with the hook of his lockstave, dragging it to himself and taking out oatbread, goat's cheese, and lavender honey. Ellie rolled her eyes and continued practicing on her own, swishing her lockstave.

The village of Cloudstone was so well hidden that Ellie still had trouble spotting it when she was out on her morning flight. She and her friends had been lucky the night they'd found the place. They'd been fleeing Goldwing knights, with no idea where they might hide. Usually, they'd been told, the clouds blanketed the mountain slopes, concealing Cloudstone entirely. But that rare night had been clear, and the lamps in the windows had guided Ellie's little band of fugitives to safety.

They'd had no idea what they'd find when they landed, and to Ellie's initial alarm, they soon learned nearly all the people in Cloudstone were members of the Restless Order.

She'd only ever met one other member of the Restless—an old woman named Granny Tam who had nearly burned Ellie and her friends alive in an attempt to rob them. But as it turned out, she'd been an exception, and the other Restless monks were quite welcoming. In fact, most of them were fugitives, people who'd fled their lives in the Clandoms for a thousand different reasons. Here in the safety of the mountains, they lived just out of King Garion's reach.

Ellie spun through the air, using her wings to thrust herself farther, then landed in a crouch at the edge of the courtyard, in front of a tall stone door carved with spiraling patterns.

"When are you going to let me go in there?" she asked.

"Not my call," said Charlo. "Only Elder Rue can invite you into the Sanctum."

"What are you people hiding, anyway?" She rapped the door with her staff.

"Skeletons and hoards of gold."

"Liar." She'd been poking around the big, solemn door for weeks, trying to sneak inside to spy on its secrets. Anything worth locking up was worth discovering, in her opinion, and her curiosity only grew stronger every day.

Charlo laughed. "The others will be down here soon for noon meditations. You gonna join us this time?"

Ellie shook her head. "I still don't understand this whole Restless Order thing. How do you stand it—all the sitting still and staring at nothing?"

"We don't stare at nothing. We stare at nature."

"It's just so . . . *boring*."

"That's because you're not staring properly."

The courtyard was surrounded by short, gnarled trees. From their branches fluttered many white ribbons, filling the air with a soft susurrus. The mountains rose sharply on every side, rocky cliffs dotted with cleverly concealed doorways leading to the villagers' homes.

Ellie whirled and spun her lockstave over her head, striking at an invisible enemy. From the ground, Charlo called, "Too slow again! If you're going to use our weapons and way of fighting, at least *try* to do it right."

"I am trying!" She wiped sweat from her forehead and performed the move again.

She was about to fly off to find lunch of her own but had to wait as a stream of Restless monks began swooping into the courtyard for their noontime meditation, all dressed in matching blue tunics and white leggings. Each carried a lockstave just like Ellie's, which they wielded with practiced ease. She paused to admire how they flew, using the hooks of the staffs to grab hold of poles anchored in the stone, allowing them to change directions in a blink. She'd been practicing that for weeks but still wasn't nearly as agile as the others.

Twig happily jumped down to join them. They nodded politely at Ellie, then seated themselves around the outside of the courtyard, facing away. Each one focused on a different object—a rock, a leaf, a crooked tree growing out of the stones—and let their gazes go vacant as they meditated.

Ellie still didn't understand most of what they did, or *why*. Still, she did appreciate their style of nonlethal fighting, and their unique weapons, the lockstaves. What she'd first taken for an odd staff she'd come to learn was a tool with many different uses, from disarming opponents to changing directions without losing speed.

Once the sky above was clear, Ellie took to the air, leaving the acolytes to their ritual. Charlo waved from the ground, where he sat cross-legged with the others.

Ellie spiraled upward, slipping from breeze to breeze; the winds around the mountains were narrow and always shifting. Flying on them was like leaping across logs floating in a river. But she'd gotten the hang of it pretty quickly, and enjoyed the challenge of reading the air around her before she maneuvered herself into its flow.

She spotted Gussie perched on a stony ledge, tinkering with her collection of odds and ends as usual. No point in waving; when Gussie was inventing, it was better to leave her to it rather than risk getting your head bitten off for interrupting.

At the peak of the highest mountain, she found Nox.

The Crow boy sat against a jagged rock, out of the worst of the cold wind.

Ellie recognized the look in his eyes and was careful as she dropped beside him. He said nothing, not even looking at her. He was staring at the eastern horizon with an intensity that made his black eyes seem to smolder, like coals that might crack open at any moment to reveal hidden fire. Out of habit, she glanced at his back, where his shirt opened around the joints of his dark wings. There was a fresh pink scar over one of them, where he'd nearly had a wing sliced off the day they'd fled Thelantis.

In his hand was the blue skystone that had caused them all so much trouble—the magical rock that had once been the eye of a gargol, the stone monsters who roamed the skies on cloudy days. That bauble was the reason they were on the run, the reason they'd lost everything. Its mysterious ability to float like a soap bubble and heal the terrible disease called wingrot made it more valuable than any gem in the world. And she knew if King Garion ever got hold of it, he'd destroy it without hesitation.

"I was talking to Gussie this morning about leaving," she said. "She says it's too soon."

Nox's hand tightened on the skystone. "We should have left weeks ago."

Ellie picked at her thumbnail. "I've been thinking. This place is special. It's . . . like a clan all its own, made of people of every feather."

She saw his jaw clench harder, but he said nothing.

"Charlo said if any of us chose to stay, they'd let us."

"So you're staying."

"I . . . haven't decided yet." Why did she feel so guilty? How could she make him see she wasn't like him—born to fly alone? "But I am thinking about it."

"What about the skystone? You said you wanted to use it to heal people?"

"I do! I just don't know *how* to do that yet, without attracting the king's attention. He's dead set on destroying it. So for now . . . I don't know. I guess I just want someplace to call home for a while."

She thought sorrowfully of Linden, her hometown, and the Sparrow clan. As much as it pained her to admit, she knew she could never return there, not after being branded a thief and thrown in King Garion's dungeons.

"Do what you want," said Nox stiffly. "I don't care. But I'm not sticking around much longer."

"I know what you want to do. And I understand. But it's so dangerous, and you're still healing."

"I made a promise to my mother. And I still haven't kept it." He finally looked at her. "I have to get her out of that prison, Ellie."

"I know."

They sat in silence for another few minutes, listening to the wind whistle over the peaks. Nox resumed staring at the horizon, in the direction of the island prison where his mother had been held for years.

She felt for him, she really did. And Ellie wasn't one to shy away from danger or noble missions—far from it. But *this* mission . . . it felt too big, too fast. The Crag was the most secure prison in the Clandoms. They were lucky *they* hadn't ended up there themselves.

A sudden flutter to Ellie's left drew her eye. It was Charlo, winging frantically toward them.

"Oh, look, it's your boyfriend," intoned Nox, his eyes narrowing. He quickly dropped the skystone under his shirt, out of sight.

"He's not my—oh, *shut up*." She shoved the Crow and then launched into the air, meeting Charlo halfway.

"What's wrong?" she asked.

He was panting, his wide wings spread on the wind. "It's Elder Rue! She wants to see you."

"*Me?* Why?" Ellie had only glimpsed the leader of the Restless Order twice in all the weeks they'd been in Cloudstone. Her impression had been of a severe, humorless old woman best avoided, which wasn't hard to do since she spent most of her time locked away in the Sanctum, doing who knew what.

"There's only one reason Elder Rue sends for anyone lower than a novice," he replied breathlessly. "It must mean she's had a vision of the future—a vision about *you*."

CHAPTER THREE
· ELLIE ·

Her heart beating fast, Ellie landed in the courtyard in a swirl of leaves, her lockstave held close to her side. Behind her, the monks gathered curiously. Apparently a vision was news worth interrupting their meditations for.

Gussie, Nox, and Twig stood off to the side. The Falcon girl lifted an eyebrow when Ellie glanced her way. Of the four, Gussie was the most skeptical about the Order and their so-called ability to glimpse the future.

Twig, who was a total believer, gave Ellie an encouraging thumbs-up.

Drawing a deep breath, Ellie turned to the great stone door that had so tempted her. Now it stood open, revealing a dark passageway into the mountain.

"Hurry, girl!" snapped an old monk behind her. He scowled and waved his hands as if to push her in. "How rude to make the elder wait!"

"All right, all right," she muttered. She handed her lockstave to Twig, then walked into the tunnel.

The coldness of the mountain's interior closed around her. She shivered and glanced back, just as the stone door began to shut. It groaned before sealing with a loud *thump* and leaving Ellie in total darkness.

That thump echoed through the passage ahead like an ominous drumbeat.

"Okay." She squared her chin and shook out her wings. "Just because it *feels* like a tomb doesn't mean it is one, right?"

Her nervous laugh fluttered weakly into the dark.

She followed the tunnel with one hand dragging along the wall, wondering how many nervous people had walked this same path before her. Did she even believe in these visions the Restless claimed to have? Charlo had told her only the oldest, most devout monks even had them. And who knew what a lifetime of staring at rocks did to a person's mind?

The darkness was so deep it felt surreal, like she'd fallen into a dream. It had been two months since Ellie had left her hometown of Linden and her clan, on a quest to join the Goldwing knights. And it had been one month since she'd learned those knights were not the heroes she'd always imagined, and that the king she'd hoped to impress was really a monster. Now here she was, a fugitive, walking deep into the heart of a mountain to hear some old seer's vision of her future.

Ellie began to giggle.

When she rounded a corner minutes later, to find a sudden gleam of light ahead, she was still giggling. Not because it was particularly funny, but because it all felt so nerve-racking and impossible, like she'd fallen into someone else's story, a place she didn't belong.

Then where do *I belong?* she wondered.

That sobered her up. It was a question she'd been dodging, a hole in her heart she hadn't quite looked directly into ever since fleeing Thelantis. She knew, vaguely, what she *wanted* to do—use the skystone to heal people suffering from wingrot. But she had no idea where to start, or how one small rock could make a real difference when so many people were sick. And she still wasn't sure where *she* fit in, specifically. Should she take the stone and travel around in disguise, finding the sick and healing them with its magic? Or should she stay in Cloudstone, and entrust it to someone older and stronger—and *not* wanted for high crimes—to see the job through instead? Charlo had been pressing her to do just that, though she had told him nothing about the skystone.

He'd told her this town was a home for the homeless . . . which pretty much described Ellie.

She'd spent the last six years knowing exactly where she belonged. Or, at least, where she *thought* she belonged: with the Goldwing knights. But that dream had turned into a puff of smoke, and now she felt like she was flying over endless ocean with no idea where to land.

Maybe Elder Rue could help.

Maybe that was why Ellie kept walking, despite her doubts about visions of the future.

Maybe the answer to that question—*Where do I go now?*—lay just around the next bend in the tunnel. Maybe Elder Rue had had a vision of Ellie joining the Restless Order, donning a blue robe and meditating on a mountain peak. The idea made her stomach churn.

At last, she stepped into a large cavern—and gasped.

Channels had been carved into the stone floor and filled with oil, which now burned with low, steady blue flames. These spiraled inward to the center of the chamber, where massive rods of white crystal jutted from the ground. Their facets glimmered in the glow of the fire, the crystals' depths sparkling. On the cavern ceiling, a massive pattern came into relief, a version of the same symbol Ellie had seen repeated all throughout Cloudstone—an inverted triangle with a spiral inside it.

A lone figure sat before the crystals, dressed in the usual blue robes, watching Ellie approach.

"Elder Rue," Ellie called out. "You wanted to see me?"

The old woman didn't reply, only stared at her expectantly.

Ellie began walking toward the center of the cavern, following the spiraling path created by the channels of blue fire. The flames rose only as high as her knees and burned without heat, so the chill of the cave still made her shiver. Around and around she walked, while Elder Rue waited in serene silence on a mat of furs.

Finally, Ellie reached the center of the spiral, and stood dwarfed by the towering crystals. After a moment's uncertainty, she slowly knelt down the way she'd seen the monks sit for their meditations, with Elder Rue across from her.

Ellie cleared her throat. "You, uh, sent for me?"

The old woman squinted at her, and Ellie frowned as she really studied the elder for the first time. Her dark skin and wings, her frizzy gray hair . . . it was all terribly familiar.

"You're not related to Granny Tam, are you?" asked Ellie.

The woman blinked, then grimaced. "Ah. I heard you met my sister down in the low lands."

"Your sister!" Ellie coughed.

"One cannot choose one's blood kin," sighed Elder Rue. "My sister left the true path long ago. Now, as for why I summoned you." She raised a hand, gesturing to the crystals behind her. "As the elder of the Restless, it is my duty to spend every waking moment meditating upon the Mountain's Heart, to glean what I may of the future."

Ellie nodded, her fingers curling into clammy fists.

"It takes months, sometimes, to catch a single glimpse of what's to come. Months of staring, pondering, waiting . . . occasionally nodding off for a few hours." Elder Rue chuckled. "Even when we do manage to see anything, it's often too blurry to understand, or it involves someone we've never seen and never will see. But once in a decade or so, if we are lucky, we might glimpse something we *do* understand."

"You saw something about me?" whispered Ellie.

Elder Rue nodded. "*You.* The Sparrow who carries one of our lockstaves—there was no mistaking you. I saw your future, child, or at least a reflection of it."

"What does that mean?"

"Our visions aren't always literal." Elder Rue shrugged. "Sometimes they require . . . interpretation."

"So what did you see?"

The Elder shut her eyes and murmured in a deep voice, "You will carry a flame through the darkness, to light a great fire. But if you drop it, or if the flame goes out . . . the sky will fall."

Then she opened her eyes and sighed heavily, as if uttering those two sentences had exhausted her.

Ellie blinked. "That's . . . it? But that could mean anything!"

"It doesn't matter whether you *like* the vision, girl," said Elder Rue stiffly. "This isn't a tavern, delivering up whatever you order."

"Sorry. I know you only get a vision every decade and all that. But . . . couldn't you be a little more specific?"

"I can only tell you what I saw, and I have." Disgruntled, the elder shimmied herself around to face the crystals again. "Considering my age, that's likely the last clear vision I'll ever receive too. Humph! Youths these days! Always ungrateful."

"I just wish I knew what it meant." Ellie sagged a little. It wasn't that she'd been hoping for something like *Go to this exact spot on this exact day and you'll meet your destiny* . . . But then, to be honest, she kind of *had* been hoping for that. Instead she had a metaphor. She didn't know anything about flames or the sky falling. How was that supposed to help?

"Well . . . I guess that's all, then," she said, rising to her feet. "Thanks."

Elder Rue said softly, "I know what it is your Crow friend wears around his neck."

Ellie froze. "I, uh, don't know what you mean."

They hadn't told anyone here about the skystone, knowing the trouble it had brought them everywhere else. In fact, they'd said little about their pasts beyond that they were wanted for theft, which the Restless Order had accepted without comment. The people here had little love for Garion, whose ancestors' harassment of their Order was what had originally driven them to live in the mountains to begin with.

Ellie and her friends had agreed to keep the skystone secret, but clearly they hadn't done a good enough job. Or maybe Elder Rue had glimpsed that in her crystals too.

Without turning around, Elder Rue continued, "We have legends about skystones in our order, you know. They're rare and sacred artifacts of great power. It's said that meditating upon one can even lead a person to Truehome."

"Truehome," muttered Ellie. "That's the place you people are trying to get to, isn't it? The reason you're always meditating? That's what that symbol represents, right?" She pointed to the triangle and spiral carved into the ceiling.

The Elder nodded. "Truehome is a state of mind—a clarity of thought and transcendence of place that brings total freedom. When you find it, it is believed that you find your*self*. It is what we Restless spend our entire lives seeking. All people are born into exile, you see, separated from their true and best existence. That is why we Restless meditate—it is a devotion to finding our way home."

That last part, at least, Ellie could understand. For the first time, she thought she might see how a person could spend their days on these mountains, staring at leaves and rocks—hoping to discover what they were meant to do, where they were meant to go.

But that wasn't Ellie's path. She belonged somewhere, she was sure, but it would have to be a place she found for herself, not some revelation hidden in the pattern of raindrops on grass.

"Did you see the skystone in your vision of me?" asked Ellie. "Is it the flame I'm supposed to carry?"

"I don't know."

"Well . . . *could* it be?"

"Perhaps."

Holding back a groan of frustration, Ellie glanced toward the cavern entrance. She wasn't going to get any more help from Elder Rue, it seemed. Whatever the vision meant, and whatever the skystone had to do with it, Ellie would just have to find out on her own. Or maybe Gussie was right and nobody could see the future. Maybe what Elder Rue really needed was a week of fresh air and sunshine to clear her head. Spending every day in a cave had to be messing with her brain.

The elder was already falling back into her trancelike state. Taking this as her cue, Ellie retraced the spiraling path and followed the dark tunnel out of the mountain.

None of the monks asked her about the vision, not even Charlo, though she could see curiosity burning in his eyes. She suspected they had some rule about speaking visions aloud, the way you weren't supposed to tell someone what you wished for on the first star of winter solstice—because then it might not come true.

But that night, as they lay in the spare room Charlo's family had offered them, Twig and Gussie pestered her relentlessly. Finally, she broke and repeated the elder's words while swaying gently in her hammock.

"Carry a flame through darkness?" echoed Gussie. "Of *course* she said that. These so-called fortune-tellers always phrase things so vaguely that they could mean practically anything. It's more proof that their visions are a crock."

"*Or*," said Twig, "she really will have to carry some all-important flame and light some all-important fire and save the world!"

Nox snorted. Ellie twisted around to peer at him, where he lay with his wings lazily dragging on the floor on either side of his hammock.

"Well, smart guy, what do you think?"

"I think no one controls my future but *me*."

"Hey, maybe the prophecy has something to do with you!" said Twig. "That bit about flames and fires . . . I mean, it would make sense, considering."

Considering, Ellie knew, that Nox was *fireproof*.

That was another secret they'd kept from the Order—a secret even bigger than the skystone. Ellie twisted again to look at Nox and saw his wings had gone stiff. He didn't like talking about his weird invulnerability to fire, and she suspected he was sorry he'd even told the three of them about it. Not that he'd had a choice—they'd all seen him run through a wall of flames and come out the other side without so much as a singed feather.

Maybe Twig was onto something.

But she couldn't see how Nox quite fit into Elder Rue's vision. And he wasn't likely to offer any ideas.

She sighed. "I guess we'll just have to wait and—"

"Shh!" hissed Twig.

They all went still, hearing the warning in his voice. Ellie's eyes and ears strained to sense whatever it was Twig had heard. But there was another sense she didn't have that the younger boy did—what she thought of as his "inner ear," which gave him the ability to feel a person's emotions and intentions. Was that what had alerted him?

"There's someone in the room with us," whispered Twig.

The hair rose on Ellie's arms. "Charlo?"

"No, it's—"

Ellie screamed as a shape lunged out of the dark, a figure way too tall to be her new friend. It was a shadow of a man, hissing with glee, his dark wings spreading wide as he grabbed Ellie by her hair.

In his hand flashed a dagger.

CHAPTER FOUR

NOX

Nox was up in an instant, wings spreading. He barreled through the air and headbutted the attacker in the chest just as the man was about to plunge his dagger toward Ellie.

With a *whoof*, the man crumpled, but he didn't fall. Instead, he dropped and rolled beneath Ellie's hammock, popping up spryly on the other side. He was grinning the whole time, as if this were all a game.

"Wanna play with the Hunter, children?" he sang in a creepy voice. The dagger danced in his grip. "A little game of death, hmm?"

Nox pulled Ellie out of the hammock. She grabbed her lockstave from the corner and held it out defensively.

"Who are you?" demanded Nox.

The man only laughed. Then, so quickly Nox didn't even have time to shout, he darted toward Gussie's hammock and slashed with his blade.

But the girl was ready, her Falcon clan training kicking in. She whipped up the hammock and caught the knife in its weave. Meanwhile, Twig scrambled down and ran out of the room, yelling.

In moments, the household woke and lanterns gleamed to life. Charlo and his parents appeared, each armed with a lockstave.

"Where is he?" asked Charlo's father, a burly blacksmith.

"There!" said Nox, pointing.

But the intruder was no longer standing there.

Skies, but the man could *move*. He'd already blended into the shadows and reappeared behind Charlo. He slashed the boy's wing, and Charlo cried out in pain.

"Stop!" roared Ellie. She and Charlo's parents all converged on the Hunter, staffs swinging, but the man ducked and rolled away.

This was no good, Nox realized. There was only one of him, but he moved like liquid, and in these close quarters they were easy targets for his knife.

"Outside!" he yelled. "Get out of the house!"

They rushed out of the cave house, taking to the air. Charlo, too wounded to fly, dropped from ledge to ledge with practiced movements, though Nox knew from experience how badly his wing must be paining him.

"Do you know this man?" asked Charlo's father, while his wife flew to ring an alarm bell higher up the cliff.

"No," said Nox. "But clearly it's us he's after."

He exchanged looks with Ellie, then they both scanned the darkness, hovering in a circle formation. The attacker had to be somewhere close. Nox doubted he'd flown all this way just to give up easily.

"King Garion must have sent him," said Ellie, swooping nearer.

He nodded grimly. "He knows where we are."

"And he'll send more. We've put Cloudstone in danger."

Nox let out a long breath, having caught Ellie's meaning. They'd have to leave. Tonight. Who knew how many more assassins were hiding in those shadows?

As long as they were here, no one in the village was safe. Charlo was already hurt, and they couldn't risk worse befalling the Order.

The alarm bell rang out and Restless monks flooded the sky, lighting lanterns strung on ropes and twirling their lockstaves. One thing was certain—few towns were as prepared to fight as this one. But Nox couldn't ask them to risk their lives for him and his friends.

"You four go to the Sanctum," said Charlo's father. "We'll seal you inside, where you'll be untouchable. We'll deal with the scum."

"No," sighed Nox. "It's time we moved on anyway. We'll draw him and any others after us."

He glanced at his friends, and Gussie and Twig nodded in agreement. Nox's chest tightened when he saw the resolution on his crew's faces. They were weary and scared, same as him, but ready to fly nonetheless.

But Ellie looked torn.

He remembered her saying she was considering staying here. In fact, her words had been stuck in his head ever since.

"Ellie?" he asked.

Finally, she nodded. "You're right. We can't draw any more trouble to this place."

Though he didn't show it, Nox felt the knot in his chest loosen in relief. For a moment, he'd been sure she would tell them to leave without her.

Not that he *cared* or anything. The Sparrow wasn't part of his crew. She'd just been in the wrong place at the wrong time, and now there was no real reason for her to stick with them.

But their brief respite in Cloudstone was over. There would be no more hiding, not for a while.

"Are you sure?" asked the blacksmith. "The Restless have a code: We suffer no harm to befall our guests."

"We have a code of our own," said Nox. "Hiding's only good until you're found."

It was one of the Talon's sayings, and it made Nox wince to recall the thief who'd been his mentor—then nearly his executioner. But he'd taught Nox how to survive, at least.

"Wait until dawn and clearer skies, then," said the blacksmith firmly. "We won't have you flying right into gargols' claws."

For the next few hours, the monks searched out the village, trying to find the assassin, but there was no sign of him. Nox, Ellie, Gussie, and Twig sat in a row on a high balcony, silent and tense, watching every shadow with dread. There weren't just silent killers to fear but gargols too. The clouds above were thin and moving quickly, but the monsters were known to hunt farther afield in the dark.

"What kind of maniac *was* that guy?" whispered Ellie. "He didn't sound like a Goldwing."

"He sounded like a monster," grunted Gussie.

"Not that there's a difference," said Nox.

"And the way he moved," said Ellie. "Did you see it? It was like he was made out of snakes."

"I know him," murmured Twig.

Nox, Ellie, and Gussie all turned to stare at the boy.

"What?" Nox gasped.

Twig lowered his eyes. His pronged marten, Lirri, lay draped over his lap, and he stroked between her horns. "It's been bothering me all night, and then I remembered. I know his voice, but it's been years since I heard it."

"Well, who is he?" asked Ellie impatiently.

"He was part of the circus I worked for. I don't know his real name; he went by the Twist because he was a contortionist. Nobody liked him. He was creepy, always playing with knives and spying on people. Then one day . . ." Twig grimaced. "He attacked one of the acrobats, for no reason. He cut the guy's fingers off. Then he ran and we never saw him again."

"I've heard of people like that," said Gussie. "They enjoy hurting people just for fun. They don't even *think* like normal people do, which makes them doubly dangerous. You can't predict what they'll do."

Nox felt sick. He'd thought he could deal with just about any threat, even Goldwings, because at least he could guess their next move.

But this Twist guy—or the *Hunter*, as he'd called himself—might be another kind of threat entirely.

"Do you think the king sent him?" asked Ellie.

Nox shrugged. "Does it matter? Either way, he's after us."

"And trust me," said Twig, shivering, "we do *not* want him to find us again."

At last the sky began to grow pink as the sun rose, though the mountains would be dark and chilly for hours yet.

With half a dozen Restless guarding them, they went to the house and gathered their belongings. Nox felt like he was waking from a dream, returning to the real world. And he wasn't entirely sorry for it either. Granted, this wasn't the way he'd *wanted* to leave Cloudstone, but he had been getting anxious to hit the open sky again.

To journey east, toward his mother.

Ellie had tears in her eyes but in her stubborn way refused to let them fall.

"I have to say goodbye to Charlo," she said when she'd finished packing.

Nox nodded. She'd grown to be good friends with the Swan boy, spending nearly every day sparring with him in the courtyard. It had begun to grate on Nox, watching them swap blows and jokes like they'd been pals for years. Was that the real reason she wanted to stay? So what if the kid could swing a lockstave? It took more skill to pick a pocket, in Nox's opinion. Not that Ellie had ever asked him to teach her *that*.

Yes. It was definitely time to move on.

"Thanks for everything," he said to the blacksmith.

The man put a heavy hand on Nox's shoulder. "Fly true. Watch the skies."

"Watch the skies," Ellie said in return. She was no longer crying but had set her face with fierce determination, as if she might fly through the mountain itself if she wanted.

There was the Ellie who Nox knew . . . and slightly feared.

Their goodbyes said, there was nothing else to do but fly and fly *fast*.

Just because they wanted to draw the Hunter away from Cloudstone didn't mean they actually wanted to *face* the assassin. With any luck, they'd lose him in the labyrinthine tangle of the mountains.

"Stay close together," shouted Ellie as they winged eastward, passing through two high peaks. The wind pushed them through, gathering strength in the open air. "We don't want to get picked off one by one."

Even with the sun rising, there were still plenty of shadowy hiding places that could conceal the assassin. They flew high, on a sharp western wind that caught their wings like sails and sent them shooting through the sky.

Far below, the pockets between the mountains filled with blue fog, and the breezes that curled through made the mists flow like water. As the sun rose higher, it was the peaks that glowed first, crowns of golden light shining around their stony summits, then slowly burning downward, as if the mountains themselves were rising to meet the day. Clear skies waited to the east.

When the Hunter attacked, it was out of the fog below, rising so swiftly and suddenly that by the time Nox spotted him, it was too late to make a plan.

"Watch out!" Nox yelled.

He did a barrel roll, narrowly avoiding the dagger the man was holding. The Hunter shot upward, flared his wings, and turned a wide loop in the sky above.

"He wants the stone!" called Ellie, swooping over. "Toss it to me, Nox. I'm the best flier!"

She was right, and he had no problem admitting it. She'd won the Race of Ascension, after all, something most high clan kids couldn't even do.

He unlooped the skystone from around his neck. The gem flashed as he tossed it. As she dove by him, Ellie caught it and soared away.

"Come and get it, if you can!" she called, taunting the Hunter.

Nox pulled a slingshot from his belt; he'd traded pickpocketing lessons for it with a seven-year-old in Cloudstone. If Ellie could keep the Hunter's attention, Nox might be able to take out one of his wings with a well-placed rock.

But as he dug into his belt satchel for the perfect ammo, he heard Gussie yell, "Nox! Look out!"

He glanced up just in time to see the Hunter diving at him.

Sucking in a breath, Nox frantically flapped his wings, stumbling backward through the air. He was too slow, and the Hunter nicked his primary flight feathers, shearing off a few barbs. It was as painless as if he'd cut Nox's hair, but the inches he'd taken off made Nox's wings suddenly clumsy.

He cursed; it'd be months before those feathers molted and regrew. It was sheer luck he hadn't lost more—or he'd be plummeting to the ground right now.

"Hey, lunatic!" Ellie screamed, waving the skystone on its chain. "*I've* got the shiny rock, not him!"

But the Hunter ignored her and swooped toward Nox again, leering as he pulled another dagger into his free hand. This one he slung, and Nox barely yanked his head back to avoid having his eye impaled by the spinning blade.

What was *with* this maniac?

"He's after *you*, Nox!" Twig shouted. "Not the stone!"

Skies, he was right. *Nox* was the assassin's real target.

He pocketed his slingshot and flew downward. His clipped feathers made speed impossible in any other direction; at least this way, his own weight would help him move faster. Maybe he could shake the assassin in the mists gathering between the mountain slopes.

The lower he descended, the choppier the air became. He looked back once, to see the Hunter giving chase, and Ellie, Gussie, then Twig trailing behind him. Ellie reached out with her lockstave, trying to hook the man's foot, but couldn't get close enough.

Looking down again, Nox yelped and rolled as a sudden prong of sharp stone materialized out of the mist. Unable to adjust for his clumsy, trimmed feathers, he couldn't regain his balance and slammed into a rock wall.

Dazed and winded, he half fluttered, half fell down the stony slope, gathering a nasty collection of cuts and bruises along the way. Finally, he crashed into a boulder and lay still, groaning. The mountain above seemed to be spinning. He tasted blood in his mouth, and the arrow wound in his shoulder, only a few weeks healed, screamed with fresh pain.

Dimly, he saw the form of the assassin growing larger above him. Wedged in the rocks, dazed and wounded, Nox could do nothing but wait for his doom. He sighed, long and slow, and thought of his mother, locked in a cell on the Crag.

She would never know what had happened to him.

She would never know how hard he'd tried to keep his promise.

He met the assassin's eyes as the man landed on the boulder above him.

"So you're the little Corvain brat?" said the Hunter, studying him as if he were already dead. "Hmm. Have to say, I'm not impressed. But who can really account for His Darling Majesty's whims, eh?"

He twirled his dagger—then paused, frowned, and looked up.

To where Ellie Meadows had appeared, red-faced and furious, on a torrent of copper-brown wings. She swung her lockstave in a mighty arc, slamming it into the assassin's temple and knocking him off the boulder.

"Ellie!"

"Nox! I got you." She reached down and gripped his arm, hauling him upright. "Wow, you really took the hard way down, huh?"

He looked over the boulder, to where the Hunter was cursing and howling, a hand pressed to his temple.

"Now, Gus!" Ellie yelled. "Nox, *move*."

She yanked him aside as, above, a great rumbling sound filled the air—and then he saw the tumble of rocks bouncing down the mountainside.

"Hurry!" Ellie panted, flying while pulling Nox along.

They dove clear of the rockslide just in time and landed on a ledge to watch the boulders wash over the Hunter. Looking up, Nox spotted Gussie and Twig silhouetted against the sky. How they'd caused the cascade of rocks, he had no idea, but he was grateful.

"C'mon," said Ellie grimly. "He's a tricky one, and we can't be sure he won't wriggle out somehow."

"Any idea why he was after you?" Gussie asked, fluttering down to join them.

"Yeah." Nox let out a long breath. His whole body ached from his fall. "He called me by my name."

"So?" said Twig. "That doesn't explain why he went after you and not the skystone."

Nox met the boy's gaze. "It does, actually. Because he didn't call me Nox Hatcher. He called me *Corvain*. That's, um, my real name. Tannox Corvain. I haven't used it since I was little."

They exchanged looks, then Ellie asked, "Which means . . . ?"

"The only other person who knows my real name is my mother," he said. "At least, that's what I thought. But this guy knew it, and I think King Garion knows it too. My mother told me to never speak it to anyone, in case they might connect me with my . . . father."

"Who was executed on account of his being fireproof," said Gussie.

Nox nodded. "My secret isn't a secret anymore. And for whatever reason, I don't think King Garion's going to rest until he knows I'm dead."

CHAPTER FIVE
· ELLIE ·

According to a weathered sign by the road, the seaside town was called Porton. Ellie leaned on the sign while she pulled off a shoe and shook out a sharp pebble.

"Do we dare go in?" asked Gussie, peering at the haphazard jumble of buildings ahead.

The structures had once been painted a variety of colors but had all faded into grayish pastels under the harsh northern winds. Ellie breathed in the salty air, her heart beating faster at the prospect of seeing the ocean for the first time.

The land here was wild and harsh, moors of rolling hills covered in short, tough grass or clusters of jagged stone. The wind blew roughly from the east, howling like a wolf. Despite the clear sky, the light felt dim and the ground perpetually damp.

They'd landed not long after leaving the mountains, to rest their wings and patch up Nox's new assortment of scrapes. He looked worse than he truly was, with the bitter exception of his clipped feathers. Ellie's own wings had tingled in sympathy. He could still fly, at least, but not nearly as fast enough as someone in his position needed to.

The king wanted his head, after all.

Ellie thought about this as she studied the town of Porton.

"We don't really have a choice," she admitted. "We all dropped our packs back in the mountains in order to dodge the assassin, so we need food and supplies."

Gussie sighed heavily; she missed her pack more than any of them, Ellie suspected, with all its bulging pockets of odds and ends she used for her inventions. All they had left was whatever had been strapped to their belts.

"And after that?" asked Twig.

Ellie shrugged and looked at Nox. He had no answer either.

They were on the run with nowhere to go. She couldn't believe they'd be lucky enough to stumble across another place like Cloudstone. And if the king really was after Nox and not just the skystone he carried, they wouldn't be safe anywhere in the Clandoms.

"One step at a time," she said at last. "We go into town, get supplies—"

"*Steal* supplies, you mean?" Nox asked, giving her a wicked grin.

She glared back. "No, I mean *buy* them." She patted the coin satchel on her belt, money earned from doing various chores for the people of Cloudstone. "We may be fugitives, but that doesn't make us criminals."

The Crow rolled his eyes.

Ellie wanted him to wait in the hills while she, Gussie, and Twig went into town, but he refused.

"I'm the best at reading people," he said. "I spent my whole life as a thief watching for trouble. Unless *you* can spot a guard in disguise from twenty paces? Or a spy shadowing you through a crowded street?"

"Fine," Ellie relented. "But I'm going too because when your thief senses fail, someone's gotta be around to whack heads." She thumped her lockstave.

Twig was happy to wait outside town, but only after the others swore to bring back nuts for his marten. Lirri gave Ellie a withering look as they walked away, as if to impress upon her the enormous importance of those nuts.

Minutes later, Ellie, Nox, and Gussie crested the last hill before Porton, and there was the sea.

Ellie stopped in her tracks, her breath rushing out of her lungs. Nox, a few paces ahead, glanced back and grinned.

"Like it?" he asked.

"It's . . . *big*."

Tall ships were anchored in the harbor, bristling like a forest of bare winter trees. Beyond them . . . water. So much water. She'd known, in theory, what the sea might look like, but the width and depth of that gray-blue expanse was enough to steal her words away. And the sound . . . the waves rushing over the rocky shoreline reminded her of home, of the wind rustling over the sunflower fields of Linden. How could two places so completely different and so very far apart sound almost exactly alike?

"Come on," said Gussie. "The quicker we get in and out, the better."

They'd rubbed mud into Nox's feathers to dull their iridescent sheen, so he looked less obviously Crow clan. But Ellie still felt nervous as they strolled by houses and shops. In her mind, every person they passed might as well have been another Hunter.

"We should have made you wear a cape," she said to Nox. "To cover your wings."

"That's the *first* way to get yourself noticed," he replied. "It's one thing walking around as a stranger, but covering your wings is like shouting *I don't want you to know who I am*."

"He's right," said Gussie. "I don't know how you country Sparrows do it, but in these eastern towns, hiding your wings is considered a sign of bad intentions, like concealing a weapon."

"The only way to hide," Nox added, "is by showing you have nothing *to* hide."

"Fine, fine," Ellie said, still looking around worriedly to see if they'd attracted any suspicious gazes.

"And stop looking around like that."

"Like what?"

"Like you're expecting a dagger in the back at any moment."

"Well, I *am*."

Porton's streets were made of cobbled bricks, and the deeper they went into the town, the taller and closer the buildings became. Ellie noticed a good many Gull clanners, their long white-and-gray wings as salty as the air, and wondered if this was their clan seat. Mixed in were at least a dozen other clans—Terns; Pigeons; Doves; tall, shaggy-feathered folk she guessed might be from the remote Pelican clan who lived on the rocky islands of the north. Everyone looked as weathered as the land, faces craggy and clothes patched. Judging by all the oilskin coats, knee-high boots, and scarves, they were mostly seafaring types, fisherfolk and clammers and traders. Maybe many of them were just passing through Porton too, but Ellie was sure she, Gussie, and Nox stuck out anyway.

Then she spotted a group that stood out even more than her own—five tall Falcon clanners were swaggering up the street, joking and picking on the townspeople they passed. They couldn't be much older than twenty. One plucked a plate of oysters from a stall and began slurping them down without paying. The small Tern clanner selling them could only stare helplessly.

Ellie's blood boiled. "Spoiled jerks."

"Who? Oh." Nox lifted his eyebrows, then nudged Ellie. "Look at you, sounding like proper street scum!"

"Um . . ." Gussie stopped in her tracks. "I, uh, I gotta go."

"Huh?" Ellie frowned. "What's wrong?"

"Agustina!"

They all turned to see one of the tall Falcons waving frantically at them.

"You *know* them?" gasped Ellie.

Gussie winced. "One of them. He's . . . my cousin."

Ellie saw the resemblance. The boy had the same dark skin and thick eyebrows as Gussie, though where hers were always scrunched together in thought, his bounced all over like they'd come loose from his face.

"Agustina Berel!" The Falconer had begun striding toward them while his friends hung back to swipe more oysters. "It's me, your cuz Finnion!"

Gussie turned away, hiding her face with her wing, but it was too late. They couldn't sprint away without drawing even more attention. "You two back off. Pretend you don't know me."

Ellie and Nox nodded and drifted away, trying to appear casual even though Ellie's heart was pounding. She pretended to look at a display of nautical charts and astrolabes in a cartographer's shop window while still watching from the corner of her eye.

Finnion jogged up and tugged Gussie's wing, grinning. "Hey! Didn't you hear me calling? It's me, Finn!"

"Hey, Finn," Gussie sighed.

"I heard you went on a farflight. It's been, what, a year almost?"

"What can I say? I decided to see the world."

Ellie remembered Gussie telling her about the high clans and their idea of a *farflight*, which was what they called it when they kicked out a kid who refused to go into the family business. Gussie had been sent away because she wanted to be a scholar, not a warrior, and hadn't been home or seen any of her family since.

Until now.

Finnion laughed. "You're so weird. I took the family ship out for a jaunt, up the coast and back, you know, to get away from it all for a while."

"Uh-huh."

"Hey, when are you coming back? You heard about your little sis, right?"

"What?" Gussie straightened, her eyes widening. "What happened to Evantine?"

"She's saying she doesn't want to go into the Martial Academy, same as you. There are rumors if she doesn't enroll in the fall, she'll get sent on a farflight too."

"What? No! Evie can't survive a farflight. She can barely walk from her room to the kitchen without stubbing a toe or spraining a wing!"

Finnion shrugged. "That's just what I heard. I figured you'd get back by then and talk sense into her. She only ever listened to you."

When his friends at the oyster stall started shouting for him, Finnion jumped. "Ah, we're due to cast off right about now. Sorry—can't miss this tide or we'll be late to this party in Petrel Bay. Hey, wanna come? It's supposed to be *wild*. There'll be dancing polar bears."

"Polar bears? Huh? No! I can't go with you, I—I have to send a letter to Evie."

"Right. Okay. Well, tell the family I said hello, and that I'm fine, and I definitely had nothing to do with the large hole in the upper deck of the ship. You tell them we were absolutely *not* playing around with cannonballs."

"Right. You got it. *Goodbye.*"

"See you. And don't forget—I *didn't* make the hole in the ship! It was, uh . . . sharks. Or pirates or something. You're supposed to be smart, you figure it out. Thanks!"

He hurried away to catch up with his friends, and Gussie stood in the street, her hands knotted.

Cautiously, Ellie rejoined her as Nox drifted back from whatever shadow he'd been lurking in.

"You okay?" Ellie whispered.

Gussie stared after her cousin, even when he'd vanished around a corner. "I'm fine."

"Your little sister . . ."

Shaking her head, Gussie replied, "Evie's an idiot. I told her the day I left she shouldn't come after me, but she's always followed me around. Her head's been stuck in the clouds since she was born."

"Do you want to send the letter now?"

"Letter?" Gussie blinked. "I can't send a letter. My parents would read it, then rip it up before it ever reached Evie. I only said that to get rid of Finn. She'll have to find her own way, like me." Gussie dropped her gaze and folded her arms, closing herself off. But her long wings remained tense, pulled so tightly together that they trembled.

Ellie could tell she was holding back her true feelings. In other words, she was Gussie as usual.

"Do you want to talk—"

"*No.* Absolutely not. Let's just get this day over with."

Ellie exchanged a look with Nox, who could only shrug. They relented and let Gussie lead the way.

In a busy market street, they found a leatherworker who sold them four plain packs; a grocer who supplied them with potatoes, greens, salt, nuts, and oats; and a cheesemonger who took their coin with only a grunt and shoved a hard yellow wedge their way. Ellie had to hunt for a while before she found the last item on her list.

"Ahh." She opened the jar of the Sparrow Farms sunflower oil and inhaled deeply. The honey-gold oil inside, scented lightly with lavender, smelled like home.

"See?" said Nox, breaking off a piece of cheese to split with her. "No problem. You've got to act like you belong, and . . ."

Ellie frowned, watching his expression change as his voice faded. "What's wrong?"

Nox's eyes had gone distant, as if he was listening.

Focusing harder on the murmur of the other shoppers, Ellie finally realized what he'd heard. There were two old Gull clanners chatting behind her, leaning on the window of a tavern with their mugs of ale.

". . . don't know why you bother with ferrying supplies to that prison, anyway, Doon. The money's poor."

"Aye, but I feel sorry for them souls locked up in there. My granddad did a turn in a cell, y'know. I figure, why not make sure they get fresh greens once a week at least?"

"But didn't you hear? The Crag's overrun with the sick. They say half the inmates have wingrot. I'm starting to think it might be contagious after all."

"Pshaw, that's just rumors. And it ain't like I go in there or nothing, just unload my crates on the dock and . . ."

"Nox!" Ellie whispered, grabbing his arm. "I know what it sounds like, but you have no idea if—"

"My mother's in there," he said in a low, tight voice.

"It's just hearsay," said Gussie. "I'm sure she's all right."

"And if she isn't?" Nox's eyes had begun to burn with an inner light Ellie had grown to dread. It meant he was cooking up some mad plan. "You heard them. Wingrot's spreading through the Crag—the disease that has only one known cure. A cure *we* happen to carry. I'm not asking you to come with me. But I *am* going."

She shut her eyes. She'd known deep down it was going to come to this eventually. Nox was set on breaking his mother out of prison, and really, Ellie couldn't blame him. She was sure she'd feel the same in his position. But the idea still made her anxious.

They'd be flying straight *toward* the very people hunting them.

CHAPTER SIX
· NOX ·

Of course it *had* to be turnips.

They were Nox's least favorite vegetable. The smell alone was enough to turn his stomach, and yet here he was up to his ears in them—literally.

He wished he'd chosen the crate to his left. He could be happily curled up with a bunch of potatoes right now, like Gussie was.

Stealing away on the vegetable trader's ship was the only plan they'd been able to come up with, and it was wildly risky. Twig had argued all the way up to the point he'd climbed into his crate of onions—all right, so maybe there was someone who had it worse than Nox right now.

"I could try to ask a whale to give us a ride," Twig had offered. "Or some friendly fish!"

But in the end, even considering Twig's strange ability to persuade animals to do what he wanted, the crates were the only real option.

Set as it was on a large rock in the sea, the Crag was impossible to sneak up on any other way. If they flew there, they'd be seen at once by any guards on patrol and probably shot down by crossbows. They'd have the same problem if they stole a boat and rowed themselves out—Gussie's idea. Nox had suggested getting themselves arrested and thrown in the Crag, but the others had pointed out that if the king was already sending *assassins* for them, they might not even make it as far as the prison.

It was Ellie who'd thought of tracking down the produce trader from the market, with his weekly delivery to the Crag a possible way in. Sure enough, when they tailed him to the harbor the next morning, they found him loading crates onto his small trading boat while telling the harbormaster he was headed out to the prison island.

With a blanket of heavy gray fog covering the sea, it was easy to slip aboard the boat and hide themselves in the crates before the trader returned from the harbormaster's office. After that came the hours-long ride, which to Nox felt like a year.

He was cramped, sickened from the reek of turnips, and in urgent need of relieving his bladder, but none of that mattered.

The only important thing was that at the other end of this wretched boat ride, his mother would be waiting.

He was finally doing it. After years of planning, hoping, and failing, he was keeping his promise and rescuing her at last. And this time, his plan didn't rely on anyone else. There'd be no one to betray him at the last minute. Nox was taking matters into his own hands, the way he should have done all along.

He just had to make it to the prison without getting seasick.

Finally, he felt the boat slow and then lightly thump against something solid. Gentle waves lapped the sides, making the vessel rock like a cradle. Moments later, he heard the sound of the trader's heavy boots and off-key whistling as he shuffled around the deck.

Nox waited, one eye pressed to a slat in the crate boards.

What was Gussie's holdup?

Had something gone wrong?

They'd wanted to pull this off without the trader ever knowing they were there, so he wouldn't get blamed for being part of their jailbreak scheme. But if Nox had to, he'd burst out of the crate and—

Bzzzzzzz!

Nox caught his breath as the sound of hundreds of angry wasps filled the air.

It had taken them all day yesterday to find the hive. Twig had lulled the wasps to sleep with a smoking branch and moved their nest into a wooden box salvaged from Porton. Then, when they'd stolen aboard the boat, Gussie had had only seconds to rig the string that ran from her crate to the lid of the box, which she'd concealed in a coiled rope.

Right on cue, the trader began shouting in panic, and Nox heard the frantic tread of his boots as he hurried across the deck. Then came the slam of the door on the boat's narrow cabin. Like most seafaring vessels, this one was equipped with a small shelter in case of a sudden storm, complete with a protective ashmark to ward off gargols.

"Go, go, go!" hissed Nox, shoving open the lid of the crate. The others were already tumbling out, wincing as they unfolded their cramped limbs and wings.

They were docked at a small pier jutting from a sandy beach, on the sheltered leeward side of the island. Above them loomed massive black cliffs. A winding staircase of stone zigzagged up the bluff to the prison, of which Nox could only see a slate-gray roof. Looking back, he could make out the faintest shadow of the shoreline they'd left.

One by one, they slipped over the side of the boat and into the lapping waves. Twig was the last one over, having remained to calm the wasps so the insects didn't turn on *them*.

Once they were all in the water, they began swimming away from the beach, keeping to the sharp rocks at the shore for cover.

"Ha!" yelled the trader, emerging from the cabin with a lit torch. He waved it at the wasps to hold them at bay. "Nasty critters, what d'you think you're at, stowing away on *my* boat?"

Nox nearly panicked, thinking the man was yelling at them, but glanced back to see he was still focused on the wasps.

"Guards," said Ellie, who treaded water ahead of him. She pointed up the stone steps, where a man and a woman, both Hawk clanners, were descending to meet the trader.

"Keep going," whispered Nox. "Let's circle to the back of the island."

"And then?" asked Gussie.

So far, everything had gone beautifully. They'd reached the Crag without being discovered, getting the trader in trouble, or even getting stung by one of their waspish accomplices.

Unfortunately, this was where their plan ended.

"We'll figure it out," said Nox.

"This is nuts. We should have waited till we had an actual plan."

"And how d'you think we could've made a plan, Gussie? Chatted up one of the guards on their day off, hoping they wouldn't get suspicious about a bunch of kids asking him to draw a map of the place with all its entrances and, oh, could he kindly please mark down where they store the keys to the cells?"

"Hey, no fighting," said Twig.

Nox sighed. He was more wound up than he'd thought. The knowledge that his mother was closer now than she'd been in years was enough to make his head spin.

"Sorry, Gus."

"Let's just not rush into this, okay?" she replied graciously.

"Of course not. We'll recon, discuss, watch the guards' schedules—"

"Or," Ellie interrupted, "we could just go this way."

She'd been swimming ahead of the others and now stopped to point at an iron grate set into the bottom of the cliffs. Seawater flowed through it, in and out with the rhythm of the waves.

"Some kind of cave?" guessed Gussie.

Ellie shrugged. "Whatever it is, I think it must run underneath the prison. See?"

She pulled herself onto a rock and kicked a pile of trash that had accumulated in the water. Onion skins, old cloths, and other garbage floated there in a gross tangle. Clearly it was waste dumped into the tunnel from inside the prison, which then washed out to sea.

Gussie gave a long sigh as she pulled herself out of the water. "This is going to be gross, isn't it?"

"You can wait here," said Nox. "Really. I'll go in and—"

"We're sticking together," said Ellie firmly, and Gussie and Twig nodded in agreement.

"You're a lunatic," said Gussie. "But you're *our* lunatic. You'll just owe me one."

"Me too," said Twig.

Nox waved his hands. "All right, all right. Look, I'll go into the creepy trash tunnel first, okay?"

"Oh, *that* was never in doubt," said Gussie.

"Can we just go?" asked Ellie. "All it would take is a guard on that cliff looking down, and we'd be stuffed with arrows."

"Lirri doesn't like this place," whispered Twig, patting the warm bulge of fur in his pocket. "It's seen too much sadness."

Nox swallowed. The cliff loomed impassively, as if daring them to try its strength. He set his jaw and waded toward the grate, the water sloshing up to his chest. The bars weren't wide enough for an adult to pass through, but with some effort, Nox managed to squeeze in. Twig and Ellie followed, but Gussie, no matter how she tried, couldn't pull her larger Falcon frame through.

"What can I say?" She shrugged. "I'm built for strength, not stealth."

"It's fine," said Nox. "Lie low and wait for us. We'll try to escape the same way."

She nodded, looking apprehensive. "Be careful. Don't do anything I wouldn't. Which means anything *stupid*."

Nox grinned. "You got it. I'll listen to the little Gussie in my head."

She snorted. "Don't take too long either, okay? I don't like the feel of this wind. Might be a sea squall coming. Oh, and take this. You're lucky it was in my pocket and not my old pack, or it'd be lost with everything else in the mountains."

It was one of her newest inventions—the illuminator, a little glass bottle filled with chalky liquid. Nox took it carefully, giving her a sincere look in thanks. He knew how much her inventions meant to her, and how hard it was for her to part with any of them.

When he shook the bottle, the liquid inside began to glow softly.

Nox led the way through the tunnel, at times wading, at times swimming when the floor dropped away. It seemed like a natural feature of the island, the walls uneven and the passage twisting, with many little tunnels branching away, far too small for them to fit through. Gussie's illuminator was their only light, and Nox was glad for it. The bottle's glow was just strong enough to see a few steps ahead, and to warn them of any low-hanging rocks so they could duck in time.

"Look," said Ellie. "Light."

They passed under a small, round grate, the holes in it not even large enough to put a finger through. Then they began passing more of them, and above some, they heard heavy breathing, footsteps, or muffled sobs.

"These must be the cells," whispered Ellie.

"Yes," said Twig faintly.

Nox turned at the quiver in the boy's voice and saw Twig's eyes were huge, his skin pale.

"What is it?" he asked.

"I . . . I can feel them. I'm not even trying to. It's just . . . their feelings. They're so *loud*."

Nox had suspected for a while that Twig's ability to understand animals' feelings might also work on people, but this was his first real confirmation of the fact. Ellie, who looked unsurprised, put her arm around Twig.

"Do you need to go back?" she asked.

He shook his head. "I want to help. If we can get Nox's mother out . . . it'll be enough to know that's one less person suffering up there."

They continued on, moving slowly so the sound of the ripples they made wouldn't alert anyone above.

"You realize what those drains are, right?" said Ellie. "I mean . . . there's only one reason they'd put them in the cells."

"I was *trying* not to think about it," Nox groaned.

"Just watch out for any, um, sudden waterfalls, is all I'm saying."

Nox winced.

He wondered how he'd know when he'd passed under his mother's cell. Had he already walked within inches of her without knowing it? Was one of the sobbing voices hers? If he did find her, then what? They couldn't fit her through those tiny drains.

There was nothing for it but to keep going and hope the answer would present itself.

And then, all at once, it did—when Nox heard his own name echoing in the tunnel ahead.

"Tell me where Tannox would go, what relatives he might hide with. Tell me, woman, or I'll have your rations suspended for a week!"

"W-who . . ." replied a weak voice. "Who is Tannox?"

Nox stopped so quickly that Ellie walked into him.

There was another opening in the roof of the tunnel ahead, still too small to fit through and offering only a narrow view of the room above.

Nox's heart pounded.

He didn't want to take another step.

But he couldn't stop himself.

Sliver by sliver, the room came into view. First there was a stone wall with manacles dangling along its length. Then there was a torch burning by an iron door.

Then he saw a chair and, in it, a small, skinny woman with ratty gray hair and tattered clothes.

Standing over her was a familiar soldier.

The Stoneslayer, Ellie mouthed.

Their old enemy. The Stoneslayer was one of King Garion's top generals, whom Nox had stolen the skystone from two months ago. He was the one who'd recognized Ellie and had her thrown into the king's dungeon after the Race of Ascension.

And now he was interrogating Nox's mother.

Threatening her.

"This is your last chance, woman!" the general roared, lifting his closed fist. "Tell us where that scum boy of yours has hidden himself, or—"

Nox's heart erupted, releasing a surge of hot, angry blood that rose to his ears and cheeks, and before he knew it, he was bellowing into the cell.

"Leave her alone, you beast! I'll tear you apart!"

His mother started, and the Stoneslayer's eyes snapped to the drain, locking with Nox's.

"Nox, no!" Ellie hissed, grabbing his shoulders and trying to pull him back. It took her and Twig working together to finally wrench him away—just a moment before the Stoneslayer's boot came down on the drain.

"Aha!" he laughed. "You fool boy! You couldn't have made this easier for me, could you?"

"Nox, we have to go," whispered Ellie, pulling at him urgently.

He was seeing red. He couldn't think beyond the need to burst through the floor and throw himself on the man who dared threaten his mother. In the back of his mind, he knew he was being stupid, that he was blowing the whole plan out of the water. But his anger burned so hot, it was like flames were rising in his throat. If he only breathed them out, he would burn down the whole island.

"Nox!" Ellie slapped his cheek in a desperate bid to get his attention.

It worked.

He blinked, then looked at her in horror. "Uh-oh."

"Uh-oh is right! Nox, we have to go *now*!"

He looked back once, to catch a glimpse of his mother. Her face was turned toward him, her eyes wide and as dark as his own. He saw her mouth his name.

She does remember me! he thought.

Then the Stoneslayer's voice rang out. "Sound the alarm! Turn out the guard! There are intruders on the island—they're in the tunnels!"

As Nox, Ellie, and Twig raced back the way they'd come, the sound of clanging bells broke out overhead and echoed through the tunnel. Even if they reached the exit, there would be guards waiting for them.

They were trapped.

CHAPTER SEVEN
· ELLIE ·

Ellie was angry. *Furious.*

Not at Nox. Yes, he'd blown their mission and was likely about to get them all captured, but she couldn't say she wouldn't have done the same thing in his place.

No, she was angry at everyone else.

The king for hunting them.

The Stoneslayer for hurting Nox's mother.

This awful, evil place for the pain and sorrow it inflicted.

And she was angry at herself, for not thinking of a better plan. For letting them attempt this impossible quest in the first place.

But Ellie had never been one to waste time second-guessing. She was a girl of action, and girls of action handled trouble as it came, one step at a time.

Right now her steps propelled her as fast as she could go, which wasn't fast at all given they were wading through waist-deep salt water. Nox and Twig sloshed behind her, panting hard.

She had Gussie's illuminator in hand; Ellie wondered if Nox even realized he'd dropped it in the water when he'd gone into his rage. Now she held up the glowing bottle and led them through the last few twists and turns in the sea tunnel. Only when she saw the glint of daylight ahead did she pocket the light.

"C'mon, c'mon," she muttered, still hoping against hope they might make it out before the guards closed in on the tunnel entrance.

They didn't.

Just as they wriggled through the bars on the drainage gate, five men dropped from the rocks above, grinning as the three kids rushed straight into their hands.

Ellie squirmed and bit down on any flesh or feathers she could find. One guard howled and let go of her while another grabbed her around the waist and pulled her lockstave from her hand. Nox was snagged by his wing, and Twig squealed as another guard wrapped an arm around his neck, putting him into a headlock. Gussie was already caught, her mouth covered by a guard's hand, her arms twisted behind her back.

Still Ellie struggled. She went limp, momentarily catching the guard off balance, and dropped into the water. He still had hold of her, but when she came up she had a mouthful of salt water in her cheeks, which she spat into the man's eyes.

He cursed, and his grip loosened enough that she was able to wrench free and throw herself sideways, crashing into the guard holding Nox. The man fell easily, losing his footing on the slippery rocks.

Nox and Ellie both shot into the air.

They rose in a flurry of wings, spiraling around each other, shooting above the cliffs and the prison. For the first time, Ellie got a good look at the place. It was as ugly as she'd suspected, a windowless gray monolith.

"They're not chasing us," she said.

The guards below were watching them, pointing, but none had taken off.

Then she heard the first hissing arrow as it whistled toward them.

Ellie threw herself into a barrel roll—a narrow miss.

The Stoneslayer stood atop the prison roof with a score of guards, all of them holding crossbows.

"Get out of range!" she shouted to Nox—only to turn and see he was already speeding away.

Toward a dark thunderhead cloud that had appeared on the eastern horizon.

"NOX!" She hurried after him, another arrow shooting past her ear. "What are you doing?"

"Keeping—my—promise!" he panted.

"They've got an entire army down there!"

"Then we need an army too!"

"What—" She cut herself off with a yelp as an arrow nicked her calf, scratching her but not impaling. Still. *Way* too close a call.

She dove, flying evasively. A moving target was hard to hit, especially if it was zigzagging erratically. But when she glanced up, Nox wasn't following suit.

Instead, he was aiming for the storm cloud on the horizon as if it were a safe harbor.

Bewildered, Ellie followed, still dodging and weaving. She glanced back in dismay at Gussie and Twig, who were held captive, and hoped they didn't think she was abandoning them. But she couldn't do much without Nox to help her, and right now he was speeding away like his wings were on fire.

"Nox, wait!"

Did he even hear her? What was he doing? What had he meant by *an army of our own*?

"Nox! Don't you see that storm! It'll be full of—"

She stopped in midair, her wings flaring.

Oh skies.

She suddenly realized what he meant to do.

And just what *army* he meant to summon.

"NO!" she screamed.

He flew on, heedless.

Gritting her teeth, Ellie hovered in the air, looking from Nox to the prison, to their two friends still held by the guards. The Crow had lost his mind, that was certain. He was going to get them all killed. This wasn't what Ellie had signed up for.

But Nox was her friend.

She couldn't let him fly straight into death, not when he wasn't thinking clearly enough to realize how stupid this new plan was.

So she put on a burst of speed, wishing she had her lockstave. How quickly she'd grown used to its weight, the comforting sturdiness of it in her hand.

The wind rolling off the storm washed over her in a sudden gust, and she rolled with it, the way Charlo had taught her in the mountains. *Don't fight the wind. Use it.*

Even when it was blowing against her, it could be ridden. She tacked, wings stretched wide, weaving right and left like a pendulum. The wind lifted her higher, and in this way, she caught up to Nox, who was still struggling headlong against the gale.

"Turn back now," she said. "Please, Nox. This is insane!"

"*You* go back. You'll only get hurt."

"Your mother wouldn't want this!"

"I'm getting her out of there, whatever it takes. Go back, Ellie!"

He was as determined as she'd ever seen him. There'd be no pleading or reasoning with him in this state. She could either turn back . . . or go with him, and try to save his stupid neck anyway.

With a frustrated groan, she kept pace with him as the storm's winds strengthened.

So this was what Gussie had meant by a *sea squall*.

The cloud over the sea was unlike anything Ellie had seen on land. The whole of the thunderhead rose in front of them, its dark depths flashing and groaning. Rumbles of thunder rolled through the sky, vibrating in Ellie's rib cage. Like a living beast, the storm moved on legs of lightning, crawling over the choppy skin of the sea.

This was total madness.

But Nox flew on, as if in a trance. And Ellie, her pulse hammering in her ears, followed.

She'd once heard an old story that claimed the gargols were created when lightning struck rock. She'd never really given that idea much credence—until now. There was no denying the raw power of that storm.

"Enough, Nox! *Please.*"

She looked back to see herself entirely enveloped by the storm. Dark gray swirls billowed and curled all around, deepening until it was as dark as night. Strobes of lightning flared within the knots of cloud, some so near to Ellie that she felt the energy on her skin, pulling the hairs on her arms and head until they stood on end. Stinging threads of rain lashed her face, and the wind buffeted her until she lost all sense of up and down.

With a panicked start, she realized she'd lost sight of Nox.

Screaming his name did no good; the storm swallowed her voice and spat back crashes of thunder.

Then she heard the screeches.

It was impossible to tell where the sounds came from, but there was no denying the source: *gargols*.

They were here, all right, enraged and shrieking. When she heard the thump of stone wings to her left, she gasped and wheeled away, into a powerful updraft that caught her wings and catapulted her high into the storm's crown.

Ellie fought to stabilize herself, her wings frantically pumping, but this was no mountain wind to be ridden. It was a beast in and of itself, a leviathan of air, tossing her about as if she were no more than a leaf. Helpless, she tumbled and twisted, blown this way and that, her wings burning from the strain of trying to fight the gale. It had her in its teeth and dragged her as it pleased.

Then, for a brief pause, all went still. She hovered helplessly in the air, walls of wind and cloud shifting around her. There was no escape from the storm, no clear path ahead. She looked about her, wings beating in desperation.

Only to see a small, soft light drifted toward her out of the tempest.

A moonmoth.

Ellie stared in bafflement at the delicate creature as it fluttered across her path; she'd only ever seen the rare creatures twice before. The moment felt impossible and dreamlike, with the storm raging all around. What was it doing here? How had it survived the storm? Where was it *going*?

The next moment, with a mighty roaring gust, the wind tossed her backward. She lost sight of the moonmoth and slammed into something solid.

Wheezing as the air was crushed from her lungs, she dropped onto bare rock, landing on her hands and knees. She immediately pulled in her wings to keep them from catching the wind. But as she fought for her breath, unmoving, she realized the air was different here, wherever she was. The wind was less intense, and the rain had stopped lashing her skin.

The solid thing she'd crashed into rose behind her, firm and tall. She felt for it in the gloomy light and stared.

"What the . . . ?" Ellie pushed herself up on wobbly legs, finding she could stand here without being blown over.

The thing was a pillar, white stone veined with gray, and atop it, there might have once been a statue, but now it was only broken, jagged rock.

Had she been blown clear to the shore? Or was this some part of the Crag she hadn't noticed?

The ground below was covered in damp moss and slabs of marble, as if it had once been a grand street. But she could see no farther than that; the clouds were thick as drapes in all directions, obscuring everything outside five paces. She took a few halting steps, her mind spinning, and then a powerful gust of wind blew overhead. Shrinking back against the marble pillar, she watched as the gale parted the clouds for a moment.

Ellie gasped.

An entire *city* rose before her.

Buildings of stone and brick towered atop hills, gaping windows like black eyes, towers broken in half, walls crumbling. Spires pierced the sky and statues stood proudly upon pedestals, though they'd been so worn down it was impossible to tell whether they were meant to be people or animals. Vines and moss grew over everything, hungrily devouring walls, seeping out of doorways.

A flash of light caught her eye, and she turned to stare at a tall tower to her right, more intact than the others. In an open chamber ringed with columns, there stood a man, his arms raised, blue light glowing all around his form. He moved strangely, in stiff, jerky motions.

Ellie took a step forward, staring hard, trying to make sense of it all.

"Ellie!"

Whirling, she spotted Nox standing some distance away, his hair and wings ruffled. He didn't seem to have noticed the man.

"Nox!" she called. "Look out!"

She pointed at the man, who now turned at the sound of her voice.

Ellie recoiled.

He was made of *stone*. From head to toe, he was a statue sprung to life, made of the same gray rock as the gargols. Even his eyes were like the monsters', icy blue skystones.

He saw Ellie and opened his mouth. No voice came out but a roar like thunder, and then he thrust his hands toward her. Lightning cracked around him in a brilliant flash, and in that brief, fierce illumination, Ellie saw them—the gargols.

They bristled on every building, crept over the leaf-strewn earth toward her. Some hovered high in the air, their great wings generating downdrafts that ruffled the leaves on the vines and trees.

There were *hundreds* of them.

Then the wind struck her.

Pouring from the stone man's hands, it crashed into her like falling boulders, hurling her backward. Her feet left the ground, and then she tumbled up and over the edge of a cliff, and fell.

Ellie twisted, trying to unfurl her wings, but she was falling too fast, the strange wind still pressing on her chest as if it meant to slam her into the ground. She could do nothing against it.

Above her, the city shrank into the sky, and below it hung enormous cliffs. It was like an entire mountain suspended up there, upside down, the peak pointing toward the sea below, the city resting on its base. And jutting from the hanging cliffs in massive, angular slabs—*skystone*.

Not the small, polished gem that hung around Nox's neck, the kind she'd seen in the faces of the gargols. These were monoliths the size of hills, glowing faintly blue and coursed with bright veins.

Of course, Ellie thought. *Skystone floats.*

All this she saw in an instant, before the city vanished, along with the great slabs of skystone, swallowed up by the clouds.

Now terror and panic clawed in Ellie's chest. She struggled with all her strength until finally she twisted free of the wind's grip. Tumbling head over heels, she opened her wings and used every technique she knew to get control of her body.

At last, her feathers flared and she steadied herself, legs and arms locked. Ellie soared in a straight line, knowing whatever direction she was flying, she'd have to eventually escape the storm.

And whatever—whomever—lurked inside it.

She knew now she wasn't back on land, or on some island. She was still in the storm, had never left it. Which meant only one explanation: The city of gargols, the stone man—they were *in* the storm, riding it atop a huge floating island like a ship on a wave.

Ellie had seen such a thing before, the last time she'd encountered gargols in a stormy sky. But that time had been so brief she'd thought it was her imagination and hadn't even told her friends about it.

This time, there was no denying the truth of her own eyes.

Now, however, was not the moment to ponder what it all meant. She was still in terrible danger, and there was no sign of Nox anywhere. Had he escaped the gargol city?

The clouds began to thin around her, lightening as she neared the edge of the storm. The wind's strength lessened enough that she could maneuver a bit more easily, and she turned to glide upside down in order to scan the sky for any sign of the Crow boy.

Instead, she saw gargols.

They were streaking after her in a V formation, a dozen or so of them all together, stone wings taut on the wind, skystone-blue eyes burning with killer instinct.

Turning over again, Ellie swallowed.

Had they followed her from the city? Had the stone man sent them?

It didn't matter.

Whatever the case, they were death, and she was their prey.

Ellie put on a mighty burst of speed while fighting to conserve energy. Her battle with the storm had left her exhausted and aching, but a new surge of terror-fueled adrenaline flushed her body. Three hard wing beats, *glide*, three wing beats, *glide*. She flew faster and faster as the clouds melted away and she streaked through open sky.

The sea glittered far below, and in the distance sat the Crag on its heap of rock. She angled for it, her heart in her throat, her every thought bent toward one purpose: *faster!*

Nox dropped out of the storm like a stone, spreading his wings just before he hit the water. The sea tossed in waves like mountains, rolling heaps of water that threatened to drown him if he didn't gain altitude. Flying desperately, his left wingtip tracing a wall of water, he lifted higher until he finally shot over the crest of the wave.

Then he spotted Ellie.

The Sparrow was diving from the sky above with a dozen gargols speeding behind her. Nox fought to catch up, lifting over another wave's peak. He kept his eyes on Ellie as she pulled free of the storm and turned to a silhouette against the pale-blue sky beyond. She flew like an arrow, straight and true, aiming for the Crag. But the gargols were gaining on her.

His heart knotted in his throat.

Nox had drawn her into this.

It was supposed to be *him* leading the gargols back to the prison, not her. She should have listened to him and stayed behind instead of throwing herself into danger right along with him. But then, was he really surprised? Ellie was not one to shy away when things got hard. And she was the stubbornest person he knew.

He would never catch up to her now, not with his clipped wing, but at least he knew where she'd go. So he focused on reaching the Crag, soaring over the angry sea with long, steady wing beats.

I'm coming, Ma.

When he finally reached the island, he found a bitter fight raging between the guards and the gargols dropping out of the sky. Landing on the top of the prison, Nox dropped to his knees and panted for breath. His lungs and wings ached and he felt he might never have the strength to fly again.

But where were Gussie, Twig, and Ellie?

Breathless with horror, he sprinted to the edge of the roof to stare down at the rocks where Gussie and Twig had been held.

No one was there. He saw only a faint shine where the contents of the illuminator were smeared across a wet stone. It must have been smashed in the scuffle.

"TWIG!" he shouted, his voice hoarse. "Gussie!"

Spotting a patch of dark hair floating in the water, he dove at once, his heart stopping. He grabbed it, pulling up the lifeless face of a guard. The man's neck had been slashed by gargol claws.

Relief hit Nox like a punch to the gut. It wasn't one of his friends. He dropped the man with a cringe, wiping his hand on his pants leg.

Then the bone-shattering screech of a gargol above spurred him to his wings again. Sick with worry, he flew desperately over the water, searching.

His reckless plan had led a horde of murderous gargols right to his friends. What had he been thinking? What if they were—

"Nox!"

Wings flaring, Nox slowed and looked up.

Ellie appeared on the rooftop above him, with Twig and Gussie beside her. Nox felt a dizzying rush of relief to see her unharmed. The Sparrow had gotten her lockstave back, he noticed, and her windblown hair stuck out in all directions.

"You *idiot*!" Ellie cried as she threw her arms around Nox and hugged him tight. He went stiff, surprised. Hugs were . . . not his thing.

"You're the dummy who followed me," he said. "I told you to go back!"

"Did you see it?" she asked. "The city in the sky, Nox! The floating island, it—"

"We'll talk about that later. What's going on here?"

"Your disaster of a plan is . . . working," Gussie said dryly. "The guards forgot all about me and Twig the minute they saw Ellie leading the gargols here. Thanks for the *warning* about that, by the way."

"Right, um. Sorry." Nox looked across the prison roof, to where the Stoneslayer and the guards were frantically firing their crossbows at the monsters. Undeterred, one of the gargols swooped in and grabbed a guard, pulling him up into the air before dropping him into the sea.

"Retreat!" the Stoneslayer bellowed. "Get inside!"

Nox turned to the others. "If most of them are out here—"

"—then the prison's open and unguarded," finished Gussie.

"Let's go!"

They sprinted, then launched into the air, landing in front of the prison's great doors. One man stood on guard duty, wide-eyed and trembling as he clutched his crossbow.

"S-stop!" he stammered.

"Gargol!" Nox shouted. "Coming this way—watch out!"

The man started, his eyes going skyward, and Ellie took the chance to swing her lockstave. It clocked the man's head, and he dropped at once, unconscious.

"Sorry!" Ellie said, wincing. "Sorry sorry sorry—"

"Come *on*." Nox shoved open the heavy prison door, just as the Stoneslayer and the rest of the guards landed behind them.

"Stop!" roared the general. "You vermin—"

Nox slammed the door shut and Gussie pulled down the heavy beam that locked it in place. The guards outside began pounding on the door, and then came the shrieks of the pursuing gargols.

The angry shouts turned to screams.

"Oh no . . ." whispered Ellie. "Those poor people."

Nox looked at Ellie's pale face. "There could be other ways in. We have to hurry."

"I'll wait here," said Twig, who looked sick to his stomach. "I can't . . . the sadness is too strong."

Gussie put an arm around him. "I'll stay with him."

Nox nodded. "You coming, Ellie?"

"Yeah," she said faintly, still looking torn about leaving the guards outside.

Nox didn't feel bad, at least not terribly so. Those people had kept his mother locked up and starved for years. They deserved whatever they got.

Taking a lit torch from the wall, he led the way deeper into the prison, through several stone rooms that must have been the guards' barracks and dining hall. Slippery steps led downward to the first level of cells.

Nox knew his mother must be on the lowest level, since they'd seen her from the tunnels below the prison. Skipping the next three floors, he only stopped when the stairs ran out.

"She's here, somewhere," he said.

"Let's split up," said Ellie, taking down another torch.

Going left, Nox wandered down row after row of cells. The rooms were tiny, dark, and reeked of filth and sweat. Voices cried out; hands pushed through bars in the doors, pleading. Some of them spoke in languages Nox didn't even recognize. The corridors were littered with dirty straw and feathers.

He tried not to look too closely into each cell. The faces and bodies inside were emaciated. Some looked like they'd been there for decades, with hair grown to their knees and wings nearly bare of feathers. He fought down nausea, tears burning in his eyes as he thought of his mother locked in this horrible place.

Finally, he came to the last corridor, where he stopped in his tracks. A sign had been nailed to the wall over the entrance.

WINGROT ROW: PROCEED WITH CAUTION.

Nox's throat closed. He rubbed the wooden grip of the torch, fighting the urge to run back the way he'd come, to shut all of it out.

Maybe she was on the other end of the floor, where Ellie was searching. Maybe he'd already passed her cell without realizing it.

Or maybe she was down this corridor, in the dark.

He forced himself forward. The smell here was worse, and he raised his scarf over his nose. In the first cell, he saw a man crumpled on the ground, his wings withered, his dropped feathers piled under his head in a macabre version of a pillow.

The rest were all the same: wings shriveled, feathers gone, skin gray and scaly. Some were worse off, their fingers and toes black and their breathing labored.

Wingrot.

Every one of them was infected with wingrot.

Nox had seen people afflicted with it before, but not this badly. They all seemed to be in an advanced stage of the illness.

One cell was larger than the rest; he could tell by the wider door leading into it. He stopped there, his heart clenching, eyes shut. He knew even before he looked that this was it—this was his mother's cell.

Her voice came wavering out of the dark. *"Nox?"*

The sound jolted him into motion. He'd brought a pair of iron pins he'd found on the trader's boat, which he used to pick the lock, then he stepped in cautiously. A bracket waited on the inner wall, and he placed the torch in it.

"Ma," he whispered.

She was on her knees, too weak to stand. He dropped down in front of her, his hands shaking as he took hers.

"It's really you," she murmured, her eyes squinting as she studied his face. "I thought . . . when I saw you through the drain . . ."

"I'm here, Ma. I promised I'd get you out, remember?"

She shuddered and leaned into his shoulder. He realized with shock that he was now taller than she was. This wasn't the woman he remembered. His mother had been tall and laughing and bright when he'd seen her last. The person he now held was like a ghost, barely held together by the dingy fabric of her prison uniform. He could feel her ribs.

"My boy." She ran her hands over his face, his hair. "So big and grown and strong. So like your father. Are you real? What are you doing in this awful place?"

"I'm getting you out of here. I'll carry you if I have to."

He put his arms around her and felt the twisted jut of her wing bones. Stomach churning with dread, he lifted his head to look.

Her feathers were gone. Her wings were crumpled against her back like broken sticks, the skin gray as ashes.

"It's all right," he whispered. "It's all right, Ma, I can fix you. See?"

He took the skystone from his shirt, and his mind flashed back to the island in the sky, floating on its glowing mountain made of the same stuff as this little rock.

"It'll help you," he said, pressing the skystone into her hand and gently curling her fingers over it. Hers were an old woman's hands, veiny and gnarled, though she wasn't much older than thirty.

Hearing a soft footstep behind him, Nox glanced over his shoulder to see Ellie had found them. She stood in the doorway, eyes wide.

"We don't have much time, Nox," she said softly.

"She just needs to be a little stronger," he said. "The stone will help. See?"

When the stone began to glow, it shone through her papery skin. Nox held his breath, his lips parting in a smile.

"It's working! It's . . ."

The stone began to flicker, then fade, going dark again.

"What? No. No, it's going to work. Just wait. I've seen it work before, Ma. I've seen it heal people."

“Nox . . .” she whispered.

He rubbed her hands. Were they too cold? Had the stone run out of power? He thought of the floating island, of all those enormous sky-stones holding it up, and cursed himself for not grabbing a piece.

“Please. *Please.* This has to work!”

“My boy . . .” His mother smiled weakly; she was so frail she was barely able to sit up. “I feel it in my lungs. Around my heart. I know what’s coming. I’ve made peace with it. I just didn’t expect this mercy, to see you one more time. But you must go, before they find you.”

“No. No no no no *no.* Ellie!” He whirled. “Why isn’t it working?”

She dropped her gaze. “Maybe . . . there’s a point where even the stone isn’t enough.”

“You’re supposed to be the one who believes in destiny and fate and all that!” he cried out. “So tell me what this is! I happened to find the one thing in the world that can save her, and it won’t work? What kind of destiny is *that*?”

“I don’t know.” A tear rolled down her cheek. “I don’t understand either.”

“Tannox.” His mother let the stone fall into his palm and put her hands on his cheeks. “My beautiful son. I’m sorry I can’t be stronger.” Her eyes moved over his shoulder, to Ellie. “What a brave girl. I can see the sunlight in you . . . Take care of my boy, will you?”

From the corner of his eye, Nox saw Ellie nod, her cheeks wet.

“Stop that. You’re coming with us,” Nox said firmly. “If this stone won’t work, we’ll get another. If that doesn’t work, I’ll find the best doctor in the world. I’ll fix this. I’ll make everything the way it was.”

“Oh, son . . .” She ran a trembling hand through his hair, the way he remembered her doing when he was very small. “We cannot move forward if we keep trying to go back.”

“I don’t want to move forward. Not without . . . I made a promise.”

“Listen to me, Nox. You must listen to me now.” She held herself up, as if pulling on the last bit of strength in her body. "They're hunting for you. The king must know who you are. Which means it's time to fly."

"With *you*, Ma. I'll only go with *you*."

"You'll go to the far south, to the jungle. There is a city there, Khadreen, where your father has some family. We should have gone to them years ago . . . We were fools. You mustn't make that mistake. Fly south, my heart."

She sagged, as if this speech had wearied her, emptied her of words.

"You . . . mustn't blame yourself." Her voice was fading. *She* was fading. "Don't . . . let your heart go cold. You are so like . . . your father . . . a flame . . . in the darkness."

Behind him, Ellie sucked in a breath.

Nox held his mother as she slipped to the floor, felt the strength draining from her body. He sobbed, the hot tears he'd been holding back now running from his eyes. His mother weighed less than Twig; he pressed her against him, as if some of his life might pour into her. But she only wilted in his arms. Her frail fingers traced the worn seam in his vest, until he pressed the skystone into her palm again. But she lacked the strength to grip it, even when he held her fingers closed for her.

"Ma." He shut his eyes and leaned his forehead against hers, willing time to turn back. For his mother to be herself again, lively and dancing in the kitchen while his father played his accordion. He remembered her fingers, deftly braiding dough into his favorite sugar loaf. He remembered her cutting his father's ruined work shirt, saving one crimson strip, which she tied around Nox's neck for a scarf—the same scarf he still wore.

When he opened his eyes again, she was gone.

Nox stared at her face, her delicate eyelids, and forgot everything else. He stared and didn't understand.

A hand closed on his shoulder. Ellie's voice reached him as if from across a great distance. "I'm so sorry. Oh, Nox. We have to go."

"Get away from me," he whispered.

She didn't let go. "I know it hurts. Believe me, *I know.* But we can't help her anymore."

"I made a *promise.*"

"So did I, to my parents, that I'd become a Goldwing knight, whatever it took. And I broke that promise, for you and Gussie and Twig." Ellie pushed her face in front of his, her nut-brown eyes blurry with tears. "Because that's what we *do*, Nox. We keep fighting: for the living, *because* of the dead."

"Don't say that word!" he shouted. "Don't you touch her!"

She stiffened. "I hear footsteps. They're coming."

"Then go, Ellie. Escape without me. I don't care—I'm not leaving."

Her grip tightened on his shoulder, then she let go and stood. He turned his face away, glad for it, wishing she'd just leave him alone. Save herself. Leave him to the Stoneslayer.

After all, what was the point of surviving now? What did *he* have to fight for? His only purpose was lying in his arms, emptied of meaning.

But instead of running, Ellie crossed the room and sat cross-legged in front of him, her eyes steady. "If you stay, I stay."

"What? Ellie—"

"That's the deal."

"You can't do this to me! It's not fair!"

"No, it's not. None of this is. If things were fair, she'd be alive. We wouldn't be criminals. My parents would be here. If things were fair, Nox, we wouldn't have to fight. But they aren't fair, and they won't be until we *make* them."

"Will you just *leave*?" he howled.

"No."

Nox stared at her, exasperated, furious. He felt the sudden urge to scream, to punch, to tear down the walls.

Didn't she understand?

He'd broken his promise.

The one and only purpose he had was gone. *This* was supposed to be his story: saving his mother, taking her far away to someplace safe. Fixing what had been broken in his world.

And now he'd failed, this time for good.

He was in free fall, wings snapped, tumbling through empty sky. Didn't Ellie see that? Ellie, with her stupid, naive need to save everyone—didn't she see that there was nothing left in him to save?

"What's it going to be?" she asked calmly.

He heard the footsteps now, moving fast, getting closer.

"I hate you," he said.

Ellie nodded.

Nox snarled. "You're as bad as the Goldwings and all the rest. You think you're so brave and noble. But you just want to be in control of everyone else, including me."

Ellie reached out. "Let go. Take my hand."

He looked down at his mother, pressed his fingertips to her cheek.

Then, next thing he knew, he was standing, Ellie gripping his arm. She pulled him out the door, and he felt such a flood of shame that he couldn't look back. Couldn't bear to see how he had left her lying there on the cold stone.

"Nox!" yelled a voice. "Ellie!"

They stepped out of the cell to find not guards with swords, but Gussie and Twig, breathing hard. Twig took one look at Nox, and his face fell.

"Oh, Nox," he said softly.

"They broke through the front door," panted Gussie. "We were searching everywhere . . . of *course* you had to be . . . on the bottom floor!"

"We're trapped?" Ellie asked.

"Not yet. I found a map of the prison. There's a back exit on this level. But we have to hurry." Gussie's eyes shifted, looking into the cell. Her gaze widened. "Oh. Oh, no. Nox, I—"

"Let's go," said Ellie, pushing them all along. "We have to outfly not just the guards, but the storm too."

"They're here!" Twig called. "Run!"

He and Gussie took the lead, but Ellie had to grab Nox's hand and pull him along. Behind them, guards rounded the corner, ablaze with torches. The general led them.

"Stop!" ordered the Stoneslayer. "Or we'll shoot!"

Nox looked back just as the first crossbow fired.

A blinding pain struck him in the chest, catapulting him into Ellie. He gasped, seeing stars.

"Nox!" Ellie screamed. She kept dragging him along, while he teetered on the brink of unconsciousness. He felt like a sledgehammer had been driven through his rib cage.

But looking down, he saw the crossbow bolt had dropped to the floor. Instead of burying itself in his heart, it had struck the skystone pendant that still hung around his neck, shattering it. Before his eyes, the shards fell free of the iron setting and floated away like glittering glass bubbles.

That was it, he thought deliriously. *My last bit of luck.*

"Nox, keep running!" Ellie urged. "We're almost out!"

The skystone was lost, and Nox let himself be dragged along.

Ellie wanted him to let go?

Fine.

He'd let go of everything. Everything but this: His mother was dead.

And it was his fault.

CHAPTER NINE

· ELLIE ·

It would be a long three weeks.

The cargo hold was roomy, at least, though they had to keep watch for sailors coming down for supplies several times a day. It had been dangerous sneaking onto the trading ship because it had meant flying over open seas at night and landing on the ship when most of the crew was asleep. Then they'd crept down the stairs to hide amid the cargo.

The hold creaked and rolled with the waves, its arched roof supported by large wooden beams. In the back, they'd found crates of cheese, blackberry juice, and other goods, enough to keep them very well fed until they reached the southern jungles. When the others weren't looking, Ellie dropped nearly her entire supply of coins into one of the crates, to assuage her guilty conscience.

As she snacked on a delicious wedge of cheddar, washing it down with juice, she studied the sea chart she had found in a box of navigational equipment. Gussie fiddled with a tin bowl and some needles, trying to make a compass but mostly just groaning as she fought back seasickness. Twig was fast asleep in a crate of hay. A cluster of white candles provided light and could be extinguished in an instant if they needed to hide.

Ellie tossed a crumb of cheese to Lirri in her ongoing mission to win the temperamental little animal over. The marten took the offering but hissed in return.

"Should I check on him?" she whispered to Gussie.

The Falcon girl glanced across the hold at the bundle of dark feathers curled in a sheepskin.

"He hasn't eaten since we landed on the ship," Ellie added. "That was yesterday."

The last time she'd tried to rouse Nox, he'd refused to even open his eyes.

"He'll come around eventually," said Gussie, but she sounded unsure. "Sometimes people just need to be left alone."

Ellie frowned, not sure she agreed. There had to be *something* she could do to make Nox feel better, or at least to get him to eat and talk again. He wouldn't even say how badly his chest hurt from the crossbow bolt that had nearly killed him. He'd been wildly lucky, but there was still a dark purple bruise on his sternum that Ellie knew had to hurt.

The loss of the skystone was a different sort of wound, but she tried not to dwell on that. What was done was done, and besides, she'd rather have Nox alive than the gem intact. Maybe that was selfish, given how many lives the skystone might have saved from wingrot. But even despite the pang of guilt she felt, Ellie would have traded a dozen skystones for Nox's life.

Sighing, she turned back to the chart. With the piece of charcoal she kept in her pocket, she drew an *X* near the unlabeled island of the Crag.

"Do you think the floating city follows the wind currents?" she wondered. "If it does, maybe its course can be charted just like a ship's. You know about all that stuff, right?"

Gussie looked at her a moment, then held up one of the sewing needles. "See this? Let's say this needle represents everything I know about science and the way things work and wind and charts and ships and how cities *don't* float." She flicked the needle, and it went spinning way into the shadows, lost in the depths of the cargo hold. "That's what all of it amounts to if the island you say you saw is real: *nothing*."

"It wasn't just me," Ellie returned. "Nox saw it too. We were both there."

"The realm of gargols," whispered Twig.

Ellie turned to see him still lying in the crate, but now his eyes were wide open, staring at the curved ceiling.

"Maybe," she said. "I mean, it was definitely infested with them. But . . . I never thought of gargols as the type to build anything, much less a whole city. And the place was obviously in ruins—walls falling down, plants growing over it all."

She jumped to her feet and began pacing. "What if that city wasn't the only one? What if there are more of them up there?"

"Then we'd have heard about them," Gussie pointed out. "I've read thousands of books, not just science but history, geography, even legends and myths. And none of them mentioned anything about islands in the sky. Do you really think there could be a whole world up there, just floating around, and *you're* the first person to see it?"

Ellie bristled a bit. "This is also the second *time* I've seen it."

"Right." Gussie lifted a skeptical eyebrow. "The first time, you just forgot to mention it."

"Um. More like you all dumped me in the woods and left before I *could*. What are the odds that the island I saw over Bluebriar Forest and the one we found over the Crag are the same? I know what I saw, Gus. I know it doesn't make sense. But it was real."

"I believe you," Twig piped up.

Ellie sighed. "Thanks, Twig."

He grinned, then stuck a stick of straw between his teeth and lay back, chewing happily. Of all of them, Twig was certainly in the best mood. They were on their way to the southern jungles, the place he'd dreamed of seeing for years—or rather, he'd dreamed of seeing the mysterious *elephant* creatures it supposedly was home to. He'd been the first to agree to Ellie's plan to sail there. Gussie still seemed unsure, while Nox had merely shrugged and gone along with whatever the group decided. He'd barely spoken more than ten words since the Crag, and Ellie wondered if he was still angry at her for forcing him to leave.

But what other choice did they have? The Clandoms weren't safe. They couldn't return to Cloudstone. Right now, the only hope they had was of following Nox's mother's last wish: to find shelter in the south, in the one land they knew of that was beyond King Garion's reach.

Maybe that was where Ellie belonged. Maybe she'd never go home again, and some new life was waiting for her in the hot jungles.

It was hard to imagine.

But with three weeks of sailing still ahead, she had plenty of time to wrap her mind around it. For now, the only thing she could think about, beyond worrying over Nox, was the city in the sky.

"I keep thinking about the Restless Order," she said. "Remember how they always talked about a thing called *Truehome*?"

Gussie looked up, frowning. "So?"

"What if . . ." Ellie paused, then shook her head. The idea forming in her mind was far-fetched and sounded ridiculous even to her. And yet . . . for some reason, her pulse was pounding in her ears. When she closed her eyes, she could see it all again so clearly: the ruined towers, buildings, streets. The glow of the skystones beneath it all.

"We have to go back," Ellie whispered.

Gussie dropped her tin bowl with a clatter. *"What?"*

"C'mon. You can't tell me you aren't a little curious. Gussie . . . this could change everything. Even if it really is just the home of the gargols, if we could learn about it, maybe we could find a better way of fighting them."

"Or talking to them," added Twig.

Ellie glanced at him, startled. That was an idea that had never crossed her mind.

"Maybe," she murmured. "The point is, until we know more, we don't know what's possible. But don't you want to find out? This could be it—the way we *change* things."

"There she goes again," said a dry voice across the hold. They all turned to look at Nox, who'd stood up. His eyes were averted, his hands curled into fists. "Ellie Meadows, on a mission to solve everyone's problems, everywhere."

"That's not fair," Ellie said.

He shrugged and walked closer, picking up a bottle of blackberry juice and drinking deeply. The others watched him in silence, even the candle flames seeming to shrink warily.

"Are you . . . feeling okay?" Ellie asked at last. "Nox, I'm so sorry about what happened. If you want to talk—"

He gave a short, acidic laugh. "I most definitely do not want to talk."

"It wasn't Ellie's fault," Gussie said. "We all did everything we could to help your mother."

"You're right," he said. "It wasn't any of your faults. It was mine."

Taking the juice, he returned to his nest of furs and sat with his back to them.

Ellie and Gussie exchanged looks.

"We've got to get him to Khadreen," Ellie whispered. "Maybe being with his family will help."

Gussie nodded, looking back at Nox with an uneasy expression. "I've never seen him like this before."

"He lost everything he had in one moment," Ellie said.

"He still has us," said Twig.

Ellie nodded but wondered if that was enough. Nox looked haunted, lost. She recognized that emptiness in his eyes because she'd felt it herself, the day she'd given up her dream of being a knight and been thrown into the king's dungeon. And long before that—when her parents had been killed by gargols right in front of her.

Yes, she knew what it was like to feel your world shatter around you.

But she'd pulled herself out of it. She'd found a new purpose in the skystone and the hope it represented—that she could make a difference in the world by healing people with wingrot. But what would save Nox from the darkness inside him?

His mother had asked Ellie to take care of him.

She'd called Nox *a flame in the darkness.*

A cold wind swept through Ellie, making her shiver. Nox's mother's words and Elder Rue's swirled her head like leaves, mingling and merging.

"Ellie!" hissed Gussie. She grabbed Ellie's sash. "Get down!"

With a start, Ellie realized the wind she was feeling wasn't just in her head. It was a draft blown in from the cargo hold doors, where a sailor was descending the steps. Gussie had already blown out the candles, and Twig pulled the lid of the crate he was in over himself.

Dropping down, Ellie crouched between two barrels and quieted her breathing.

The sailor rooted around a crate for a while, found what she wanted, then plopped down to enjoy her spoils—a large flagon of cordial. Suppressing a groan, Ellie wished she'd chosen a more comfortable hiding spot. The sailor was obviously not going anywhere for some time.

It would be a long three weeks.

CHAPTER TEN
· NOX ·

"*O**i!* Stowaways!"

Nox startled awake, disoriented. The floor was rolling—no, the *ship*, he remembered. They were on a ship to the south, following his mother's final wish.

He groaned and sat up, peering at the Albatross clanner looming over him, hands on hips.

"Up with you, lout!" the man growled. "All of you!"

Ellie, Gussie, and Twig hauled themselves up, chagrined. They'd gotten lax about splitting watch duty, as they'd learned the sailors' schedules and found they never entered the cargo hold after dark.

But tonight must have been different.

"We're up, we're up," Ellie said.

"Up on deck," ordered the sailor, roughly shoving Twig toward the stairs. "You'll be lucky if the captain doesn't tie your wings and send you to the sharks!"

Nox glanced at Ellie, who caught his look and returned it with a small nod. As the sailor began walking, Ellie stuck out her lockstave and tripped the man. He fell with a shout, and at once the four of them lifted up and away, slinging packs over their shoulders and flying through the cargo hold to the door.

"Oi!" The sailor cursed as he stumbled up, but Twig had tossed a coiled rope over him, and his legs were tangled. "Stop!"

They raced up the steps, burst onto the deck, and took to the sky.

The other sailors began shouting but were too late to stop them. The foursome rose through the billows of the sails and shot into open air, carried aloft by a strong sea wind. It was predawn, the horizon barely red.

"Land!" Gussie said, pointing.

That must have been why the sailor had been in the hold. They were nearing harbor, making preparations to dock.

A few sailors took off after them, shouting angrily, but didn't give chase for long.

The day was young, the air warm. Nox glimpsed a scattering of white clouds on the far horizon, but otherwise the sky was clear. His wings stretched wide, working out the stiffness of three weeks of disuse. He rued his clipped flight feathers, struggling to balance.

They flew toward the strip of land on the horizon, with the wind swelling under their wings. Twig whooped and began windhopping, shutting his wings and falling from one breeze to another.

At least one of them was glad about their current course.

They landed at last on a shore of white sand, where gentle waves rolled and broke. At the top of the beach, a tall forest rose in a tangle of glossy, broad leaves, palm fronds, and ropy vines. The plants all looked strange to Nox.

"The jungle," said Twig, wide-eyed. "Do you see any elephants?"

Ellie laughed. "Not yet. But we'll keep watch."

"Fascinating," said Gussie, picking up a hard green fruit. "Coconut, I think."

"Well," said Ellie, scanning the trees. "Now we just have to find Khadreen, and your family, Nox."

She gave him a hopeful smile, but he only nodded once and looked away, his stomach turning with a mixture of irritation and nervousness.

It was strange, the idea of there being other Corvains out there. His father had never spoken much of his family, and Nox didn't know what to expect if he did find them. He wasn't sure he *wanted* to. What would they think of him—a thief, a fugitive, a freak, who'd let his mother die in prison, who'd stood uselessly by as his father was executed? Why would they want anything to do with him at all?

Ellie would never understand his worries. She naturally expected the best out of everyone. And if anything went wrong, they could just launch some wild plan to make it all right.

Nox knew now that no matter how hard they tried, some people were born to shatter everything they touched.

The image flashed in his mind: his mother lying broken in her cell while he ran to save his own skin.

Gritting his teeth, he pushed it away.

After taking time to rest their wings, they took off again, this time to fly along the coast. They glided on the shore winds, in search of anything that might point them toward Khadreen.

Even the air in the south felt different, warm and heavy. It smelled sweetly of jungle flowers and salt. The water was so clear that even from the air, Nox could see schools of bright fish darting in the shallows, chased by lithe gray sharks. Farther out, where the water darkened, dolphins leaped and raced, to Twig's overflowing delight. He kept wandering off to explore, catching up only when they were nearly out of sight.

After an hour of searching without finding anything of interest, they landed on the beach to catch their breaths.

"Three weeks of no flying," panted Ellie, leaning on a palm tree, "really throws you out of shape, doesn't it?"

Gussie sprawled on the sand and groaned, but Twig was still out at sea, swooping over the waves to peer at the fish below. Breathing hard, Nox waded into the shallow water and reached down to cup his hands, eager to splash away the sweat on his face.

But just as he reached down, something zinged past his ear.

With a shout, he stumbled back, blinking in confusion at the spear that had sprouted out of the water.

"What the—" Whirling, he looked all around until he spotted her: a slim girl about his own age, standing high above on a leaning palm. She wore a knee-length dress with a tasseled skirt and brightly patterned wraps, her feet shod in scrappy leather sandals with flowers painted on them. Her skin was as brown as the coconuts dangling from the palm, and her black hair swung in dozens of tight braids plaited with ribbons and fresh flowers.

Ellie and Gussie spotted her a moment after, and all three of them gathered quickly, Ellie with her lockstave at the ready, Nox with his slingshot.

"She tried to spear me!" Nox said. "You saw it!"

"Actually," said the girl brightly, "I saved your life."

She jumped down from the tree, spreading the most colorful wings Nox had ever seen. The undersides were brilliant yellow while the top feathers were a shocking clash of scarlet, gold, and cerulean.

The girl swooped over the water and plucked her spear up, then landed in front of them. Impaled on her spear was a wriggling fish with a bulbous, ugly body.

"Stonefish," she said, twirling the spear and the fish stuck on it. "If you'd taken one more step, you'd have cut your foot on his spines, y'know. His venom would've killed you in minutes. Painfully."

Queasily, Nox glanced at the placid clear waters with new respect.

"Thanks," he muttered.

"Who are you?" asked Ellie.

The girl suddenly frowned, her eyes narrowing. She lowered the spear, squirming stonefish and all, toward them. "Depends. How do I know you're not pirates, here to plunder my village and steal our jewels?"

"Um." Ellie shrugged. "Because we're . . . not?"

The girl eyed her a moment, then broke into a wide grin and raised her spear again. "Works for me! And lucky for you because we haven't got any jewels anyway. Though it *would* be exciting to be attacked by pirates, don't you think? I've been practicing with my spear. I'm sure I could take out at least twenty of them all on my own. I mean, did you *see* that throw?" She twirled the speared fish. "Right through the eye! Okay, maybe I got a *little* lucky, actually. I'm not usually on target on the first try. I guess that means *you* got lucky too." She laughed at Nox's look of horror, then paused. "Wait. What were we talking about? Oh yeah! Who *are* you people?"

At that moment, Twig landed on the sand between Nox and the girl, breathless and bright-eyed from chasing dolphins.

The girl gasped. "Whoa! Nice wings."

Twig stiffened. Nox knew he was sensitive about his bicolored wings, which he'd been relentlessly bullied for all his life. But then he remembered Twig once telling him how in the south, bicolored wings weren't considered bad luck, but good. After his initial shock, Twig's pale cheeks flushed red and he grinned shyly.

"Thanks. I'm Twig. That's Nox, Ellie, and Gussie, and *that*... is just cruel." His eyes fell on the speared fish. "Poor thing. He's hurting. You should at least put him out of his pain."

"Oh my skies, you're right! Sorry. My granna says once I start talking, I stop thinking. She's right, y'know. One time I was cutting plantains and chatting with Gade—he's the son of the Quetzal clan chief, *soooo* handsome—anyway, and I didn't even realize I was cutting through the actual table until—oh!" Her eyes went round. "I'm doing it again, aren't I? Wait, what was I gonna do before I started talking?"

Wordlessly, Twig pointed at the fish.

"Oh! Right!" She waded into the water and laid the fish on a rock, then finished it off with a swipe of a small dagger she took from her belt. "That's dinner, then! Yum. Stonefish stew is the *best*, unless you cook it wrong and then, y'know, it'll kill you. Do you guys want to come over for dinner?"

"Uh . . ." Gussie lifted a finger. "You're Macaw clan, aren't you?"

The girl cleaned her blade and sheathed it. "Yep! I'm Tariel. My village is around the bend there. It's called Brightbay. It's the Quetzal clan seat, y'know. Have I told you about Gade? Oh, wait, I did. Anyway, you can meet him when you come for dinner. We're pledged to be married one day, only he doesn't know it yet." She flitted into the air, twirling her spear. "This way! C'mon! Granna will want to start cooking right away when she hears there are guests. Stonefish stew takes *forever*, on account of having to remove the venom and all, but it's worth it! I mean, unless you cook it wrong. Then, well . . . y'know." She put a hand around her throat and mimed choking to death.

With that, she swooped away, darting up the beach on her rainbow wings.

"And I thought *Ellie* talked too much," groaned Gussie, earning a sour look from the Sparrow.

"We're . . . going for dinner, then?" Twig looked flabbergasted.

Nox shrugged. "Guess so."

Brightbay turned out to be a sprawling town of wooden houses with thatched roofs, shaded by tall, tranquil palms. Shrubs exploded with vibrant blossoms in pink and orange, and vines with purple flowers crept up the walls and spied through cloth-covered windows. Between the trees were strung ropes, from which there hung paper lanterns of every color, or bright tassels that shimmered in the breeze. It was so utterly unlike any place Nox had seen, and yet the sounds of the village were familiar: a dozen chattering conversations, the screams and laughter of fledglings testing their wings, the clatter of cookware. In the center of the village a great bed of coals glittered, and over their heat turned several spits heavy with crisping meat.

Many of the residents had the same red, blue, and yellow wings as

Tariel, but he saw snowy whites, dark browns and golds, blacks, pure yellows, and every other hue imaginable. But the most numerous clan represented had to be the Quetzals: glossy emerald and black.

"This way," said Tariel, landing on springy grass. "Everyone will stare at you, but ignore them. They're just being nosy, probably wondering why three northie kids have turned up out of nowhere. Actually, now *I'm* wondering that. Maybe I should have asked that first. Why are you here, anyway?"

"It's a long story," said Ellie. "Let's just say . . . we're on our way to visit family."

Nox felt the stares immediately, and his feathers bristled. They might have been beyond King Garion's reach here, but it still felt wrong to walk straight through a town without any attempt to hide their identities. He'd spent his whole life trying to *avoid* attention, but now there wasn't a pair of eyes that didn't turn his way. Ducking his head, he resisted the urge to draw his wings around his face.

"Cool wings!" shouted a Macaw fledgling, running up to jog beside Twig. "I never saw lucky wings before. Can I touch them?"

Twig blinked, looking stunned. "Uh . . . I guess."

"Don't be rude, Seff!" Tariel ordered. "That's my little cousin Seff. Granna says he has absolutely no boundaries. *I* say he has absolutely no brains. Shove off, Seff, this is important business we're on and these are very distinguished guests."

"Are they northies?" Seff peered closer. "My friend Klo says all northies are kneelers. I don't know what a kneeler is, but it sounds stupid. Are you all stupid?"

"Oh sacred skies, Seff, *go away* or I'll club you with this stonefish!"

With an impish grin, the fledgling scurried off, fluttering his small wings but not quite making it into the air.

"He's the *worst*," complained Tariel. "I'd say he's not always like that, but he's *always* like that. Come on, Granna's place is just over there."

The house she led them to was set between two rows of palms, with a wide front porch and tasseled ribbons strung along its roof. A red dog lay sprawled on the woven mat in front of the door, and Tariel had to push it out of the way with her foot so they could enter. The dog yawned and barely cracked an eye.

"That's Tuber," Tariel said. "Granna says he's worse than useless. She'll be in the back at her wheel. This way!"

As he stepped inside, Nox noticed the ashmark drawn in fresh soot over the doorway; even here, the symbol was used to ward off gargols.

The interior of the house was cool and breezy, with rooms separated by colorful cloth curtains. Mats and cushions on the floor provided seating while the center of the room was dominated by an iron cookstove whose chimney rose to the apex of the domed roof.

Tariel led them through the house and out a back door, where they found a wide awning roofed with palm leaves over a cluttered workspace. Pots, bowls, and plates were stacked at wild, teetering angles, and absolutely everything was spattered with mud—including the round old woman bent over a spinning wooden disk, her foot working quickly to spin another disk below it. Mud caked her arms up to her shoulders, and dried in streaks on her apron and face. Her hands worked a lump of wet clay set on the upper disk, shaping it as it spun round and round.

"Your grandmother's a potter?" asked Gussie.

"Of course!" Tariel shrugged as if that were obvious. "We're Macaw clan. Pottery's our legacy."

"Wow," breathed Twig, his eyes wide with awe. "It's so *messy*. I've gotta try it."

"Granna!" Tariel shouted over the noise of the spinning wheels. "I caught a stonefish for supper! Oh, and I found these lost northies and invited them over."

The old woman looked up, squinting. Her foot fell still and the pottery wheel began to slow. “What’s this?”

Nox braced himself, waiting for her to demand to know who they were, what their business here was, tell them that they weren’t welcome in this place.

Instead, she stood up, spread her plump, muddy arms, and pulled them all into a massive, sticky hug.

“My dears!” she cried. “Welcome, welcome, welcome! Stonefish stew for us all, and if we’re lucky, we might even live through the first bite!”

CHAPTER ELEVEN
· NOX ·

These people were nuts. All of them. From Granna to Tariel to the broody Quetzal clanner Gade and his noisy father and three noisy sisters, who were also, apparently, invited to supper. For good measure, Nox threw Ellie, Gussie, and Twig into his assessment.

All of them were happily tucking into stew made of deadly fish, shoveling it into their mouths as if it were sugared cake. They sat in a circle around the stove in Granna's house, cross-legged on cushions with their bowls lifted to their chins. Gade was a thin, pale boy with long black hair and dark emerald Quetzal wings, and he seemed completely oblivious to Tariel's fluttering eyelashes and wistful sighs as she gazed at him.

"What's wrong?" asked Tariel, pulling her attention from Gade long enough to blink at Nox. "You don't like my granna's stew?"

Every person in the room stopped eating and stared at Nox.

He gulped. "Uh . . . no, it's great."

"Then why aren't you eating it?"

"Uh . . ."

He glanced around till his eyes met Ellie's. She glared and jammed a finger toward her own bowl, then at her lips, in silent command.

Drawing a deep breath, Nox raised the bowl, shut his eyes, and braced himself.

The first taste was . . . salty. Tangy. A little spicy.

Delicious.

And he didn't immediately drop over dead.

Taking that as a good sign, he slurped down the rest of the stew, though every bite of salty white fish meat still went down his throat with a shiver.

"To Nox!" said Tariel, raising her bowl in a toast. "After all, he was the one who found this tasty meal for us. With his *foot*."

The Macaw and Quetzal planners fell into peals of laughter, except for broody Gade, who sighed and gazed off into the corner. Nox's own friends joined in, as if *they* wouldn't have just as easily stepped on the fish.

Nox hid his blush by lifting his bowl up to his nose while he drank.

After dinner, Gade's three sisters—all under the age of ten, each louder and more raucous than the last—dragged Twig outside to show his wings off to everyone they knew. The others followed and watched from the front porch.

Nox had to smile. He couldn't remember the last time he'd seen Twig so deliriously happy. The people of Brightbay treated him like royalty, plying him with snacks and little clay animals in exchange for a chance to admire his bicolored wings.

"Good for him," said Gussie, leaning on the porch rail beside Nox.

"Yeah. He needed this."

"What about you?" asked Gussie. "How are you holding up?"

He shrugged. "We just go where Ellie tells us, right?"

Gussie frowned. "Look, I like Ellie. She's tough and brave and loyal. But she's not our leader, Nox. You are."

"Not anymore. We're not the Talon's crew now, Gus. You don't have to follow me anywhere. All that ended when the Talon betrayed us."

"Nox, did it never occur to you that the reason I followed you in the first place had nothing to do with the Talon . . . and everything to do with *you*?"

He turned to look at her, a little shocked. It was as much emotion as he'd ever seen Gussie display.

"Do you even *want* to meet your family in Khadreen?" asked Gussie.

He stared at the sea glittering below. Sunset had turned the waters bloodred, and the waves broke golden on the sand. All through the village, people began lighting the paper lanterns and tall torches driven into the ground, until Brightbay shone with orange and yellow light. Voices floated on the salty breeze, everyone settling onto porches, hammocks, or mats spread on the grass for an after-dinner laze.

"I suppose I have to," he muttered.

"Because Ellie says so?"

"No . . . well, maybe a little. But also because if I don't, I'll always wonder what they're like."

She nodded.

"What about you, Gus? I haven't forgotten about what your cousin said in Porton. I know you're worried about your little sister."

Gussie's eyes pinched. She was silent a long moment, until Nox thought she wouldn't answer.

But then she said softly, "She's . . . not like me. She cries when she sees a dead butterfly. I should never have left her in the first place."

"You had to do what was right for you. Maybe she's tougher than you think."

He could tell she was unconvinced, but she nodded.

"You're a good person, Nox Hatcher." Then, to his total shock, she reached out and squeezed his hand, only for a heartbeat, before turning and going inside. But coming from Gussie, it was enough to leave Nox speechless.

Even if she was wrong.

"Nox!" Ellie came running up, breathless, with Tariel skipping behind her. "You'll never believe this, but Tariel and her granna are going to Khadreen tomorrow! They said it's only a two days' flight."

"I dunno why you didn't just tell us straightaway that's where you were headed," said the Macaw girl. "We're not *going* to Khadreen, just passing through it on our way to the Clay—that's the Macaw clan seat, out in the western jungle. We're going for my Seed Ceremony. It's a Macaw clan thing, you know, coming of age and all... Big deal actually. You guys should come!"

"Isn't this *perfect*, Nox? It's almost like fate."

"Right," he said, feeling a nervous tug in his gut. He'd imagined there would be more time before he had to face his father's family. But a two days' flight?

Tariel cheered. "Now I only have to convince Gade to come. I just *know* when he sees me become a grown-up he'll finally confess his true feelings for me." She sighed and stared across the green, where Gade slumped against a tree, plucking boredly at some sort of stringed instrument. "Isn't he dreamy?"

"A real charmer," said Ellie, giving Nox a look of suppressed laughter.

"So which one of you confessed love first?" asked Tariel. "It was Ellie, wasn't it? Or does Nox have a hidden romantic side?"

"WHAT?" said Ellie.

Nox blanched. "Oh, we're not—"

"I'm only twelve! And anyway, I'd never—"

"Yeah, I'd rather die!"

Ellie stopped, mouth half open, and looked at him. "You'd rather *die*?"

His face caught fire. "Huh? I mean, I thought we were—I thought you— Oh skies."

"Wow," said Tariel, shaking her head and giving him a look of pity. "You really know how to ruffle a girl's feathers, Crow. If my Gade ever said something so stupid, I'd pour pine sap on his wings while he slept."

"Not a bad idea," muttered Ellie, staring at Nox through narrowed eyes.

He took a step back. "I'm gonna . . . I think I better go."

Hastily taking flight, he perched himself atop a tall broad-leafed tree, only to find it already occupied by a collection of grubby fledglings.

One pointed a wooden sword at him. "Oi! Northie! You wanna sit, you gotta pay the toll!"

Nox laughed. "How much?"

"A million gold bits!"

"Or a plate of Granna's coconut sweets," a little Quetzal girl piped up.

The leader frowned, shoving the sword so it prodded Nox's chest. "Make it a *million* plates!"

The others cheered in agreement while Nox laughed again and raised his hands in surrender. "All right, all right, you—"

He was cut short by a sudden resonating tone that sang through the village. The fledglings all straightened, eyes wide.

"The weather bell," whispered the Quetzal girl.

Another peal rang out, followed by one more.

"Three bells," said the fledglings' leader grimly. "That means big clouds moving fast. We have to go."

They all dove from the tree, flying back to their homes. Below, the people of Brightbay scattered, gathering possessions and herding one another indoors. Nox leaped off the branch and flew higher, into the open sky, and saw the danger the bell had signaled: a massive cloud system was rolling in from the south, over the top of the jungle. A great rush of wind swept toward him, bending the treetops.

Diving to the ground, he dropped onto Granna's porch just as Ellie and the others were going in. Tariel retraced the ashmark over the door with fresh soot.

"Hurry, young ones!" Granna said. "Close the shutters."

The walls of the house, which could be slid open to the warm outside air, were quickly drawn shut and secured. Granna lit lamps of oil in coconut shells and set them around, and they gathered near the center of the house.

Tariel leaned into her grandmother, eyes shut. Nox realized the girl's wings were trembling.

"Shh, little one," Granna murmured, stroking Tariel's feathers. "This will pass. It always does."

Twig put his head on Ellie's shoulder, while Lirri curled in his lap. They sat in silence, listening to the wind grow stronger. The shutters rattled, and something heavy hit the roof, making them jump.

"Just a branch," murmured Granna. "We are safe inside."

Tariel suddenly burst into tears.

"Her parents were killed by gargols," Granna said, patting Tariel's back. "Her mother when she was eight, her father a year later. The clouds come quickly on the coast, and sometimes there isn't enough warning."

Nox glanced at Ellie, remembering that her parents were also killed by gargols. The Sparrow girl's eyes widened, and she scooted to sit by Tariel, wrapping an arm around the girl and whispering something to her. The Macaw girl sniffled, then turned and hugged Ellie.

Granna began to sing, her voice a bit wobbly but her notes sweet.

High above in skies of blue, that is where I once met you.
Where the wind is wild and sweet, there we once spread our wings.
We loved our island in the clouds.

Nox lifted his head, his lips parting slightly as he stared at the old woman.

Fair she was, that land of ours, how her towers touched the stars,
Before the stones rose up to crush, and the lovely voices hushed,
We lost our island in the clouds.

Shifting his gaze to Ellie, he saw the Sparrow staring back at him. She'd heard it too.

"Granna," Ellie said, "that song—what does it—"

SCREEEEECHHHHH!

Tariel shrieked and curled into a ball on the floor as the gargol's scream tore through Brightbay. The thin shutter walls did little to dampen the sound. Lirri vanished into Twig's shirt, and Gussie grabbed hold of his arm. As another scream followed the first—different in pitch, likely from a second gargol—Ellie and Nox jumped to their feet. Ellie had her lockstave in hand, and she gave Granna a worried look.

"It's all right," Granna said, stroking Tariel's hair. "We are safe indoors. We have always been safe indoors. The ashmark protects us."

"They're close," Ellie murmured. "Very close."

A loud crash sounded outside, as if a tree had been knocked over. The wind howled, turning frenzied as it battered the walls and pulled at the thatch. Drafts curled through any opening they could find, and half the coconut lamps flickered out. In the dim remaining light, Ellie and Nox moved closer together.

"Something doesn't feel right," whispered Ellie.

He nodded. He sensed it too—a wildness to the storm, a fury in the gargols' screeches that set his teeth on edge.

"They sound angry," he said. "Well. More than usual."

"We should know." She gave a wry half grin. "We're making a habit of running into them."

"They won't bother us if we're inside."

"I know. But still . . . something's not right."

They flinched as another loud crash sounded nearby, then a whole series of them, grinding, ripping . . . screaming.

"That's not gargols," Ellie gasped. "Someone's out there!"

Nox shook his head, taking the slingshot from his belt. Gussie and Twig stood to join them.

"Don't go outside!" Tariel wailed. "Don't open the door!"

At that moment, the door began rattling as someone pounded on it from the outside.

"Someone needs help!" Ellie cried.

"It could be a gargol's trick!" Tariel said.

"That's not how the creatures work, dear," said Granna. "Quickly, Ellie, let them in."

The Sparrow ran to the door and yanked it open, and three wild-eyed Quetzal girls fell into the house. As Ellie slammed the door shut, the girls ran to Granna, sobbing and unintelligible.

Nox recognized them from dinner—they were Gade's little sisters.

"Calm down, dears!" Granna soothed them. "Tell me what happened."

"It ripped through the roof!"

"It took Papa! And it hurt Gade!"

"Gade told us to run, so we did!"

"Is Papa dead, Granna? Is Gade?"

They dissolved into wails, falling onto the old woman. Granna looked over their heads, her eyes grave.

"This has never happened," she said, looking stunned. "Never."

Nox and Ellie exchanged looks.

So they'd been right. Something was different about this attack.

"No!" Nox said, when he saw Ellie start for the door. "You can't go out there."

"We have to check on Gade."

"No," said Granna firmly. "No one leaves this house. Especially now."

Ellie pressed her lips together, clearly about to argue, but Nox gently put a hand on her shoulder.

"Please," he said. "Not this time, Ellie. *Please.*"

She relented at last, her eyes glittering with tears. Slamming her staff into the floor, she strode instead to the shutters, slipping a finger through them just enough to peer out. Nox leaned over her shoulder to look.

The entire roof of the Quetzal family's house had been torn away and now lay in clumps of thatch, wood, and rope on the ground. The porch roof had partially collapsed, blocking the door.

"Gargols don't *do* that," Ellie whispered. "They just don't. It's . . . it's against everything we know about them. Why are they cheating, Nox?"

"I don't know. Maybe it was one rogue gargol, who doesn't act like the rest. Or . . . maybe they're changing the rules."

She looked up at him, her face set into hard lines. "If that's true, then nowhere is safe anymore."

CHAPTER TWELVE
· ELLIE ·

The following dawn brought a red sky above a village in mourning.

Ellie stood on Granna's front porch, watching the procession of Quetzal clanners laying flowers around the house of their fallen chief. Nox, Twig, and Gussie stood nearby, silent. None of them had slept, but that couldn't fully account for the weariness in Ellie's body.

The Quetzal chief had been found on the shore and carried home to await burial. Gade's sisters sat beneath a palm, surrounded by family and friends. The boy would be named the new chief, Ellie had heard, but not until he'd healed. Apparently the gargol that had torn into their home had ripped off his wings, and he was currently unconscious in the local healer's house.

Ellie gripped her lockstave in her free hand and looked up at the sky. The sun hadn't fully risen yet, and a few wisps of cloud still spread from east to west like streaks of blood.

"So much pain," whispered Twig, trembling. "So much confusion."

Ellie squeezed his shoulders. "I thought you only felt other people's emotions when you wanted to? Can't you shut it out?"

He shook his head. "I can't explain it, but it's been getting stronger. I used to be able to tune it out, but now . . . it's like a song that's always stuck in my head."

His words tickled the back of Ellie's mind.

The rules are changing, she thought. She still wasn't sure what the words meant, or why they kept coming into her mind. What *rules*, really? Who said the gargols had to work a certain way, or that Twig's odd ability to sense emotions couldn't evolve?

But Ellie was full of foreboding, and she felt the same tingle at the back of her neck she got when she was flying, the one that told her the wind was about to change a moment before it did.

Granna's door burst open and Tariel ran out, her face twisted with anger and her colorful wings half spread. Granna was right on her heels, looking tired.

"I'm not leaving!" Tariel shouted. "How can I leave when Gade is lying there hurt? When his father's funeral is tomorrow? How can I possibly care about some stupid ceremony now?"

"Tariel." Her granna took her shoulders. "This isn't just about attending your Seed Ceremony. What happened here is important, do you understand? If the gargols are changing the way they hunt, we have to tell people. The chiefs in Khadreen and the Clay need to know."

Tariel sniffed, looking down at her sandals.

"I know it hurts," Granna said. "But someone has to be the messenger."

Tariel turned away, her wings tight. "At least let me say goodbye."

"Of course."

Tariel flew in the direction of the healer's house. With a sigh, Granna turned to Ellie.

"We're leaving in an hour, if you still wish to travel with us."

Ellie nodded.

They set out quietly, winging away from the sea and over the jungle. For an old woman, Granna set a sprightly pace, and the first few hours passed in silence as they alternated between flight and rest. When they stopped, they drank and ate quickly, staying high in the treetops.

"There are leopards down there," said Tariel the first time they rested, nodding toward the jungle floor. "And snakes. And spiders. Basically lots of ways to die."

"What about elephants?" asked Twig eagerly.

Tariel smiled, but it fell short of her eyes. "They're farther inland, near the mountains."

"Let's keep moving," said Granna.

Ellie could tell the old Macaw was worried. When they'd met her yesterday she'd been bubbly and cheerful. Today her face was grim, and she spoke little. Her mood spread to the others, and they flew in a cloud of tense silence.

An hour to dark, they finally pierced the jungle canopy, heading for a wayhouse Granna said would shelter them through the night.

Ellie could see why they stayed above the treetops; the jungle was nothing like the forests back in the Clandoms. Flying through them was nearly impossible, with all the vines and spreading branches knotting together. It was an impenetrable tangle, which they had to navigate by flitting from branch to branch rather than flying openly. This was a place riotous with life and greenery and strange sounds. The whir of insects was nearly deafening. When Twig spotted a tiny blue frog, he laughed in delight, until Granna snapped at him not to touch it, lest its poisonous mucus knock him flat. He flew more warily after that.

"Here we are," said Granna. "I'd like to see a gargol knock through *these* walls."

She landed on a bank plush with emerald moss, beside a thin, filmy waterfall that sprang out of a high cliff face. Leaning against the cliff, covered in mats of flowering vines, was the wayhouse.

"Oh skies," breathed Ellie, her eyes widening. "Is that . . ."

"Yep. We've seen one of these before," said Gussie.

"It's just like the tower in the woods!" It had been months ago, but she still remembered the strange tower they'd found one night in the forest, when they'd been desperate to escape a rainstorm and any gargols it might hide. There'd been no explanation why a tower might be there, fallen deep into a ravine, and Ellie had barely thought of it since.

But there was no mistaking that this tower and that one—hundreds of miles apart—were made of the same stone, and in the same style. The only difference was that this was vertical, leaning against the mossy cliff.

The interior was also in better shape. Clearly it was used often, because the floor was swept dirt, and a stack of firewood had been set against the wall. Like the other tower, its interior woodwork had long since rotted away, so where there may once have been a winding staircase and many floors above, there was now only a cavernous cylinder of stone, broken by a few small windows that let in thin rods of sunlight. The whole place hummed gently with the sound of the waterfall outside.

"Look," said Gussie, pointing. "Murals, just like the ones we saw before."

The tiled murals were almost too faded to see, but just like in the first tower they'd stayed in, these showed people in flight, swooping through towering cloud formations.

"Flying in clouds," Ellie murmured. "And no gargols in sight."

"Who built this place?" Gussie asked Granna as they took wood for the fire. A pit built of stones was in the center of the tower.

"Ancestors, of course," said Granna. She settled down by the firepit with a groan, stretching her wings. "From before the Migration."

"The what?"

"It's an old legend," Tariel explained. "About when the gargols first appeared and the war we fought against them."

"They won," said Granna. "Our ancestral cities fell into their stony claws, and the clans were forced to leave, to found new cities and villages."

"You think these towers are remnants of some ancient civilization?" asked Gussie. "But that doesn't make sense. I've never read about any such thing, and I've read—"

"Let me guess," chuckled Granna. "A hundred books?"

Gussie scowled. "More like *thousands*."

"An ancient civilization," murmured Ellie. She knelt to light the fire, striking the tinder and flint she'd purchased back in Porton. Watching the flames leap up, she said, "Towers of stone found in the wilderness, as if they'd been dropped there . . ."

"What are you scheming up?" asked Nox.

Ellie shook herself. "Your song," she said to Granna. "The one you were singing before the gargols attacked last night . . . It mentioned islands in the sky."

"Yes." Granna's eyes twinkled in the firelight.

"We've been to them."

Now Granna blinked, sitting up straighter. "Excuse me?"

"Nox and I, we've seen them. We *landed* on one, in a great storm. It was an island atop a cloud, and there was a ruined city there teeming with gargols."

Granna and Tariel exchanged a look. "Well. I've never met anyone who's claimed to actually have laid eyes on one, but . . . yes. Our legend does speak of a land hidden in the clouds."

"Truehome," said Ellie, rising to her feet and clenching her hands.

"Not a name I've heard." Granna scratched her chin thoughtfully. "To us, the place has always been *Tirelas*."

A shiver went through Ellie's wings.

The word resonated through her, clear as a bell, setting off a riot of whispers in the back of her mind. She saw she wasn't the only one affected. Gussie sat up, Twig let out a soft sigh, and Nox went pale.

"That word . . ." Ellie stared at the old Macaw. "I've never heard it before and yet . . . I feel like I have. It's like a memory . . ."

"Tell us the story," said Gussie. "The whole thing."

"Yes, please," said Ellie.

They all gathered around the growing flames. A meal of dried plantain, rice balls, and nuts was shared among them, as outside, the daylight began to fade.

"As the Macaws have always told it," Granna began, "our ancestors once dwelled in a mighty civilization, a place of freedom and exploration and limitless skies—a land high above the ground. These islands were vast and diverse, some desert, some hot and humid, some forever blanketed in ice. Every clan had their own island, or perhaps an entire archipelago, floating on a sea of clouds. Together, they raised glittering cities, centers of commerce, art, and politics."

Ellie drank in the words as if they were rain and she a field in drought.

"But," said Granna, "it was not to last. It's said these cities glowed at night, so brightly, so magnificently, that the very stones of the ground became jealous. They rose up, gargols, to drive our ancestors out of their homes, to exile them to the lands below."

"Exiles," breathed Ellie. "Just like the Restless Order says. Only they meant it . . . what's the word?"

"Metaphorically," Gussie said.

"Right. That." Ellie nodded to Granna. "What happened next?"

Granna shrugged. "That's it. That's how we came to live where we do now, the skies forever closed to us. The gargols' jealousy keeps us imprisoned on the ground."

"What about a stone man?" asked Ellie. "When I was up there, I saw a stone man with eyes like the gargols. He threw a wind at me—like some kind of sorcerer."

"I don't know anything about stone men," said Granna. "Though I could tell you a story or two about men with *hearts* of stone." She burst into laughter.

Agitated, Ellie jumped up and began pacing. "It all makes sense. The Macaw legend and the Restless Order's beliefs . . . they match up perfectly, like two pieces of the same puzzle."

"So?" said Nox.

"So!" Ellie stopped and blinked at him. "*So*, don't you see, this changes everything!"

"What does it change? So what if we did once live in the sky? We don't anymore and nothing's going to change that. Maybe the gargols did drive our ancestors out. Again . . . *so what*?"

"Why are you arguing with me about this?"

"I'm not arguing. I'm just saying it doesn't change anything. Ellie, come on. You're always reading too deep into things."

"Excuse me!" Ellie's face grew hot. This was so typical of Nox! Always taking the opposite side, just to make her angry. "Like what?"

He shrugged, looking like he wished he'd kept his mouth shut. Well, too late for that. "You know . . . the whole prophecy thing, for example."

She'd *known* he was going to bring that up again. She'd practically thrown out an invitation. "I never said I believed it, only that—"

"And what about the King's Ladder?"

Flinching, Ellie shot back, "I don't see what that has to do with it."

"You built your entire life around a book."

"And I threw it away to save *your* mangy feathers, remember?"

"I'm just saying, when you go in for something, you go *all-in*. There's no shallow end of the lake with you. It's in-over-your-head or not at all."

"And what's wrong with that?"

He shrugged and bit his nail, refusing to say more.

"Gussie gets it. Don't you?" She whirled on the Falcon.

"Um . . ." Gussie glanced between them, looking like she'd rather run outside and risk her chances with the gargols. "I mean, maybe Nox is right? Not that I don't see the enormous academic ramifications of a floating archipelago, mind you. It *would* explain why so many history books stop about a thousand years back, without much to say about our ancient ancestors beyond hypotheticals. But pragmatically speaking—"

"Ugh! Never mind." Ellie turned to Twig. "What about you?"

"Me? What? Um . . . can I sit this one out?"

Granna raised her hands. "Now, now. Let's all settle down. Nox has a point—things are as they are. We Macaws have known about these islands in the sky for generations, but what does it change?"

"Change . . ." whispered Ellie. "That's got to be it, though. *The rules are changing.*"

They weren't listening to her anymore. They'd moved on to discuss tomorrow's journey, and Twig wanted to know if they might see any elephants. It was as if none of them even *cared* about the revelation humming in Ellie's very bones.

But then . . . what, exactly, *was* she trying to say?

She wasn't sure, except it seemed like if it was true, and if their people *had* once lived on islands high above in the sky, it had to matter. It had to *change* something. How could they go on as normal, knowing they weren't where they belonged? Knowing something—some*place*—precious had been stolen from them?

Or maybe only Ellie cared. This wouldn't be the first thing the gargols had stolen from her. They'd taken her parents, and she could never make that right.

But what if there were some island up there, drifting on the wind, a place her Sparrow ancestors had called home . . . ?

Too deep in thought to be angry at Nox, she sat down and finished her dinner, staring at the fire, reliving the memory of those few moments she'd stood in that ruined city.

Tirelas.

It was true. All of it. She *felt* it was true, in a way she'd never felt anything before, even if the others didn't see it or didn't care to.

"We're . . . not where we belong," she murmured to herself, and the words rang in her heart like a bell's toll.

CHAPTER THIRTEEN
· NOX ·

Despite how much he'd been dreading this day, it was almost a relief to Nox when they reached Khadreen. At least it was enough to shake Ellie out of her stubborn silence. She'd barely said two words since last night. He figured she was still angry at him. Not that he didn't deserve it; he'd known he was riling her up. But honestly, sometimes she just found his nerve and *pressed* . . .

He still wasn't entirely sure why her notions about the islands in the sky—this Tirelas—bothered him so much. He got an uneasy feeling when he thought of the place, and not just because of the gargols they'd found there. All he knew was that it felt like bad news, like a tall, dark door that, once opened, would unleash a storm of trouble.

"You coming?" he called to Twig, who flew some distance behind them.

Twig waved in response. The journey seemed to be taking a toll on him, and he'd been lagging behind since morning. Or maybe he was just really focused on looking for leopards. Either way, they had to slow to let him catch up.

Then Granna led them over the last hills and to the city that waited.

Unlike Thelantis, Khadreen had no wall around it, and no guards to prevent people from flying in. It was a sprawling, low-built city clustered around three tributaries, which met in one wide, slow river. Also unlike Thelantis, there seemed to be no organization to the neighborhoods and districts. Most of the buildings were wooden, with thatched roofs, and markets crooked through the streets beneath canopies of brightly colored fabrics.

"There is a saying you must remember," said Granna as they banked lower, in preparation to land. "There is no king in Khadreen."

"Who's in charge?" asked Ellie.

"No one. There's no governor, no council, no guard. Each clan has a claimed neighborhood, and they might keep peace within their own boundaries, but stepping from one street into another could take you into an entirely new set of rules. When in doubt, it's best to be polite and quiet. Mind your business and everyone else will mind theirs."

"A city with no laws!" Gussie exclaimed. "Sounds like chaos."

"On the contrary, you'll be surprised to see how civilly everyone gets on. Not that there aren't scuffles from time to time. Certainly alliances form between some clans, while feuds between others make for . . . interesting developments. But for the most part, and aside from some shady wheeling and dealing, Khadreen gets on well enough." She paused, then added, "The city has its own way of dealing with troublemakers."

"What's that?"

"Well, imagine a gang of Macaw planners roughed up a crew of Nightjars. The next day, all commerce and clientele in the Macaw businesses would stop. No shoppers, no traders, no one to dine on our delicious coconut pies or purchase our pottery. We would be shunned until we made reparations—as we would rightfully owe."

Nox surveyed the vast, dusty city and felt his stomach tumble over. Did he really have family somewhere down there?

"Is there a Crow neighborhood?" he asked.

"I don't believe so. Those without a clan section of their own can usually be found in one of the older, more central streets. Such merchants and craftsmen can often make an alliance with a stronger clan for a percentage of their profits." She smiled encouragingly. "If your people are here, young man, Macaw clan will know of them."

Despite her assurances that Khadreen was one great orderly system, the skies above it were certainly not. People flew in all directions, without any sort of pattern to their routes. They had to fly in a wild, zigzagging course, dodging groups of green-winged Parrot clanners, hot-tempered Kingfishers, Sunbitterns with their wings patterned like great eyes, boisterous Hoatzins hauling nets filled with reeking garbage, which Granna said they turned into the finest compost in the south. Many of the clans Nox didn't recognize at all, and their languages were as varied as their feathers.

He remembered Tariel telling them earlier that day that only a few of the southern clans—including the Macaws—spoke what they called *tradesong*, the common language used between clans to communicate and trade goods. To Nox, it had only ever been *the* language, the one everyone in the Clandoms spoke. But here, it was one of dozens of tongues, and the words a clan used with one another might be entirely different than the ones they used with outsiders.

At last, they landed in a bustling avenue lined with multicolored canopies. This was clearly the Macaw clan's territory; nearly all the vendors and craftsmen had the same rainbow wings as Granna and Tariel, though most of the shoppers looked to be visitors from other clans. While the stalls boasted a wide variety of wares, by far the most common was pottery, the Macaws' specialty. Nox spotted half a dozen potters within a stone's throw, bent over wheels and lumps of clay.

"Granna Tarkin!" someone called out, and soon the words rang down the street as people flocked to Granna's side. They hugged the old woman and pinched Tariel's wings, admiring their growth. Nox guessed that Granna was quite the popular figure among her own clan; everyone seemed eager to speak with her.

Pushed back by the wave of Macaws, Nox, Ellie, and Gussie found a shady spot to sit, and gratefully accepted cold coconut water from a beaming vendor.

"No, no!" she said, refusing their coin. "Any friend of Granna's is a friend of ours."

"Where's Twig?" asked Ellie.

Nox looked around, wondering if some animal had caught Twig's attention. But then he spotted the boy across the street, sitting against a wall with his eyes shut.

A flutter of unease drove Nox to his feet. Handing his drink to Gussie, he said, "I'll get him."

Twig stirred when Nox prodded his leg. "Huh?"

"Come on, we have drinks and shade. What's wrong?"

Twig blinked hard, then shook his head. "Nothing. Just tired, I guess."

Odd. Of all of them, Twig was always the one with energy to spare. Nox took his hand and hauled him up, then brought him to the others. He started looking better once he had a cold drink in his hand, and Nox supposed it might be the heat getting to him. Twig *was* on the small side, and his pale skin was already red from sunburn.

Nox turned his attention back to Granna, who was telling the crowd about the gargol attack on Brightbay. They listened in horrified silence, then, when she'd finished, all scrambled to speak at the same time.

"Hush, hush!" Granna ordered. "You first, Red."

A Macaw clanner stepped forward, and at first, Nox did a double take. The woman had no wings—only a short cape that covered her back. But when she moved, the cape fluttered and he caught sight of two stumps on her shoulder blades . . . where her wings had been cut off.

"You're not the only one with a story like this, Granna," Red said. "Since two weeks ago, we've been hearing reports of gargols smashing through houses. We've even heard of attacks happening in broad daylight—no cloud in sight."

"There was a bad storm five nights ago!" shouted another Macaw. "Word has it they tore apart a whole row of houses in the Sunbittern neighborhood. Two people died."

Everyone was nodding, then more tried to share their own stories.

Nox turned back to his friends. "You hearing this?"

They nodded gravely.

"Attacks in broad daylight," Ellie whispered.

"It wasn't just one rogue gargol," Gussie added. "They're changing their behavior."

Hearing his own name mentioned, Nox turned to see Granna pointing his way. At once, the Macaw named Red waved her hand.

"I know who he's looking for! The Corvain shop—it's over in Ibis clan territory."

Nox's heart flipped.

They were really here.

His family.

"Nox, that's great news!" Ellie said, jumping up. "Oh skies, you must be so excited!"

Excited? More like so-nervous-he-could-puke.

Not that he'd ever, ever admit that to Ellie Meadows, of course.

"These old wings need a break," said Granna. "Tariel, you and Red take Nox to his people. But I want my goodbyes first!"

She hugged each of them, made sure their satchels were stuffed with food, and made them promise to stop in if ever they passed by Brightbay again.

"And," she said in a lower voice, "if you ever need shelter, you'll have friends in the Macaw clan. Just fly toward Elephant Rock to find us."

"Elephant Rock!" exclaimed Twig.

She gave him a knowing smile. "Anyone in the jungle can point you to it, just ask. I . . . get the sense you four aren't heading back to the Clandoms anytime soon. Just know if you need it, the Macaws will look after you. I'll see to it."

"Thank you," Nox said quietly, wondering how much the woman had guessed about their situation.

Tariel and Red waved at them to follow, and they took off at a brisk walk. Twig trailed behind, until Nox tugged his arm so he wouldn't get separated in the crowd.

"Are you sure you're okay?" Nox asked.

"Just tired," he sighed.

Nox kept an eye on him as they walked; it was better than thinking about where they were going, and *who* they were going to meet.

But the thoughts crept in anyway.

How many Corvains were there? Did he have aunts and uncles, a horde of cousins? Did any of them have the same fireproof-ness he did? How would he even go about asking a thing like that? Would they ask him about his mother? What would he say?

He didn't realize how hard he was clenching his teeth till his jaw began to ache.

Red and Tariel led them through a wide plaza where many street performers were putting on little shows. Knots of spectators gathered around each one, and the music of many different instruments and songs mingled together in the air. As they walked, Nox watched a team of fire dancers turning cartwheels while juggling blazing torches, without a burn on them. They had the bright pink wings of Flamingo clanners. Their skill protected them from the flames, he thought bitterly, not some mysterious family curse.

"Nox!" Ellie shouted, waving a hand in front of his face. "Hello?"

"Huh? Are we there?"

"No, I said *get down*!" She pulled him to the ground, and he blinked and realized Gussie and Twig were already sitting behind a bunch of other people. They were pretending to watch a puppeteer with a dangling doll that, Nox realized, was likely meant to be King Garion of the Eagles. Tariel and Red were standing by, looking confused.

"What's going on?" he asked.

Ellie pointed. "*Trouble.*"

Two men were walking through the crowd, immediately identifiable by their long white cloaks and the golden embroidery on their tunics.

Goldwing knights.

"What in the skies are they doing *here*?" Nox whispered.

"Could be any reason," Gussie said. "Or . . . they could be looking for us."

"No one in the Clandoms knows where we are."

"Unless someone saw us steal aboard that Albatross ship," she pointed out. "Or they could have been here for weeks, waiting in case we turned up."

He watched the two knights warily. They were certainly looking for *someone*, judging by the way they scanned the crowd. They weren't there on a holiday.

The people of Khadreen seemed as suspicious as Nox, and he saw heads turn as the knights strode by, eyes narrowing.

"Friends of yours?" asked Tariel.

"Don't worry," said Red. "Nobody in Khadreen trusts those guys. They're Garion's pet dogs and we know it. The Eagles have few friends in the south. If they're looking for you, they'll have to search long and hard before anyone points them your way."

A pair of Parrot fledglings wandered up to Twig and shyly asked if they could touch his wings. He didn't seem to hear them, and Gussie shooed them away.

Nox frowned at Twig, not liking the way he stared vacantly ahead.

"The knights are gone," Tariel announced, peering through the crowd. "It's safe to keep walking."

The plaza ended in a tangle of narrow streets, which Red navigated with ease. But now they walked more quickly, heads down, watching for trouble. Nox's guard was up again; he hadn't quite realized he'd lowered it so much since arriving in the south. But knowing the king's men were here was enough to make him immediately paranoid again.

"Watch it," said Red when an out-of-control donkey cart came speeding across the path in front of them. She stopped so suddenly that Nox walked into her, his shoulder bumping the stony stumps of her wings.

"Sorry!" he said, backing away. "Sorry, I didn't mean to . . ."

"It's all right. It didn't hurt," she sighed. "I know you're wondering about my wings. *Those* did hurt, and sometimes still do. Phantom pains."

"Were they amputated?" asked Gussie.

Red nodded. "It's how we deal with wingrot in the south. Cut it out the moment it's detected, and you might stop it from spreading."

"That's . . . brutal." Ellie looked horrified.

"Yes, but necessary. I might not be alive today if I'd tried to keep them." Red's face went hard. She cleared her throat. "We're almost there. Let's keep going."

Nox tried to imagine making such a choice—keep your wings and risk your life, or cut them off altogether. He shuddered, hoping he never had to be faced with such a decision.

Then they turned a corner and Red stopped again. This time, it was to point to a small candle shop across the street.

"There it is," she said.

Nox stared, his throat going dry.

Above the shop's door swung a small wooden sign, which read TANRA CORVAIN, CHANDLER. Below it was carved a curling ashmark.

"That's them, Nox," Ellie said, nudging him with her shoulder. "Your family. Ready to go in?"

Of course he wasn't ready. He wanted to lift into the air and fly as fast as he could in the other direction.

But after trying and failing to swallow the nervous knot in his throat, he nodded. "Right. Let's go meet my family."

CHAPTER FOURTEEN
· NOX ·

The shop door opened with a soft creak, revealing a room untouched by the chaotic noise of the street outside. No one was at the counter, nor were any customers milling around.

The others stood quietly by the door, waiting as Nox walked around the shop, staring.

The air smelled of beeswax and brass, from the hundreds of candles displayed on shelves and tables. Every shape and size imaginable, some were even carved like elegant figurines—snakes, trees, sharks. Tapered candles hung from the wall by their conjoined wicks, in a rainbow of colors. The sound of softly bubbling wax wafted from a row of small cauldrons along the back wall, hung over a stone hearth warm with glowing embers.

"Hello?" said Nox. "Tanra Corvain?"

"No, no," said a shaky voice from a back room. "It's only me these days. My name's Jaff. How can I help . . . *Ashren*?"

Nox started at the name. He turned to the curtained doorway at the back of the shop, where an old man now teetered through. He was bent over, leaning on a cane, his beard thin and straggly. His dark Crow wings were shot with gray. As he peered rheumily at Nox, his head and hands trembled with palsy.

"No . . ." said the man. "Too young. But the image of him . . ."

The knot in Nox's throat tightened. "I'm Nox. Ashren was my father."

The old man's eyes widened. He stumped forward on his cane to take a closer look. "Nox?"

"That's right."

The old man smelled of his candles; wax had spattered and hardened on his work apron. *"Tannox?"*

Swallowing, Nox nodded.

"Skies and stars on high . . . my grandson." The old man reached up a shaking hand and pressed it to Nox's cheek. His head came only to Nox's chin. Nox went absolutely still, his heart hammering.

"I thought I was the last," whispered the old man. "I thought I was alone."

Across the shop, Ellie took a step forward, as if about to speak, but Gussie caught her arm and pulled her back.

Nox barely noticed. He couldn't stop staring. The longer he looked, the more familiar Jaff's face became. With a start, Nox realized he saw his own father in this old man, the warm brown eyes that betrayed his every emotion, the line of worry between his eyebrows offset by the lines of laughter at the corners of his lips.

"My grandfather," he whispered.

How stupid he suddenly felt, for ever thinking he didn't want this. For nearly walking away from it.

His grandfather pulled him down into a hug that belied his frail limbs. Nox, who considered hugs to be only slightly less threatening than a dagger to the throat, didn't immediately react.

But as the old man's warmth seeped into him, Nox's stiff muscles began to melt. He slowly lifted his arms and hugged him back, his eyes blurring with tears.

"More cake!" announced Nox's grandfather, plopping down a plate heaping with oozing chocolate lumps. "You're too thin, boy. And too pale!"

Nox stared in dismay at the food but dutifully picked up his fork. "Thanks, Jaff."

He still couldn't bring himself to call the old man *grandfather*. He might have Nox's name and his father's face, but he was still a stranger.

The old man, on the other wing, seemed to have no such reservations toward Nox.

Jaff Corvain's first reaction—after the bone-splitting hug—had been to close his shop, pull Nox and his friends upstairs to his living quarters, and then proceed to lay out a feast. The room was tight, serving as a bedroom, kitchen, and living space, but they all packed in as best they could around the small table.

Unfortunately, his grandfather's skill at cooking beeswax did not seem to extend into the kitchen. The cake was on the . . . salty side, and the fish he'd served before that had been seasoned with an adventurous blend of cinnamon and parsley. But he'd been so proud to present the dishes that not even Gussie had dared voice her objections. Of course, Nox's murderous look of warning might have also had something to do with silencing her complaints.

Nobody insulted his grandfather.

Even if the man cooked like he'd never actually *tasted* food.

"I wrote to your father a hundred times, begging him to move down here." Jaff poured hot water over a bowl of leaves; the resulting tea, at least, smelled palatable enough. "He was so stubborn. Said everything was fine, that there was good opportunity in the Clandoms. Pah! There's never been anything in the Clandoms for the Corvains but bad luck. And that goes for those of us who loved them too. Me, your mother."

Nox stared at his cake, his stomach souring in a way that had nothing to do with the salty flavor. *Nothing but bad luck.*

"So Nox's Corvain blood came from his grandmother, your wife?" asked Ellie.

He glanced at her sharply, knowing what she was digging for—information about his fireproof-ness. He already knew his grandmother had had the trait, but beyond that, he didn't know much at all about the Corvains.

"Tanra," sighed Jaff. "Yes. Tanra Corvain, my wild girl with a heart full of sky."

"What happened to her?" Nox asked quietly.

"She disappeared in the Clandoms, long before you were born." He sighed and crossed the room, returning with a small framed painting. "This shop was her dream. That's why I kept her name on the sign. I've only kept up with it in her memory, and because the only dream I'd ever had was *her*."

A moment of silence followed. Nox took the painting and stared at the woman in it, a young Crow woman with serious eyes and a smirking mouth.

"The symbol on the shop sign," he murmured, tapping the apron she wore, which also had the ashmark embroidered on it.

"That's the Corvain family crest," said Jaff.

"It looks like an ashmark," said Ellie.

He nodded. "I always said so myself. It's here too. She built this table herself, my clever Tanra did." He patted the tabletop, where the symbol had been lightly carved into the wood. "She said it always looked like a flame to her—and that's what gave her the idea to open a candle shop."

"My father had that symbol tattooed on his arm," said Nox. "I thought he got it as protection against gargols. He never told me it was a family thing."

"Yes." Jaff chuckled. "I remember when he got that tattoo. Tanra was appalled."

"The king's knights killed my father," said Nox.

Jaff's eyes pinched. He looked away. "Yes . . . I heard it from an old friend in Thelantis. He told me your mother had been imprisoned, and you'd been taken too. I gave up on you as lost, my boy, and for that I am sorry. Had I known . . . I would have come for you." He dipped a cup into the bowl of tea and pressed it into Nox's hands. "But you found your way to me on your own. You are certainly a Corvain, with gumption like that."

Nox shook his head. "Ellie, Gussie, and Twig are the real reason I'm here."

"All the more proof." His grandfather beamed at them. "A true Corvain can always be found surrounded by loyal friends."

"Jaff, just before we left the Clandoms, we were attacked by an assassin sent by King Garion. We think . . . he was targeting *me*. Specifically. Why would he do that?"

Jaff stared at him for a long moment.

"Well, now," he said slowly. "I'd guess that's because he knows who you are . . . and what you can do."

"Stand in fire and not be burned?" Ellie piped up.

Nox shot her a dark look.

"What?" she said. "C'mon, Nox. If we can trust anyone, surely it's your own grandfather."

Jaff gave her a sidelong look. "Yes, that would be reason enough for an Eagle king."

"But *why*?" Nox blurted out. "I'm not all that dangerous! So what if I can't catch fire? I did far more damage as a thief, and he never sent assassins after me for that."

"Thieving, eh?" Jaff's eyebrows arched. "Humph. We'll discuss *that* later. As for your king, well. The Eagles have hunted Corvains for generations. Your father wasn't the first they executed. *Why* they are obsessed with your particular family, I cannot fathom. It was a question your grandmother sought to answer. In fact, she was traveling to find those answers when she vanished."

"You think the Eagles got her?"

"I think either way, the Clandoms are bad luck for Corvains. You'll stay here with me, Nox. I'll teach you candle making, and you'll never have to look over your shoulder again."

Nox thought of the two Goldwings they'd seen only hours ago, but decided to say nothing. He didn't want to spoil this evening, even if it meant pretending he had any interest in being a chandler.

"So we're the last of us," he said. "You and me."

"Yes, as far as I know. Tanra never told me of any other—"

"Twig!"

They turned at Gussie's shout, Nox's heart skipping a beat when he heard the alarm in her voice.

Twig had slumped face-first onto the table. At first, Nox thought he might have fallen asleep, but though his eyes were shut, his teeth were gritted together.

"It hurts," Twig whimpered.

"Quick, lay him over here," said Jaff.

Nox and Gussie lifted Twig easily enough and set him on a narrow bed beneath the window. Twig was shivering, his skin hot to the touch.

"He's sick." Nox stared in bewilderment. "He's been acting strange all day, but . . . what is this? Heatstroke?"

"I know a doctor," said Jaff. "I'll fetch her—"

"No," said Gussie. She'd gone very still, her hand on Twig's shoulder. "I know what's wrong with him."

"Well?" said Ellie.

Grim-faced, Gussie turned Twig onto his side, revealing his wings. She gently parted their feathers until their bases were visible.

Nox's heart stopped.

The skin around Twig's wing joints was grayish and scaled.

Gussie let go of his wings, her eyes sliding shut as she whispered, "Wingrot."

"This would be no problem if we still had the skystone," Ellie groaned.

"Sorry."

"I'm not blaming you, Nox. It was just bad luck."

She paced on the flat roof of the candle shop, her wings ruffling in the rising breeze. The sun had begun to set and the sky glowed orange, lighting the mountain range in the distant south like a row of bonfires. Nox stood pensively on the corner, staring across the city. Gussie had remained inside with Twig, to wait for Jaff to return with the doctor.

"Maybe you *should* blame me," he said. "You ever notice how often the words *bad luck* have come up lately?"

"Huh? What's that supposed to mean?" She shook her head. "Let's focus on the positives: We caught it early. It's only barely spread to Twig's wings. Which means we have *time*."

"Maybe a week," he replied. "I've heard it spreads faster the more you use your wings. We've been flying for two whole days."

"Remember, we *know* how to cure it."

"But the skystone—"

"So?" She put a hand on his shoulder, forcing him to turn and meet her eyes. "Nox, we know where the skystones come from now. Isn't it obvious what we have to do?"

He pushed his hand through his hair, sighing. "I know."

Ellie glanced down at the street, where most of the vendors had packed up their stalls, carts, and blankets of wares, but a few still remained, bargaining or chatting. "There's your grandfather with the doctor."

They flew down to meet them. The doctor was a middle-aged Kingfisher clanner, her feathers a rich, dark teal. She introduced herself as Dr. Alceda, then followed them grimly upstairs.

Twig was awake now, but still groggy with pain. Dr. Alceda knelt by his bed and took out a linen bag full of small green leaves.

"Maticca leaf," said the doctor, pushing them into Twig's mouth. "For the pain. I'm afraid that is the only medicine I can give him."

Ellie nodded; she knew there was only one thing that could truly help Twig now, and it wouldn't be found in a doctor's satchel.

"Do you wish me to perform the surgery here, or at my infirmary?" asked the doctor.

She was met with silence, as the others stared in confusion.

"The . . . surgery?" said Gussie.

"Of course. There is only one treatment for wingrot."

Ellie gasped, remembering what Red had told them—and the bony stumps of her amputated wings.

"No!" she cried. "There's not going to be any surgery!"

"Absolutely not," Gussie agreed, squeezing Twig's shoulder.

Twig's eyes went wide. He thrashed his head, managing a weak, "No way."

"I'm afraid this is not optional," said the doctor crisply. "It's how we do things in Khadreen."

"Well, we're not from Khadreen," said Nox. "And you can't force Twig to—to go through with something like that."

"Ahem," said Jaff. "Nox . . . she's right. This is the only way to be sure your friend survives."

"We have a cure!" Ellie said. "We just need time to find it."

The doctor raised a skeptical brow. "There is no cure for—"

"But there *is*. We've seen it work before."

"Once," Nox added softly. "It doesn't work *every* time."

He was thinking of his mother, Ellie knew. She put a hand on his arm. "You know that case was different. Twig's is still early."

He nodded, but his eyes lowered to the floor.

"This won't stand," said the doctor, tying her satchel shut. "Having a case of wingrot will cause unrest in the city. People don't like knowing someone's infected near them."

"Just like in Thelantis," muttered Nox.

"It's not contagious," Gussie pointed out. "There's nothing to be scared of as long as people don't get superstitious and understand the facts."

The doctor peered at her. "You're a girl of science, I see. Good for you. But you must know that not everyone will see things as you and I do. If word spreads about his infection, I cannot stop them from storming this place and dragging him out. If I won't perform the surgery, *they* will, and I trust you see why that would be the worst-case scenario. Better to trust him to a professional, if it's going to happen either way."

"No one will know," said Ellie. "We'll keep it quiet until we've gotten the cure."

The doctor shrugged. "Don't say I didn't warn you. Whatever this cure is you think you've found, it won't work. I've seen more and more cases in the past few months, and nothing's made a difference. I don't know how you do it up in the Clandoms, but at least with *our* way, fewer have to die."

She left, shaking her head all the while.

"Jaff," said Nox, "please don't tell anyone about Twig. *Please.* We just need time to get the cure."

"What cure, Nox? What in the skies are you talking about?"

"It's . . . hard to explain. But I swear, we know what we're doing."

He traded a look with Ellie, and she understood he didn't want to say anything about their intentions. Of course not. What sane adult would just *let* them fly into a gargol-infested cloud?

"You're making a mistake," Jaff said. "Nox, the longer you wait, the more danger this boy's life will be in."

"Maybe the doctor's right," whispered Twig. "I don't want you risking your lives for me."

"We'll be fine, Twig," Nox said gently. "We just have to wait till the conditions are right, and we'll get what you need."

"And just *what* are you getting?" asked Jaff. "What cure? What's this mad plan you're brewing?"

"I'll explain everything soon, I swear."

His grandfather threw up his hands. "Why, *why* must you have that thick Corvain skull? Why couldn't you have inherited your mother's more sensible point of view?"

"Normally, I'd agree with you about the thickness of Nox's skull," Ellie said, drawing a scowl from Nox. "But he's right this time. We know what we're doing, and we can save Twig."

"Please, Jaff."

The old man looked at each of them, before pausing on Nox. "You're being very mysterious. But what can I do when you look at me with your father's eyes?"

"Thank you. I swear, this will all make sense soon."

But their chance, as it turned out, wouldn't come nearly as soon as Ellie had hoped. The next day dawned bright and sunny, as did the next three days after that. Every morning they flew to the roof and scanned the sky in all directions. It was the first time Ellie had ever been desperate to see a thundercloud.

But none came.

Hot, hazy doldrums set over Khadreen.

And Twig worsened.

"It's spreading fast," Gussie said on the fourth night. She showed Ellie Twig's wings again. The boy was half asleep, dazed on maticca leaf. His wings were starting to lose feathers, the gray scales gaining inches along his skin by the day.

"Oh, Twig," Ellie sighed, stroking his fluffy orange hair. "Maybe we should just fly until we find clouds."

"I'm starting to think so too," said Gussie. "But what if we fly three days in the wrong direction and miss a storm? What if someone finds out about Twig while we're gone and drags a mob up here?"

She was right. It was too risky to leave Twig alone. And Ellie wasn't entirely sure she trusted Nox's grandfather. Not that she thought he'd betray them out of malice, but out of concern. He really thought amputation was the only answer, and she knew he was just waiting for them to come to the same conclusion. What if he took matters into his own hands while they were gone and summoned the doctor back with her bone saw?

Ellie shuddered.

"We have no choice but to wait," she said.

Another two days passed with no change in the weather.

In the evenings, after he'd closed the shop, Jaff set out waxes and wicks and cauldrons and bottles of scent, determined to teach Nox his trade. Together, they spent hours dipping, stirring, and carving new candles. Ellie curled up on the chair behind the counter and watched, trying not to feel jealous.

Was this where Nox belonged? It certainly seemed that way. And what about Ellie?

On the sixth afternoon, feeling restless, she wandered upstairs to where Gussie had taken over the dining table. She'd assembled a new collection of parts for some invention. Ellie had no idea what she was building, but she seemed very focused.

"Gussie." Ellie sat at the table and toyed with a wooden cog. "What'll you do after this? After we heal Twig, I mean. If Nox stays here with his grandfather, will you stay too?"

Gussie shrugged. "Khadreen seems nice enough. I might look around and see if there's a clockmaker or someone who needs an apprentice. Don't much care what the work is, so long as I get to invent things. Don't touch that!"

She snatched the cog from Ellie's hand and plugged it into her unfathomable tangle of parts.

Ellie went to Twig's bedside and put a hand on his forehead. His fever came and went, and right now he seemed to be sleeping peacefully. He'd been awake most of the day, tottering around the room and pretending he wasn't in pain, but they'd all seen right through him. His marten, Lirri, was snuggled under his chin like a scarf, and for once, she didn't try to bite Ellie when she ran a finger over her soft fur. The little creature only gave her a solemn stare. Ellie figured she was as worried about Twig as the rest of them.

Struck with a sudden need for fresh air, Ellie told Gussie she'd be back soon and jumped out the window, spreading her wings. She took a long, slow lap around the city, keeping an eye out for the Goldwing knights they'd seen earlier. But if the men were still in Khadreen, they were lying low.

The wind shifted suddenly and pushed a column of foul smoke her way. Choking on the stinking fumes, Ellie was forced to land until she could catch her breath.

"What is that smell?" she gasped, taking shelter in the shade of a vegetable seller's stall, in what looked like Parrot clan territory.

The woman in the stall stared at her impassively. "It's the wings, of course."

"The . . . what?"

"The burn pit, for the wings they cut off the sick."

Ellie stared at the woman, then stumbled toward a barrel and vomited into it.

"Hey!" The Parrot clanner jumped up, livid. "That my potato stock!

You're going to have to pay for the whole lot, you—what's your clan, anyway?"

"Oh . . . could I work it off instead? Do some chores? I don't have any—"

"You'll pay in coin or you'll pay in feathers!" snapped the woman. "We'll see how much property you can destroy with your wings clipped, missy!"

"Sorry!" Ellie gasped, sprinting away and taking to the air. Blushing with shame, she sped quickly away. She didn't have the money to pay for one potato, much less a whole barrel. What few coins she'd made in Cloudstone she'd left on the cargo ship, in payment for the food they'd taken.

She landed back on the candle shop's rooftop, out of breath and sick to her stomach. No matter how hard she coughed, she couldn't get the taste of that acrid smoke off her tongue. How many pairs of wings had they burned to create such a plume? How many people in Khadreen were really infected with wingrot? She'd seen a few wingless people walking around, but there had to be far, far more. From what she'd heard through the street chatter below the candle shop window, nobody seemed to *talk* about wingrot. Nox's grandfather had mentioned it was a taboo subject. Unless they were actively dragging some poor sick person off to have their wings amputated, the people here didn't like to acknowledge the disease's existence at all.

Their attitude toward wingrot was only slightly better than Thelantis's, where the sick were pushed out of the city altogether, to either recover or die alone.

Desperate for a cup of water to wash away the awful taste in her mouth, Ellie walked to the edge of the roof.

But before she could flutter down to the window, a sudden boom shook the city.

Ellie gasped and looked up.

Thunder.

And there, on the southern horizon—a dark, towering cloud.

CHAPTER SIXTEEN

· NOX ·

The wind hit them first, a great tidal wave that nearly sent them tumbling. Nox set his jaw and tilted his wings so the gust lifted him rather than bowled him over.

To his left, Ellie took a slight lead, her smaller frame more agile on the gales that rocked the sky. On her other side, Gussie stretched her wide Falcon wings, struggling almost as much as Nox.

Each of them gripped a length of rope, tethering themselves to one another lest the storm tear them apart.

"We have to be quick and quiet," Ellie had said as they'd prepared.

Nox's grandfather had watched, aghast, as they stood on his rooftop and strapped on weapons and equipment. In addition to his slingshot, Nox had a chisel and hammer in his belt, borrowed from his grandfather's candle-making supplies, and an empty satchel for carrying the skystone back. Ellie had her lockstave, of course, but also the Goldwing dagger she'd stolen back in Thelantis. She'd given her second dagger, an older but sturdy blade, to Nox, which he kept tucked in his inner vest pocket.

Gussie carried . . . well, they still weren't sure. She'd refused to say what the contraption was, but it resembled a crossbow. Instead of arrows, she had a sack of small paper tubes reinforced with candle wax that the bow could launch. But since she hadn't tested the invention yet, she'd refused to say what it would do *if* it worked.

"I cannot let you do this," Jaff had said. "This is lunacy, Nox!"

“We don’t have a choice. We have to save Twig.”

“But *why*—”

“We’ll be back as soon as we have the cure. You’ll see. It’ll all work out.”

Nox wished he felt the same confidence now.

Because he was pretty sure this was the stupidest thing he’d ever attempted in his life. Even more stupid than luring a pack of gargols out of the storm to attack the prison. When he’d done that, it had been on a whim, and he’d expected the cloud to hide a handful of gargols—not an entire city of them.

This time, he knew exactly how much danger they were flying into. And yet they were doing it anyway, like fish trying to infiltrate a den of sharks.

But for Twig, he’d face a *hundred* gargols if he had to.

He still remembered the day he’d first met the kid. Twig had been curled up in a drainage tunnel under Knock Street, fast asleep, when a sudden deluge had flooded the city. Nox had been asleep in a doorway, until something bit his ear—Lirri, chittering frantically on his shoulder. Bewildered, he’d watched the little marten run across the drenched road to scratch at the sewer grate, where Twig had gotten trapped in the rising waters and was drowning. Nox had pulled him out and slapped his back till he coughed up the water and opened his eyes.

Ever since then, he’d made sure Twig had food and shelter and didn’t get himself stuck in any more drains. He’d told himself it was just because Twig’s ability to communicate with animals was a handy tool for a thieving crew’s arsenal, but in truth? A part of him had come to see Twig as his little brother—another clanless outcast with nowhere to go.

“Rain!” Ellie called in warning, a moment before the first drops stung Nox’s cheeks.

Still they hadn’t reached the thunderhead itself. It loomed ahead, taller than any mountain, swirling like black ink in water. Nox couldn’t help but see it as a living, breathing beast, spitting lightning and roaring out thunder, daring them to come nearer.

For Twig, he reminded himself.

He had to do this.

He couldn't fail someone else. He couldn't be Twig's bad luck too.

"Updraft!" Ellie stiffened her wings. "This is it—here we *goooo*!"

A mighty rush of warm air suddenly lifted Nox. It was all he could do just to stay level, keeping his wings taut. The updraft sucked them toward the cloud at a speed their wings alone could never match—and there would be no escaping it now. They were caught in the current, the storm inhaling them into itself.

They gained altitude so quickly it made Nox's head spin. He fought to stay conscious, fought to stay aloft. If his wings buckled now, the torrent would toss him for miles. Riding that wind was like trying to run atop a landslide. There was nothing for it but to stay upright and hold on for dear life.

The current sucked them into the thundercloud, and the rope around Nox's wrist went taut as Ellie and Gussie were pulled in opposite directions. Holding tight, he peered upward, the speed and force of the wind bringing tears to his eyes. There was nothing to see; the clouds thickened until he could barely make out Ellie, and Gussie was lost to sight entirely. The black belly of the storm flashed with lightning, drummed with earsplitting thunder. The noise was so loud Nox almost didn't hear the screech of a gargol hidden between crashes.

The monsters were here, all right.

But what if there was no island?

What if the one they'd seen over the Crag had been the only one of its kind, and they were risking their necks for nothing? It was the biggest gamble, that they'd fly through the storm and find nothing, and return to Twig with no cure after all. Then he would lose his wings and—

"Oof!" Nox slammed into solid ground.

The rope on his wrist went slack as Ellie landed beside him.

"We made it!" she shouted.

Shaking away the stars dancing in his eyes, Nox looked around to see vague lumps of stone all around. His feet had found bare dirt stripped clean by the wind.

"Skies above," said Gussie, reeling in rope as she approached them. Her eyes nearly swallowed her face. "It really does exist."

"There are steps over there," Ellie said. "Come on. And keep quiet. There could be gargols anywhere."

They crept from stone to stone, keeping low and never speaking above a whisper. The island was mostly rock and bare dirt, with a few scraggly, tough plants sprouting here and there. The stone steps Ellie had spotted were barely that; time had worn them down, split them open, until they were no longer usable. In some places, rockslides had washed away the steps completely. It seemed to be leading up a great slope, the top hidden in clouds.

They climbed where they could, flew where they could not. The higher they went, the weaker the wind got and the thinner the clouds. They were, he realized, climbing out of the storm itself. The world grew gradually lighter, more sunlight reaching them through the haze.

Nox began to get the feeling that something had happened to this place to leave it in such a state—not just time, but some ancient battle. There were places where the hillside had been blasted open, leaving craters the size of houses. The more the clouds thinned, the more that was revealed. Old, crumbling walls had once terraced the slope, and they passed the remains of fountains, pools, and statues, all weathered down like melted wax.

"This place used to be pretty grand," said Gussie, pointing to a fallen stone arch, the faintest outline of intricately carved patterns still visible on its surface.

"There!" Ellie scrambled up a jumble of boulders to point at a symbol on one of the columns—a spiral inside an inverted triangle. "Remember this?"

"The Restless Order's mark," said Gussie, nodding.

"The mark for *Truehome*," Ellie added. "This really is where our ancestors lived!"

"Yet we've never heard about this place," muttered Gussie. "Not in any books or . . . It's almost as if . . ."

"As if someone didn't *want* us to know about it," finished Nox.

Gussie looked at him and nodded grimly. "I think someone's been rewriting our history, or at least leaving out a very significant portion of it. That's the only thing that would explain the total lack of knowledge of this place."

"The Eagles?" guessed Ellie. "But *why*?"

Gussie shrugged. "It would explain why the Macaws still talk about Tirelas. They're outside the Eagles' control. All I know is, if they think this place is important enough to hide, then it's definitely worth exploring."

"Do you think this is one of the old clan seats?" asked Ellie. "Maybe the Falcons lived here, Gussie."

"Whatever it was, someone made a mess of it on their way out." She paused to pick something out of the dirt. "And they didn't go peacefully either."

"Ugh!" Nox grimaced. "Is that a *skull*?"

She nodded, turning it in her hands as if it were a book. "See this hole in the bone? This person probably died from something sharp impaling their head. Looks about the size of a gargol's claw."

Ellie shuddered. "Put that down and let's hurry, before *our* skulls end up like that."

As if to prove her point, a screech rang out. It was impossible to tell the direction, but it sounded close.

"Gargols," Nox muttered.

They climbed faster. Nox panted, focusing more on the climb now than their strange surroundings. His heart stopped every time one of his shoes knocked a pebble loose and it went tumbling downhill.

Then, almost all at once, they emerged from the top of the storm cloud and found themselves in bright daylight.

Blinking hard, Nox waited for his eyes to adjust.

"Whoa," said Ellie. "*Whoa.*"

CHAPTER SEVENTEEN
· NOX ·

The rocky, scorched slope fell away behind them, and ahead stretched a gentle plain of grass beneath a bright sun. The storm still raged below, thunder grumbling, but this green expanse floated peacefully above it all, a whole different world. Here, breezes tumbled through the grass, gentle as kittens.

Looking back, Nox saw the crown of the thunderhead surrounding them like a dark, angry sea, swirling with malevolent mists, nibbling at the edges of the island.

He took a first hesitant step into that green expanse, only to hear the grass all around them start rustling. He tensed, expecting trouble, as all at once, thousands of glowing lights burst up. Freezing in place, his eyes wide, Nox watched as their shimmering wings filled the air.

"Moonmoths!" exclaimed Ellie.

Nox thought at once of the forest glade where he'd first seen a pack of the little moths break from their chrysalises and take flight. These were the same, their papery wings and velvety antennae softly gleaming with light. He and Gussie and Ellie watched in awe as the moonmoths swirled around them in a dazzling murmuration, before fluttering down into the grass again.

"So this is where they go," Gussie murmured. "Guess that's one ancient mystery solved. They must lay their eggs on the ground before migrating back to the sky."

"If only Twig could be here," sighed Ellie. "He'd love to see them again."

Reminded of their mission, Nox nodded briskly. "Right. Let's find a skystone and get out of here. Those moths make this place even creepier."

"There's a building over that way," Gussie said. "Or . . . there used to be."

"C'mon," said Ellie. "Let's check it out."

A current of unease rolled through Nox. "Last time, we saw skystones *under* the floating island, not on top of it. Shouldn't we be going the other way?"

"And miss a chance to find out more about this place?" said Gussie, who was apparently completely on Ellie's side now.

"She's right," said Ellie. "Besides, do you see any gargols up here?"

"We heard one less than five minutes ago!" he protested. "What's to stop them from coming up here?"

"Scared?"

Nox nearly pulled his hair out. "Of *course* I'm scared! Only an idiot wouldn't be scared! We're miles above the ground, riding atop a storm filled with—aaaand you're walking away."

Muttering beneath his breath about the stubbornness of Sparrows, he jogged to catch up to the girls. Moonmoths fluttered irritably out of his path, trailing pale, glowing dust.

The building turned out to be a crumbling disappointment. Whatever the place had been, it was once vast and no doubt impressive, but there wasn't much left now except weathered blocks of stone, laid out in a rectangle. Grass, chunks of masonry, and little else remained.

"It's gone," he said. "Nothing to see. Can we get back to our actual mission now?"

"Wait." Gussie rubbed her cheek, thinking. Then she walked across the ruin and stopped. "Aha! It's not gone. It's just sunken into the ground. I figured that might be case. Centuries of erosion by storms and wind weakened the foundations, and the whole thing caved in on itself."

"Great. Mystery solved. Now let's—"

All at once, Gussie vanished.

Nox and Ellie rushed forward, staring down the hole the Falcon girl had dropped into.

"This way!" Gussie called, the echo of her voice indicating she'd found some kind of underground chamber.

"I don't like this, Ellie."

"Yeah, but . . . aren't you a *little* curious?" She grinned and dropped down into the dark.

"Twig is waiting for us, you know!" he shouted into the hole.

No one answered. He saw a flare of light below as Ellie lit something.

Grumbling, Nox shimmied himself onto the edge of the opening, then dropped.

He flapped his wings thrice before he landed on a stone floor. Ellie and Gussie were walking away, Ellie with one of Jaff's candles in her hand in a little brass holder.

"Wait!" Nox called, running after.

They walked down a long, large passageway, easily wide enough to spread their wings in. The walls were solid stone brick, and the sound of dripping water echoed in the darkness ahead.

"This place is *huge*," said Ellie.

"It's definitely constructed the same way as the towers we found on the ground," said Gussie, rubbing the stone walls. "This has to be Tirelas."

Ellie smiled at her, linking arms. "So you believe me *now*, Agustina Berel?"

Gussie snorted and pulled her arm away. "I haven't made up my mind about all of it yet. Let's gather more information before you get all smug."

The deeper they delved into the ruin, the more Nox began to relax. This place wasn't so bad. It wasn't teeming with gargols, anyway. At least not yet. And it *was* kind of fascinating.

"Murals!" Ellie said, passing the torch over massive mosaics on the walls. "Just like in the towers."

"Better preserved too." Gussie tapped the tiles. "And different scenes."

Instead of happy people flying around, these murals depicted grandly dressed men and women in long robes.

"Kings and queens of Tirelas, I bet," Gussie said. "See the crowns on their heads? Could this have been some kind of royal palace?"

"Why are they all on fire?" asked Ellie.

Each of the figures stood in a ring of flames, eyes closed and wings spread.

Nox shrugged. "Looks like some kind of funeral ritual."

"And yet . . ." Gussie tapped her lip. "See the inscriptions below them?" She ran her fingers over the strange letters carved into the wall. "'*Birth of Aronika, Queen. Birth of Aronidas, King. Birth of . . .*' Well, you get the idea."

"Birth?" echoed Ellie. "I thought it was a funeral thing."

"Maybe it means birth into the next life or something."

"Check out their wings."

Flakes of gold in the paint caught the light, and the murals seemed to spring to life. The wings especially began to glow, the red and orange paint of the feathers bright with bits of reflective gold.

"So beautiful," murmured Ellie, running her hand over the tiles. "Their wings are like living fire. Wonder what clan they were?"

"Orioles?" said Gussie. "Or some branch of the Parrot clan?"

"Hmm," said Ellie, looking unpersuaded.

When they came to an old cave-in, the passageway blocked by rubble, they doubled back until they found a door they'd missed. It was cracked open just enough to shimmy through.

"Great skies," Ellie gasped.

Her candle wasn't nearly bright enough to illuminate the chamber in which they now found themselves. The air was cooler, less stale than in the corridor outside. Nox took a few steps forward, each footfall sending out a chain of echoes.

Columns vaulted upward, holding up a ceiling lost in shadow. The floor was tiled in more mosaics, bright sunbursts with more flecks of gold shimmering in the paint.

Nox leaned forward, peering hard into the darkness ahead.

"Put out the candle, Ellie," he said quietly.

"Why? What is it?"

"Just put it out."

Ellie blew on the candle, extinguishing the flame.

At once, the chamber lit up.

Even Nox gasped as blue light shone from every corner, from the ceiling, from high on the columns. It was as bright as if the full moon were shining down, enough to turn the room silver.

Skystones.

They were everywhere, in every shape, size, and form.

They were worked into the mosaic floor, inlaid into carvings on the columns, glowing blue swirls of light. From the arched ceiling hung enormous chandeliers with hundreds of crystals dangling like teardrops. Along the walls, large, uncut slabs of the stuff rose from recessed channels that might have once been full of water.

The chamber was *massive*, even larger than Nox had imagined. Twelve rows of columns, every one covered in glowing patterns of blue skystone, stretched to the right and left, and marched away toward the far end of the room.

There, in the distance, rose the brightest cluster of skystones, rising in great crystals around a grand marble throne.

Nox walked forward as if in a dream.

He doubted even King Garion had a seat as fancy as this one. The back of the chair was sculpted like a magnificent set of wings. The skystones framing it were so smooth and polished that Nox's own reflection stared back at him.

The throne was set atop thirteen wide steps, their edges worn smooth. Not, he guessed, by time but by pairs of feet going up and down. Across the top step was engraved a line of script. Skystone had been inlaid into the letters, so the words glowed blue.

"'Here am I of ashes born,'" said Gussie, reading the inscription, "'ruler of all Tirelas, uniter of the people of the sky, crowned chief of the royal clan . . . Phoenix.'"

"Phoenix clan?" said Ellie. "Never heard of a Phoenix clan before."

"They must have been to Tirelas what the Eagles are to the Clandoms."

"You mean spoiled, corrupt rats in fancy clothes?" Nox snorted. "Maybe it's a good thing they're not around anymore."

"Who says they aren't?" said Ellie. "If there's one thing this place is telling me, it's that we don't know *what* we don't know. I mean, clearly this isn't just some gargol nest. It was once a great civilization, just like Granna said. This place was *ours*. And we were pushed out of it by the gargols." Her voice rose, shaking with anger. "*Truehome.* That's what the Restless called this place, even if they didn't know the whole story. And the gargols took it from us—our true homes, our true history!"

"Shh," Nox warned. "We don't know that there aren't gargols still creeping around this place. You wanna start a whole new war with them?"

"*Start?*" Ellie stared at him. "Nox, don't you get it? The war never ended! We're still fighting it, a thousand years later. And the tide is turning—against us. Gargols attacking in daylight, tearing through the walls that once protected us. Don't either of you see what's happening? They want to *wipe us out*. They started here, on these islands, which were once ours, they drove us to the ground, and now they're still hunting us!"

"Let's not jump to conclusions about motives," said Gussie. "We still don't know—"

SCREEEEECHHHHH!

The sound ripped through the throne room, rattling the crystals.

"They found us!" Ellie gasped.

"Back to the door!" said Gussie.

"Wait." Nox launched into the air. "Don't forget about Twig!"

He flew to the closest chandelier and grabbed hold of one of the skystones dangling from it. It broke off with a tug. "Got one!"

"Here," said Ellie, hovering beside him and holding open her belt satchel. Then she grabbed another crystal and pulled it free.

"What are you doing? We only need—"

"Don't be stupid, Nox. This is our chance, don't you see? If these things can heal wingrot, we're taking as many as we can carry back home with us."

Relenting, he helped her fill her bag, then his own and Gussie's. Once they had as many as they could fit, they winged toward the door.

Only to have it explode in their faces.

CHAPTER EIGHTEEN
• ELLIE •

The explosion of rocks sent Ellie tumbling backward, to collide hard with a column. She fell to the floor, dazed, as two enormous gargols came scraping and screeching into the room on their stony claws.

Scrambling upright, Ellie tucked herself behind the column and pressed a hand to her racing heart.

There was nowhere to fly. Nowhere to hide.

They were trapped in this room with two of the biggest gargols she'd ever seen.

Glancing to her left, she saw Nox and Gussie crouched behind the next pillar, looking as panicked as she felt.

Their bodies crunching and grinding, rock against rock, the gargols climbed over the rubble. One screeched again and rammed its head into a column; the stone buckled, then gave way under the second blow. Slabs of ceiling fell with deafening crashes, destroying the mosaic floor.

Taking advantage of the chaos, Nox and Gussie sprinted to Ellie.

"This is bad," Ellie gasped. "That was the only way out."

"Throne rooms *always* have a secret back door," Gussie said. "Kings and queens don't want to be trapped in here either."

"How are we supposed to find—"

They all screamed as the column above their heads splintered under the second gargol's claws.

"Fly!" shouted Nox.

They took off as the column crumbled, smashing the floor where they'd been standing.

Nox went left and Gussie right, while Ellie flew toward the throne. The doorway they'd come through was obliterated, and instead of leaving a gaping hole they could escape through, the ceiling had caved in and sealed off the exit entirely.

If Gussie was wrong about a secret exit, then this place had just become their tomb.

The only advantage they had was that the gargols were too big to fly between the columns. The great *dis*advantage was that the monsters only had to be patient and tear the place down piece by piece until there was nowhere left to fly at all.

"Nox!" yelled Gussie. "You look for a way out. Ellie and I will distract them."

"Yeah, sure, sounds fun!" Ellie called. It made sense, though; with his clipped wing, Nox was the slowest of them and wouldn't give the gargols much chase.

Swooping in a wide arc, Ellie waved at the gargol to the left. This one had a head like a boar's, each of its wings the size of a ship's sail.

"Hey, ugly! Over here!"

With a roar of rage, the gargol hauled itself in her direction.

So now they were getting gargols' attention *on purpose*. Great. Super. This was definitely going to end well.

The gargol might have been slower on the ground than Ellie in the air, but its reach was extensive. It knocked over columns like they were made of grass. Ellie yelped and rolled as one fell her way, then frantically dodged the stone blocks it pulled down from the ceiling.

Across the throne room, Gussie was in the same predicament. Columns toppled around her, and her Falcon wings made her less agile than Ellie in dodging them. Her gargol—a long, sinuous monster with a lizard-like head and spines down its back—hissed and climbed the walls in an attempt to swat her out of the air.

"Anything, Nox?" Ellie yelled.

The Crow boy was searching the back wall, to no avail.

"Keep looking!" Gussie screamed, barely avoiding her gargol's next swipe. The monster was backing her into the corner. Was it intelligent enough to actually have some kind of plan?

Not that Ellie had time to mull it over. Her own gargol had figured out it could pick up chunks of rubble and hurl them at Ellie. Its aim was devastatingly good.

Ellie flew as fast as she could, weaving between columns, rolling, diving, and fluttering to avoid the hurtling boulders. Then, hearing a scream from Gussie, she spun to see the Falcon girl pressed into the corner with nowhere else to fly.

"I'm coming, Gus!" Ellie winged across the throne room, her heart in her throat. She was halfway there when she heard Nox shout.

"I found it!"

Her head turned—and a stone claw knocked her out of the air.

Ellie hit the ground for the second time, only now she found herself pinned by the boar-faced gargol's claw. It pressed her into the floor, until the stone around Ellie cracked. She couldn't breathe. She gasped, her vision darkening, unable to even cry out for help. All she could see was the monster's gaping jaw, the gleam of its tusks. It screeched, the sound smacking into her with physical force.

Then it raised its claw and brought it crashing down again.

Out of breath, helpless, Ellie couldn't scrabble away in time. Its claw landed on her left leg, and she heard her bones crack.

The pain followed a moment later, a hot, screaming tidal wave that took complete control of her body.

She screamed.

As red stars burst in her vision, Ellie waited for the gargol to finish her off. She was utterly broken, unable to defend herself even a little. Her lockstave had rolled away; the skystones she'd collected spilled out of their satchel, many crushed to dust. Those that weren't floated up and away.

Time stopped as Ellie looked up in the face of the monster. Its stone eyes lacked pupils, robbing it of any semblance of personality. It was like being killed by a mountain or a tree or some other soulless force of nature. Those eyes gazed at her with complete indifference, totally immune to mercy.

But the final blow never came.

Instead, with a loud *crack*, a rainbow-colored cloud exploded in the creature's face.

Ellie blinked, wondering if her dazed brain was seeing things.

Then another cloud burst, and another, pops of bright colors that filled the air with smoke.

Someone grabbed Ellie and began dragging her across the floor. The friction against her shattered leg made her nearly black out with pain. She tilted her head back to see Nox.

"Hold on," he said. His face was grimed with dust and sweat. "I'll get you out of here, Ellie. Just hold on."

Her eyes slid to the corner where Gussie had been pinned, but the Falcon girl wasn't there. Instead there was only a bright cloud of red smoke.

Then she saw her—winging through the air, aiming her funny little crossbow. It was armed with one of the paper tubes, which she shot at the lizard-faced gargol. The tube popped in a burst of blue smoke.

So *that's* what Gussie had been doing, helping herself to Nox's grandfather's supply of chalk pigment. She'd made miniature smoke bombs that exploded into opaque, colorful clouds—obscuring the gargols *and* the kids trying to escape them.

"Gus, let's go!" Nox called.

Gussie fitted one last tube into her crossbow and fired it, then flew to help Nox. Beneath a dazzling rainbow of smoke, they pulled Ellie past the throne and its array of skystones, and through a hole in the floor where a set of narrow steps had been concealed.

Her leg slammed painfully on the stairs, and she cried out. Gussie scooped her up all at once, grunting at her weight.

"Run, Nox!" she gasped. "We're right behind you!"

"This could lead to a dead end," he warned.

"We don't have a choice!"

They raced through the dark, lit only by the occasional bulge of skystone set into the walls. Ellie drifted in and out of consciousness, lost in a sea of pain. They might have run for ten minutes or an hour; she couldn't have said the difference.

Then, at last, Gussie carefully set her down. They'd reached a wall, and the Falcon girl now helped Nox search for a lever or handle that might open the way.

Ellie slumped, staring at her leg. A skystone glowed in the passage ceiling, just enough light to reveal that her foot was jutting in a direction it definitely wasn't supposed to go.

She bit her lip and looked away.

"Found it!" Gussie said, pushing at the wall. With a grind and a crunch, a door began to open. Beyond it swirled the storm, growling with thunder. They must have descended back into the clouds.

A flash of lightning illuminated the passage for a heartbeat, and she saw a glint from something wedged in the corner. She reached out, her hand trembling.

"Can you fly, Ellie?" Nox asked.

"She'll have to," said Gussie. "Use the rope. We'll carry her between us, so if she falls, we can at least do something."

Ellie grabbed the thing in the corner, but in her daze barely comprehended what it was. She stuffed it into the satchel where she'd had the skystones, while Nox and Gussie sorted out the rope.

Minutes later, they had a sort of harness fashioned around her, with an end for each of them to hold.

Behind them, the passage shuddered. Dust rained from the ceiling.

"The gargols," Nox said grimly. "They're smashing the passage."

"It's now or never," Gussie said, and she jumped.

Ellie was pulled out behind them. With a yelp, she tumbled into the storm. The escape tunnel had taken them to the underside of the floating island, where she saw the great mountains of skystone that bore up the entire landmass. The blue glow illuminated the clouds and shimmered around the three small figures as they fell.

CHAPTER NINETEEN
• ELLIE •

The flight back to Khadreen passed in a blur for Ellie. If it weren't for Nox and Gussie supporting her, she knew she would never have made it. Pain consumed her like fire, her shattered leg completely useless. Every bump in the air sent a new spike of agony knifing through her body.

When they reached the candle shop, they hurtled through the window and landed in a heap, Ellie too racked with pain to even scream. She lay on the floor, tilting toward unconsciousness, the room spinning around her.

"Jaff!" Nox cried. "We're back! Why is the doctor— Wait! NO! *Get away from him!*"

Nox's shout shocked a bit of clarity into Ellie. She lifted her head to see that Dr. Alceda was leaning over Twig—a bone saw in her hand.

"No!" Ellie gasped. "Nox—!"

The Crow boy lunged toward the doctor, knocking her aside and wrenching away the saw.

But the floor was already littered with brown and white feathers.

"I had no choice!" Jaff said. "Your friend took a bad turn while you were gone, Nox. I waited as long as I could. The boy was delirious with fever and pain. He would have died—"

"His wings!" Nox cried. "Why couldn't you have just waited? I have the cure! I have it *right here*!"

Ellie lay back, her head clunking on the floor. Her chest felt as if it were caving in, sinking through the floor, dragging her into a red sea of pain.

They were too late.

When Ellie next woke, the room was quiet, the windows shut. She lay for a moment in a fog of confusion, her tongue glued to the roof of her mouth and her body heavy as stone.

Her leg still hurt, but in a distant, vague sort of way. She guessed she'd been drugged, probably with something stronger than just maticca leaf. Something soft had been spread beneath her and a pillow put under her head.

It took her several minutes to find the strength she needed to sit up. Propped on her elbows, she looked down to see her leg wrapped in a splint, with boards strapped from her ankle to her thigh. The foot was no longer pointing the wrong way, but the longer she looked, the more it began to hurt.

Blinking away tears, Ellie lifted her eyes to the bed where Twig lay still, fast asleep.

His feathers had been swept away.

Nox sat in a chair by Twig, slumped over the foot of the bed with his head resting on his arm, sound asleep. Gussie was on her pallet in the corner, a bundle of striped wings. Nox's grandfather had been sleeping in the shop below, where she guessed he was now, but there was one more person in the room—wide awake.

"Don't move," whispered Dr. Alceda. She sat at the table, looking far from tired. An oil lamp burned low by her elbow, and judging by the quill and paper before her, she'd been writing down notes.

"How is he?" Ellie asked, her voice dry as sand.

The doctor glanced at Twig. "Recovering. I know this is difficult to understand, child, but it was the best thing—"

“Stop,” Ellie whispered, her voice knotting. “Just *stop.* We got the skystones. We could have saved him.”

“Ah. The stones.” The doctor had one in her hand, Ellie realized. She released it and watched it float gently toward the ceiling before catching it again. “A fascinating anomaly, these. Your friends told me they came from *islands in the sky*. That old Macaw legend, I suppose. I’m not entirely sure whether to believe you, but I plan on keeping one of these for further study.”

“It’s true. You’d have seen it heal Twig too, if you hadn’t been so eager to—”

“You think I enjoy my work, girl?” The doctor’s voice turned cold. “I don’t. I got into this job to help people, not to remove their wings. Yet that is what I must do, day after day. It’s getting worse out there. This time last year, it was a new case every week or so. Now it’s *dozens* a week.”

“We can stop it. If people would just *listen* to us—” A sudden splinter of pain shot up her leg, and she whimpered.

Dr. Alceda was at her side in an instant, shaking a small bottle. “You’re due for more maticca extract. It’s far more potent in this form than raw, and it’ll knock you flat again. You need the rest.”

“My leg . . .”

“I’m not one to soften the truth,” said the doctor. “Your leg is broken in several places. It will never heal straight.”

Ellie stared at her, chest tight.

“You will be lucky to walk again,” said the doctor. “But you won’t run.”

The room tilted. Ellie lay back, her hands trembling. She stared hard at the ceiling for several long moments, until she’d pushed down the sobs in her throat enough to speak.

“What about flying?” she whispered.

“You’ll learn to adjust for the leg in the air, but it will take time. Your wings are all right, though you’re bruised all over. I heard you flew into a storm and ran into gargols—no surprise there. You three are lucky to be alive at all. That was mightily foolish."

Ellie felt a warm tear run down her temple.

Lucky.

She'd been within a heartbeat of becoming a Goldwing knight, just weeks ago. Her greatest dream had literally been within reach, until she'd sacrificed it to protect Nox, Gussie, and Twig from King Garion. She thought of the moment she'd stood before the whole of Thelantis, a victor in the Race of Ascension, proud and strong and as tall as any Sparrow had ever stood.

And now here she lay, broken and bruised, a fugitive in exile.

Stubbornly, she brushed away the tear. Self-pity wasn't her style, even now. What did she have to cry about, really? She was alive. She had her wings.

Her leg was nothing compared to what Twig had been through.

His wings . . .

Oh skies. They'd been so close. So very close to saving him.

Now he would never fly again.

Pain and fury clashed in Ellie's chest until she gasped aloud, a long, wordless sob.

"Drink this," said the doctor, tipping the bottle to Ellie's lips. "Sleep deeply, little Sparrow."

"I figured it out," Ellie said. "The reason Tirelas matters."

She and Nox sat on the roof of the candle shop. It had been one week since their wild flight into the storm, and this was the first time she'd been outside since. She'd floated on a maticca-extract haze for days, and she was sick of it. At least the raw leaves didn't knock her out cold. The flavor of the one she was chewing turned her stomach—it tasted like old lemon peels—but if she went even an hour without it, the pain in her leg would have her screaming.

Again.

There had been complaints from neighbors.

Getting onto the roof had been an ordeal and a half. She couldn't fly yet, so she'd had to recruit help from Nox and Gussie, who'd managed to lift her up and onto the rooftop. She'd tried so hard to hide the pain that had caused, biting the inside of her cheek, that she could still taste blood on her tongue.

"Of course you did," Nox said, sitting hunched beside her, his arms wrapped around his knees. "Go on, then. I know you're going to tell me anyway."

"You have to see it too," she said. "I can't believe we didn't realize it sooner. The skystones, the way they heal wingrot . . ."

His lips pressed together and he looked down at his chewed fingernails. After a minute, he said quietly, "I put it together too. I'm not a total idiot, you know."

"Of course you're not." Ellie pointed to the sky. "Anyway, it's obvious that Tirelas is where we came from. It's where we *belong*. What's more, our wings, our flight, are tied to the skystones. I talked to Gussie about it and she agrees."

Gussie had taken to the idea with such alacrity it had startled Ellie, since the Falcon girl had seemed so reluctant to admit the skystones' power to begin with. She'd called it a *mineral deficiency*, and theorized that whatever the skystone was made of, it was obviously integral to the geological makeup of the sky islands. And geology—she'd explained in slow, simple terms so Ellie could keep up—was linked to *ecology*. In other words, the mineral properties in skystone were likely found throughout all the flora native to the islands, leached through the plants' roots in tiny, trace amounts.

Therefore, everything the clans had eaten when they'd lived in the sky would have had a tiny bit of skystone in it—and somehow, that mineral had strengthened and sustained their wings. Gussie's best guess was that it had something to do with making their bones lighter and stronger at the same time, so that their wings supported their weight. The less skystone in their systems, the weaker and heavier their bones became—until they began to break down altogether.

Ellie squeezed her eyes shut, thinking of Twig.

He'd barely said two words all week. He sat inside, cold and vacant, Lirri whimpering in his lap. Already small to begin with, he looked even smaller without his wings—a pale, gray ghost with eyes like great empty holes.

Shuddering, she opened her eyes again and gazed at Nox.

"We've gone so long without being close to skystones," Ellie said now, "that our bodies have started paying the price. We're changing, losing our wings without it. Gussie and I think that even if we brought down bags and bags of skystones, it wouldn't be enough. In the end, we'd still lose our wings."

Nox's feathers ruffled. "Even if *we* don't get wingrot . . ."

"Our kids might, or our grandkids. In fact, they'd almost definitely get it, and we'd always have to be raiding sky islands, risking death, to get more stones. Either that . . . or we do what Dr. Alceda did to Twig. We start cutting off our wings ourselves."

She shuddered as her mind flashed to a future in which every child's wings were shorn off before they could even fly, to protect them from ever catching wingrot.

To ground them forever.

Oh, Twig.

"We're meant to be skyborn," she whispered. "But Gussie figures in just a few generations . . . we'll become earthbound. Permanently."

"Let me guess," Nox said hollowly. "You have a plan."

"What choice do we have? Lose our wings—or fight for them?" She drew a deep breath. "We have to return to the sky, Nox. It's where we belong. No more people should suffer like Twig has. We have to go *home*."

He stared across Khadreen, and the forest of plumes rising from its many chimneys. Ellie watched him anxiously, wondering if he'd agree. Did he see what the future held for their people, if they didn't act soon?

"But Ellie . . . we're just kids. We can't take on every gargol in the sky. Look what happened to Twig. To your leg. Haven't we lost enough already?"

"Of course we could never retake Tirelas with just the four of us." *Three* of us, she amended to herself. Twig would be flying nowhere. "That's why we need . . ." She pressed her lips together and swept a hand at the city. "Well, *them*. We need them to know what we know, and to make the same choice we're making: to go home, whatever it takes."

The warm wind ruffled her feathers.

"We still have two bags of skystones," she said. "All it will take is using them to heal people of wingrot, then telling them where the stones came from. They'll see what to do from there, I just know it. We'll take the fight to the gargols at last, once enough people realize that's the only way to save ourselves."

"And the ones who don't care?" he said. "The ones who shrug it off and say, better to be grounded than dead? The ones like my . . ." He twisted his neck, his barely contained fury pulsing in his temple. Ellie could hear his teeth grinding together.

She knew what he wanted to say.

The ones like *his grandfather*.

Ever since that awful night, when they'd found Jaff and the doctor standing over Twig, Nox had turned a cold shoulder on the old man.

Ellie's heart ached for him, that he had come so far to find his one last family member, only to have this seemingly irreparable rift open between them. Nox's expression alone made it clear that as far as he was concerned, what Jaff had done to Twig was unforgivable, no matter his reasons.

"It's not just Jaff's fault," Nox said after a long, tense silence. Skies, how empty his voice sounded. "I should have told him about the skystones before we left, instead of waiting to prove it after we'd returned."

"Twig is *not* your fault," she said firmly. Then she shook her head. "Anyway, as I was saying before, nobody would rather sacrifice their wings than face the gargols."

"Of *course* they would, Ellie. It's the way people work. They'll take the safest course of action, the most comfortable one, every time. If that means losing their wings, they'll do it. Most people aren't heroes."

"I don't believe that. Maybe some won't care, but most will. I believe the right people will do what's needed."

"You have a lot more faith in them than I do."

"Well, then maybe . . ." She looked at Nox, her heart beating harder. Words thickened in her throat, needing to be said, but she wasn't sure she dared. She knew how he'd react.

But he *had* to know the whole story—and the last, most dangerous truth she'd kept to herself. She'd been turning it over in her mind for days, trying to find the courage to tell him what she'd discovered on the island in the sky.

But would he even listen?

Her next words might end their friendship forever.

"Nox . . ."

"Hmm."

"There's one other thing. One other . . . person, who I think can convince them better than anyone."

Frowning, Nox tossed a nut at her. "If you say King Garion—"

"No," she laughed. "But . . . you're not too far off. What I mean is, I think we need a leader. Someone linked to Tirelas like no one else. Someone whose very existence changes everything."

"Ellie . . ." he groaned. "Whatever lunatic idea you've cooked up, just spit it out."

"Okay." She inhaled, held her breath. And when she spoke, she let it all out in a rush. "I think we need a Phoenix."

He scoffed, popping another nut into his mouth and crunching it. "Right. The supposed kings and queen of the islands in the sky. You want to find this long-lost Phoenix clan, let them magically fix everything?"

"I don't need to find them," she said softly. "Because I think I already have."

She turned to the satchel she'd brought up with her, the same one she'd carried to Tirelas on their last raid. The skystones had all spilled out when the gargol had attacked her, but she hadn't returned totally empty-handed. There'd been the shiny thing she'd found in the escape tunnel, moments before they'd dived off the island.

She took it out now, held it reverently between her hands.

Nox stared, then slowly put down the bowl of nuts. "Ellie. What is that?"

"Isn't it obvious?" She gave him a weak smile. "It's a crown, Nox. The kind a king or a prince might wear."

It was ancient; there was no denying it. The golden band, composed of three intertwining strands, was tarnished and worn. But the exquisitely cut skystone set at its center was still bright, its color clearer and purer than any other she'd seen. When she tilted the crown, the stone glimmered like a diamond. Around it, the gold filigree had been wrought to resemble flames.

But the most astonishing thing about it wasn't the pureness of the gold or the brightness of the skystone, but the simple emblem engraved on the headband, just under the gem.

Nox stared at it.

"That . . ." He shook his head slightly but seemed unable to tear his eyes away. "It's just an ashmark."

"What if it's not *just* an ashmark?"

"Ellie . . ."

"The Corvain crest," she whispered, running her finger over the lines that she'd always thought looked like an open flame. "Nox, it's carved onto the candle shop sign. Onto the table your grandmother built. You said your father had it tattooed on his arm."

She watched the blood drain from his face. "Yeah, but that doesn't mean—"

"What if the ashmark and your family crest aren't two different symbols? They look identical. Do you think that's just a coincidence? What if, all this time, even after we forgot Tirelas, forgot our *home*, a part of it still lived on—in the symbol we draw over our doors and windows to keep us safe? The symbol . . . of an ancient royal clan."

Nox jumped to his feet, his face twisting with anger. "Ellie, *stop*. You're doing it again—pushing things on people, trying to control everyone around you. You're making things bigger than they really are. That crown is nothing. It's just an old relic. We'd be better off selling it."

"Nox." Her grip tightened on the crown. "You're *immune to fire*. So was your grandmother and your father. And those Phoenix royals in that mural we saw—their wings looked like fire. You saw it too. Or do you really think that's just another coincidence?"

"That doesn't prove anything!" he cried out, desperation in his voice.

"But it answers our questions, doesn't it? Why you have that gift—and why the Eagles have hunted your bloodline for generations. Because they know, Nox. They know who you are, who you're descended from. You're not a Crow at all. You're a *Phoenix*."

"Do my wings look like they're made of fire?" he asked, unfurling his dark feathers. "Do I look like those snooty high clanners on those palace walls? No."

"Maybe the Phoenix part of you is hidden. Maybe there's a way to unlock it."

"Enough!" With a snarl, he slung himself into the air, flying high over the city.

"Nox, wait!"

Ruing her injured leg, she could only watch as he winged away. He'd reacted just as she'd feared he would. A part of her wished she'd never said anything at all.

It had been days since she'd put it all together in her head, linking the present to the past. He might not believe it, but she had never been so certain of anything in her life. She'd shattered her leg to uncover this truth. That had to mean it was important, right?

Looking down at the crown, Ellie felt a stir of whispers.

Elder Rue's voice: *You will carry a flame through the darkness, to light a great fire.*

Her thumb ran over the engraved flames on the crown.

But if you drop it, or if the flame goes out . . . the sky will fall.

For weeks, Ellie had wondered what her destiny was, where she might belong. And the answer had been beside her the whole time—black-haired, black-winged, sulky and aggravating and brave and more loyal than he'd ever admit.

Nox.

He was the flame. This crown was proof. He was supposed to lead them to their true home in the sky, where they'd be healed. Where they'd be who they were meant to be.

That had to be worth every risk . . . even if it meant losing Nox's friendship for a time. Maybe he wouldn't believe her yet, but Ellie would make sure he did. She'd make him understand, and together, they'd change everything. Even if he hated her for it, she had to help him find his true path, for everyone's sakes.

It was, after all, her destiny.

Nox had never been so furious in his life.

How dare she.

How dare she?

He stood by the bank of the Khadreen river, hurling stones into the water with all his strength. A few Flamingo kids had been swimming in the shallows, but when they'd seen Nox's face, they'd taken off in a hurry.

Ellie Meadows was the most controlling, manipulative, *delusional* girl he'd ever known. And he'd once known a Jay girl who liked to dump buckets of wet pig dung onto people's heads just for a laugh.

Ellie was worse.

Ellie went around dumping *destinies* on people.

"Stupid, stupid, *stupid*!" He chucked three more rocks into the water.

All of this was just part of Ellie's need to play hero. It was the same reason she'd conned him into guiding her through the Bluebriar Forest to Thelantis, so she could become a Goldwing knight. She wanted so badly to be like a character in one of her stories, saving the day, changing the world, watching everyone cheer for her.

Well, not Nox. He was no leader. He was not descended from some fancy-feathered royal clan. And he was *certainly* no hero.

Just ask his mother.

Just ask Twig.

All he wanted was to be left alone.

Why couldn't she understand that? Why couldn't she just *leave him alone*?

"Girl problems?" asked a voice.

Nox turned to see one of the Flamingo kids hadn't fled, but sat higher up on the bank, knees against his chest.

"Uh . . . Yeah. Kind of."

The kid nodded sadly. "Me too."

"What are you, six years old?" asked Nox.

"Eight." The boy scowled. "She broke my heart, y'know. Broke it right in half. I gave her a pretty rock with her name painted on it, and y'know what she did? She gave it to *Tarik*. Just 'cause his wings turned pink already." He looked sadly at his own plumage, which was still the dull gray of a fledgling Flamingo.

"That's rough, kid," Nox said. "But just you wait. My ma told me the longer feathers take to turn, the stronger they're meant to be."

The words left him hollow. He wished he'd kept his mouth shut. He looked down at his hands, remembering how soft and fragile her skin had felt. How weak her bones.

With a shudder, Nox waded into the river and cupped cool water in his palms. He stared a moment at his reflection, then splashed the water over his face.

But it didn't wash away the prickling question crawling over his scalp.

Ellie's theory, wild and impossible as it sounded, did answer a lot of questions. Which didn't make it *true*, he reminded himself, just *believable*. And that was almost as dangerous. Because she clearly believed it, and if he knew anything about Ellie, it was that she'd cross the world—literally—if it meant proving a point. He'd seen her do it before. This time would be worse. This time, *he* was the point she wanted to prove.

Dashing a hand through the water, he turned and waded to shore to pull his boots back on. It would soon be dark, and he'd have to return to face Ellie sooner or later. The candle shop was simply too small to avoid both her *and* Jaff.

Thinking of the old man made his fists curl and his head hot. Jaff was not his grandfather anymore, not after what he'd done to Twig. Nox was finished with him, and any hopes he'd had of staying here, of finally having a home again, had been severed as cleanly as Twig's wings.

They never should have come to Khadreen. He was sick of this place, sick of flying, sick of always making everything worse. And furious as he was at Jaff, he knew the real blame for Twig's lost wings lay at his own feet.

It was *Nox* who had left Twig alone. *He* had trusted Jaff, like a fool. Well, he wouldn't make that mistake again. The minute Ellie and Twig were well enough, they'd leave this place far behind.

"I'm back," he called when he walked through the shop door a short while later. He let it swing shut behind him.

Only it didn't.

Instead, a boot shoved in, keeping the door open. Nox whirled as two tall Hawk clanners strode in, their Goldwing cloaks rippling behind them.

"Told you it was him," said the first, grinning at Nox through his curly red beard.

The second, a pale man with a shaven head, lifted a paper with Nox's likeness sketched on it.

"Yep, it's him. The king was right—the little rat did run all the way to the jungle."

Nox moved quickly, sprinting for the stairs, but they caught him before he reached the first step. The bearded one tackled him to the ground, crushing the wind from his lungs.

"Gus!" he wheezed, lacking the breath to shout. He knew the Falcon girl was upstairs, but his voice wouldn't carry.

"Hush, rat!" The knight clamped a hand over Nox's mouth, then dragged him up. "What do we do now? The king wants him alive."

"Sure, but accidents can happen," said the bald knight, grinning nastily. "And that way, he'll be easier to carry."

They said nothing about the skystone that King Garion had originally been hunting Nox for. They didn't even look for it, or mention Ellie, Gussie, and Twig.

It really was Nox they were after, and Nox alone.

They know who you are, Ellie had said. *Who you're descended from.*

Shaking the words away, he slammed his head backward, right into the knight's nose. The man cursed but only gripped Nox tighter.

"Yeah, do it now!" he said. "Before the rat—"

"Hello?"

They all looked up to see Twig standing on the stairs, barefoot and blinking.

Nox bit down on the knight's hand, and as the man howled and released him, he shouted, "Twig, get out of here!"

The knight rapped Nox's skull with the hilt of his dagger. Nox stumbled to his knees, dazed. He waved at Twig, trying desperately to make him run, but the kid only walked closer.

"Would Kassia want you to hurt a kid?" Twig said, speaking to the red-bearded knight.

Nox, his head spinning, frowned in confusion and looked over his shoulder.

The man was still holding the knife, but instead of carrying out the awful deed, the knight stared at Twig with a stunned expression.

"Your wife, Kassia. She believes you're a hero," said Twig, taking another step. He gazed at the knight with sharp intensity. "She believes you protect kids like your son, Tam. He's thirteen, just like Nox here. What would Tam think of his dad, if he saw you now?"

"How do . . . ?" The knight's face drained of color. "Who *are* you? Where are your wings?"

Twig took another step, then shifted his strange, burning gaze to the bald man. "And you. You like hurting people, don't you? Because of the way *he* hurt you. Your father. He made you feel worthless and small, and now the only way for you to feel big is by making *others* feel the way you did."

"The boy is a sorcerer," gasped the bald knight. "He's using some kind of magic on us! We'll take them both out!"

But now they were too late. Twig had bought Nox time to scramble away, and he raced up the stairs, pulling Twig with him.

"What in the skies was that, Twig?"

Twig swayed unsteadily, his face creasing as if his head ached. It was then that Nox realized he had a skystone clutched in his hand, its light faintly pulsing.

Hearing the knights running after them, Nox began shouting. "Gussie, Jaff!"

He burst into the living quarters, where Gussie was bent over the table she'd requisitioned for inventing. Jaff was stirring what promised to be another awful soup.

"Get out, get out!" Nox shouted, just as the knights burst through behind him.

Pushing Twig toward Gussie, he turned and threw a chair, which the men dodged. The bald one drew his sword and swung at Nox's head.

When Nox ducked, the blade swished through empty air—to slice open the oil lamp Gussie had lit.

Oil spilled across the floor, immediately catching flame.

Fire, Nox thought with dismay. *Why's it always got to be fire?*

A blazing wall sprang up between him and the knights. It was barrier enough to give him time to jump out of the window behind Gussie and Twig, Jaff just behind him. Nox had the forethought to grab their satchels but had time for nothing else.

The knights retreated back down the stairs; Nox saw them spill out the front door, coughing. The flames were spreading quickly, and already a brigade was forming in the air as the Ibis clan took flight. They began tossing buckets of water on the shop and the buildings around it. Everything in Khadreen was made of wood; their response was immediate and organized, but with an edge of desperation.

Gussie landed on a rooftop nearby, carrying Twig, while Jaff joined the water brigade.

Suddenly, Nox remembered Ellie, whom he'd left stranded on the rooftop.

"Skies!" Wheeling in the air, he tore back to the shop and landed beside her.

"Nox!" She was crouched on her good leg, as if she'd been about to take off. "I saw them come out of the shop. This is bad."

"Hold on to me."

He scooped her into his arms, struggling a little. She was small, but heavier than she looked.

"Ready?"

"My lockstave!"

He bent enough for her to grab the staff. She carried it everywhere, even when they were supposed to be safe.

"Go!" she shouted.

Nox leaped off the roof, spreading his dark wings. He sank quickly, landing in the street beside Gussie and Twig, nearly dropping Ellie.

"There he is!" shouted a voice.

Nox whirled to see the knights charging toward him, blades drawn. He couldn't very well take off and leave Ellie and Twig defenseless. So he grabbed Ellie's lockstave and drew his own dagger, prepared to fight them both.

But he never got the chance.

Out of nowhere, a jumble of pink wings filled the street, accompanied by whirling flames.

"Get out of here, kids!" shouted one of the Flamingo clanners.

They were the fire dancers from the square—only now they looked ready to do far more than dance with the blazing torches they carried.

"We don't suffer northie bullies here!" bellowed the tallest of them. And with that they stormed the knights, yelling wildly and twirling their flames.

Taking advantage of the distraction, Nox and Gussie managed to carry both Ellie and Twig to a nearby rooftop, out of sight and reach of the knights. In moments, the Flamingos had chased them off. Nox could track their pursuit by the light of their torches as they hounded the panicked Goldwings through the streets.

"Those," gasped Twig, "were the *awesomest* people I've ever seen."

"Gotta give you that one," Nox panted.

He dropped to a crouch and watched the skies, looking for any telltale white cloaks. But if any other knights were around, they were keeping well hidden, probably warned off by the Flamingos' fury.

"What happened?" Gussie demanded. "Where did those jerks come from, anyway?"

Nox told her about the knights bursting into the shop, then faltered when he came to the part where Twig had interrupted them.

As if knowing why he was hesitating, Twig said, "It's all right. I don't care if they know."

"Know what?" asked Ellie.

"Ever since you brought these back . . ." Twig held out the skystone, and Lirri scurried out of his sleeve to gnaw on its hard surface. "I've been keeping one with me, in case . . . Well, my wings didn't grow back, but it's strange. Remember how I told you everyone's feelings have been getting louder lately? I think it's because we carried that skystone around for so long, and it started affecting my ability. A few days ago, I realized when I hold one, other people's emotions get so strong I have to *work* to shut them out. And I can hear a lot more about them, even their . . . memories."

Ellie looked at Nox, who shrugged and turned away. He didn't understand Twig's ability and didn't really want to. Nox was the only other person he knew of who had something . . . magical about them, and Twig's odd talent just served as a reminder of his own fireproof skin. Which, of course, brought his mind back to Ellie's wild ideas about Phoenixes.

"Maybe," Ellie said, shifting her attention to Gussie, "skystone doesn't just work on our bones."

Gussie sighed. "At this point, I don't even know what to think anymore. You could be right. But this isn't the time to hypothesize."

"Gussie's right," said Nox, leaping on the change of topic. "We're not safe in Khadreen anymore. Now Garion will *know* we're here."

As he watched Tanra Corvain's beloved shop go up in flames, he felt like his heart was being hollowed out.

Another home lost, another life destroyed by Garion's obsession with his family.

As if reading his thoughts, Ellie laid a hand on his arm. "He'll never stop, Nox. Nowhere will be safe, not until things change for good."

He pulled his arm away, his jaw tightening.

Or until I'm dead, he thought. *This happened because of me.*

"What now?" asked Gussie. "We can't stay here. As soon as the knights report back to Garion, this city will be crawling with his spies."

It was Twig who offered the solution: "The Clay!"

"What clay?" asked Ellie.

"*The* Clay. The Macaw clan seat. Remember what Granna said? We'd always be welcome there, if we needed a place to run."

Nox raised an eyebrow. "Are you saying that just because Tariel told you they have elephants there?"

"Well, yes," said Twig. "But do you have a better idea?"

Nox didn't. He looked down at his grandfather, who stood in the street beside an empty bucket, his wings sagging as he watched his home burn. A heavy roof beam fell in the candle shop with a crash, sending sparks out the charred windows.

The shop was gone. The wooden sign his grandmother had carved, with the troublesome Corvain crest, fell with a groan into a heap of burning coals.

"It's a good plan," he murmured. It would mean saying goodbye to the only relative he had left, but after what Jaff did to Twig, Nox didn't think he'd be shedding many tears over the old man.

"We'll have to find a cart and donkey," added Gussie quietly. "For Ellie and Twig."

"We don't even know where this Clay place is."

"Near Elephant Rock," said Ellie. "Granna said anyone in the jungle could point us toward it."

It seemed there was no other choice. Khadreen was no longer safe. Still, Nox didn't like it. They were being driven farther and farther back, like animals herded into a trap.

Sooner or later, they would run into a corner they *couldn't* escape.

CHAPTER TWENTY-ONE
· ELLIE ·

"Ready?" Tariel said, grinning. Her hands were clasped over Twig's eyes.

"Oh skies!" gasped Twig. "I can't believe this is happening!"

Twig looked like he was about to explode. Ellie laughed, watching him bounce from foot to foot.

"And . . . *ta-da*!" Tariel dropped her hands.

Twig's eyes went huge, then huger, until his eyeballs seemed on the verge of popping out altogether.

"They're so . . . *big*," he gasped.

A dozen elephants waded through mud, using their long trunks to dig up clay and dump it into baskets held by Macaw clanners. Ellie was impressed; the creatures were not only enormous—some of them carried as many as six Macaw fledglings, giggling and whooping, on their backs—they were also deeply intelligent, following the complicated instructions given by their handlers.

The Clay had turned out to be full of surprises, and not just for its herd of elephants. The place was a marvel of architecture, the city built inside enormous kapok trees, with hollowed-out tunnels and chambers that grew and shifted with the trees themselves. And of course, there were the nearby clay deposits that the clan mined to fuel their pottery industry, with the help of their gigantic gray pets.

"Can I ride one?" asked Twig.

"Sure," said Tariel.

Twig walked toward a great tusked male, made a little jump, then froze.

Ellie's stomach turned over as she realized he must have tried to take off—then remembered he couldn't. His shoulders sagged and his hands curled into fists.

"Oh . . ." Tariel glanced at Ellie in panic. "Um, it's fine, I'll get someone to lift—"

"I can *do* it!" Twig said sharply.

Ellie put a gently restraining hand on Tariel's arm and said quietly, "We've learned to let him work things out for himself."

She watched curiously as Twig put a hand on the great elephant's leg; the top of the kid's head barely came to the animal's shoulder. But then the elephant lowered itself on one knee, and Twig was able to climb up onto its back.

"Whoa," said Tariel. "He's a natural."

"That was nothing," said Nox. "You should have seen the time he charmed a mossbear."

"A what?"

Ellie smiled, watching Twig sprawl across the elephant's back, his expression genuinely happy for the first time since his wings had been amputated. "I'm glad we came here."

Tariel grinned. "C'mon. I'll show you around town. I haven't been back here since I was ten, but I remember *all* the places we can steal snacks from, *and* where the cutest boys go to swim. Of course, my heart will always belong to my beloved Gade, but my *eyes* . . . well, they do get lonely. You know what I mean, right, Ellie?"

"Me?" Ellie squeaked. "Um. The snacks sound great, anyway."

The last time they'd seen the Macaw girl, the gargol attack on Brightbay had left her withdrawn and shaken. But now Tariel seemed to be her usual self again. When Ellie and her friends had turned up in the Clay that morning, Tariel had squealed so loudly a flock of butterflies shot out of the bushes. After dealing out generous hugs, Granna had tasked her with looking after their guests.

Leaving Twig to his elephants, they followed the track through the jungle that led back to the village center. Ellie hobbled along with the help of her lockstave, which she used as a crutch, and bit her lip every time a current of pain went shooting up her leg.

The Clay was hidden deep in the jungle, at the foot of what Tariel called the Old Man Mountains, or just the Old Men.

"It's said if a young man starts climbing one, by the time he reaches the top he'll be an old man," she'd explained, which sounded about right to Ellie. The Aeries in the Clandoms looked like anthills compared to the great rocky peaks rising out of the jungle. Elephant Rock was a massive, triangular crag that jutted out of the mountain just north of the Clay.

Ellie'd marked the rocky range as they traveled to the Clay, thinking of how easy it might be to hide in those peaks—forever if they had to. And she'd had plenty of time to ponder it. Between her broken leg and Twig's still-healing wings, they'd had to travel from Khadreen by donkey cart. It had been an agonizingly slow journey, taking more than two weeks when they could have easily flown it in four days.

As she walked, Ellie's hand wandered into her pocket, and to a paper envelope sealed with candle wax.

It had been there ever since they'd left Khadreen, given to her by Nox's grandfather. Nox's parting with Jaff had been cold, a single "goodbye" that had left everyone feeling chilly. But afterward, when Nox was distracted with Twig and Gussie, Jaff had pulled Ellie aside.

"Will you keep an eye on my grandson, young Sparrow? I know he doesn't want to speak with me, and I deserve that. I just hope one day he can forgive me."

Ellie had nodded stiffly, still angry with the old man herself. She couldn't look at Twig without feeling a rush of fury and guilt. They'd been *so close* to saving his wings.

Jaff continued, "Nox is a good lad, but I worry . . . He has the same mood as his father and grandmother, you know. Not a day goes by I don't wish I'd gone with Tanra on that last trip. If I'd known how her thoughts were eating her . . . Well. Nox is the same. He takes his troubles and buries them deep and pretends all is well."

He took an envelope from his pocket and pressed it into her hand. "I don't know if it'll help or hurt him, but when you feel the time is right, will you give this letter to Nox?"

Ellie looked down. "If it's an explanation for what you did to Twig, I don't think—"

"No, no. It's from Tanra. She left it for me to find after she went north. I don't need it anymore; the words are sealed in my memory by now. There's something trapped in Nox's soul, just as there was in hers when she left. I hope . . . I hope her words might reach him, if nothing else can. I'm not sure anything I say right now will get through to him."

Ellie had nodded and carefully put the letter in her pocket. She was bewildered by when the *right time* might be to give such a thing to Nox. But there was no doubting the curiosity now nibbling at her mind. On the journey from Khadreen, she'd resisted the temptation to open it but still found herself touching the envelope every now and then.

After making their way up one of the great kapoks, following twisting tunnels carved through the tree's living trunk and popping into different chambers to steal honey-glazed nuts, fruit skewers, and candied pork, they found themselves a quiet perch on one of the tree's upper branches. The kapok's limbs were as wide as roads, and they could stretch out without fear of toppling off.

"There are five main trees in the town," said Tariel, pointing them out. "And that long building over there is the pottery."

"What's that?" asked Ellie, pointing to a cluster of thatched houses far below.

Tariel's expression shifted to unease. "That's the chophouse. Well, that's what people call it, but only in secret. We're *supposed* to say infirmary."

"Then why would you call it the—*what*?" Ellie looked at Nox, who'd interrupted her with an elbow in her side. Then she saw him flick his wings, giving her a meaningful look, and she gulped.

"Oh. Right." She stared at the buildings, wondering how many people had had their wings severed in there. *"Right."*

Tariel looked up at her change in tone. "What? Don't tell me you want a tour of the chophouse, because there is no way—"

"It's not that," said Nox resignedly. "She's plotting something."

Ellie turned to Tariel. "Remember when you asked us what happened to my leg?"

"You still haven't told me! Does it have something to do with those northie brutes who burned down Nox's grandfather's place?"

"No. But I think it's better to *show* you what happened." Ellie put her hand on the girl's shoulder, trying to silently persuade her to focus long enough to see how important this was. "We need your help, Tariel. Can you keep an ear to the ground, and let us know the *minute* any Macaw clanners are taken to the chophouse?"

"Uh . . ." Tariel glanced between them. "What's this about?"

"You'll just have to wait and see."

Nox sighed. "When Ellie's being dramatic, it's best to just go along with it."

"Yep," said Gussie.

"Hey!" Ellie pouted. "I'm just saying, people generally don't believe us until they see with their own eyes that— Well, you'll see." She gave Tariel a quick smile.

"O . . . kay." Tariel squinted suspiciously. "This is all sounding very mysterious." Then her eyes popped wide, and she grinned ear to ear. "And I *love* mysteries! Granna always says I have a nose for sniffing up things I shouldn't. It was me who caught Franka kissing a Gull sailor on the beach, when everyone knew full well she was meant to marry Loren, y'know. I *knew* there was something off about that Quetzal girl. Nobody puts on their best dress *and* spritzes with hibiscus perfume just to 'go look for pretty seashells.'"

Ellie held back a groan. She had to wave a hand in front of Tariel's face just to make the girl stop talking. "Right, well, you put those powers of yours to work and come find me as soon as you hear of a new case of wingrot. Got it?"

Tariel saluted. "I won't let you down! So long as you three come to my Seed Ceremony tonight."

"All right," said Ellie. She honestly *was* intrigued by the whole idea of the ceremony.

"Oh, and don't forget to wear something old and gross."

"Uh . . . why?"

Tariel grinned. "I guess you'll just have to *wait and see*."

By nightfall, the Clay was ablaze with torchlight.

Ellie walked in a long procession of Macaws, down a narrow jungle path lined with oil lamps in pretty clay jars hung in the trees. She shivered, wondering how they felt safe enough to be out at night. Then she looked up—and saw the dozens of Macaws perched in the treetops, keeping watch on the skies.

"Where's Tariel?" she whispered to Granna, who walked ahead of her.

"She's being prepared for the ceremony," said the old woman.

The clan gathered in a clearing, where the Macaw chief waited atop an elephant decked in flowered garlands and beads. Benches of hardened clay provided seating, and Ellie found herself between Nox and Twig.

"Ugh," said Gussie, lifting her foot. "Why's it so mucky?"

The ground was squelchy with mud. Ellie, who'd come barefoot, wriggled her toes in it.

She leaned forward to catch Granna's attention. "What *is* a Seed Ceremony, anyway?"

"Ah. Well, as you may have seen, we Macaws put great significance in raw clay. In the ceremony, clay represents each of us and the possibilities we hold. A lump might become a handful of beads, or an urn, or a brick in a wall. Its purpose is known only to the one who shapes it, the potter. And so Tariel comes forward tonight to learn her place in the clan. She will receive, in short, her destiny."

"Destiny," whispered Ellie, turning to the scene before them with a hammering heart. "Do only Macaw clanners get to do it?"

Granna arched a curious brow. "Yes, generally."

"Oh." Ellie tried not to look disappointed. In the Sparrow clan, there was no ceremony to determine your destiny. Everyone just became farmers like their parents. If she'd had some ceremony that told her clan she was destined to be a Goldwing knight, would they have supported her, instead of trying to clip her wings? But then, that hadn't turned out to be her destiny after all.

No, her destiny was bound to the skystones in her satchel, she was sure.

And possibly to the boy beside her.

It had been two weeks since she'd told Nox her theory, but neither of them had mentioned it since. He didn't *want* to believe it, but what she couldn't figure out was if he *might*. Certainly he had no interest in discussing it with her, and she knew better than to push too hard.

But how long was too long?

If he really was the descendant of the Phoenix clan—and perhaps the last of them—then he was the key to saving them all. He could become the kind of person others would follow. But how could she make a hero of a thief? How could she persuade a boy who lived in the shadows to step into the light?

Drums began to sound, beating a soft, repeating tattoo, and a Macaw blew into a long flute that released long, rich notes. The ceremony was beginning.

The benches encircled a kind of arena, the center of which featured a pedestal of stone. Torches blazed all around the perimeter, and the air shimmered with drifting sparks. High above, Macaws swooped and sprinkled handfuls of flower petals over the crowd.

"Here she comes," said Granna, beaming.

Down an aisle between the benches, Tariel came prancing in a gown as colorful as her wings. She was clearly enjoying the attention, blowing kisses and twirling, pausing to do a little dance. Halfway down, she stopped to give an enormous, flourishing bow to the people seated on each side.

Granna groaned and pressed a hand to her face.

Finally, Tariel reached the center of the clearing and stood before the pedestal, bouncing. Her hair had been pulled up and wrapped in cords of white flowers.

"Tariel of the Macaws," said the chief, a tall woman with black hair braided in a crown. "Why do you come here, before all these witnesses?"

"To know my destiny, Chief," Tariel said in a clear voice. "I've only been waiting my whole life, y'know. And technically I turned thirteen three *weeks* ago, but Granna had to stay in Khadreen longer than expected, which was fine, obviously, I mean, she had important business to take care of. And I do wish Gade was here. Gade's not a Macaw, obviously, but he's still the handsomest and bravest—"

"Ahem."

Tariel swallowed, giving the chief a sheepish grin. Meanwhile, Granna looked ready to bury herself—or Tariel—in the mud.

The chief sighed. "Well, Tariel, let your destiny be known." She raised a hand, and an elephant lumbered forward, carrying a bowl in its trunk.

"So clever," said Twig. "Did you know elephants have feelings almost as strong as ours? I met one today who—"

"Shh," Ellie whispered.

The elephant set the bowl on the pedestal, and Ellie craned her neck to see what was inside it.

It was a bunch of small shells made of hardened clay.

"The seeds of destiny," whispered Granna.

As the elephant backed away and the drums started up again, Tariel made a show of picking one of the shells. She tapped her chin, started reaching in, changed her mind, and walked dramatically around the pedestal.

"Oh, which to choose?" Tariel cried out, wringing her hands in anguish. "Which to choose?"

Granna watched through her fingers, looking mortified.

"Oh, pick one already!" someone shouted. "Let's get to the good part!"

Tariel turned toward the heckler and poked out her tongue. Then, without even looking, she plucked a seed of destiny from the bowl. She placed it on the pedestal, picked up a small silver hammer, and brought it down on the clay, cracking the shell open.

Everyone leaned forward, the drums falling silent.

Ellie held her breath, watching as Tariel peered inside the two halves of the clay.

Then Tariel grinned and held up the broken pieces. "I am Tariel of the Macaws, and I will be a tailor like my mother was! I will learn the art of cutting, sewing, and dyeing, and people will come from all across the south just to buy my clothes!"

The Macaws cheered, several rushing forward to scoop Tariel up and set her on their shoulders. They paraded her around while she waved and blew kisses.

Granna stood and clapped, beaming with pride. "You kids ready?"

"Ready?" echoed Ellie.

"Tariel didn't tell you?" She bent down and scooped up a handful of mud. "After the ceremony comes the initiation."

"The what?"

"It means the fun part." With a wide, wicked grin, Granna flung the handful of mud straight at Ellie's face.

Gasping, Ellie wiped mud from her cheeks and stared in shock at the old woman, who cackled and bent to scoop up another handful.

All around them, Macaws were howling with laughter as they threw handfuls of wet, thick mud on one another. Ellie ducked with a yelp as a clod flew over her head.

"They're insane!" Gussie cried. "Get me out of here!"

"Are you kidding? This is *the best night of my life*!" crowed Twig, and he hurled mud across Gussie's front. She squealed and volleyed back, spattering his mouth and chin.

In seconds, the somber Macaws had turned into a chaotic jumble of screams, laughter, and flying globs of mud. It was complete mayhem.

Ellie picked up a handful of mud and turned to Nox, grinning.

"Don't you dare," he said.

She grinned wider.

"Ellie! No! Stop!"

Letting out a whoop, she smacked her mud-filled hand right onto his face. Nox yelped and stumbled back.

"That's it!" He plunged a hand into the mud. "You're going to regret that in exactly five seconds!"

Shrieking, Ellie tried to hobble away but couldn't get far on her one good leg. Nox opened the back of her shirt, beneath her wings, and let the cold, slimy mud run down her bare back.

"Nox! I'll smother you for that!"

She chased him as best as she could, and within minutes they were covered from wingtip to toe. She could barely tell her own friends apart once they were all drenched in mud.

Then a hand grabbed her arm, whirling her around. Prepared, she let her handful of mud fly—and splattered it all over Tariel.

"Oh!" she cried. "Sorry! I thought you were—"

"Never mind that!" Tariel said. "You said to come running the minute I heard about . . . you know. Well, I did! Y'see? I told you there wasn't a bit of gossip I couldn't eavesdrop on. Did I tell you that? Well, anyway, it's true. One time, I was—"

"Tariel! Just spit it out!"

"Right. Sorry. What I came to tell you is, there's this woman, Liriel—I know, I know, sounds like Tariel. It's a Macaw clan thing. Oh, and Liriel? She's the chief's *niece*. I guess they wanted her to have one last night with her friends before . . . well."

"Tariel!"

"Sorry! What I mean is, Liriel's wings are sick. Her mother just left to take her to the chophouse." Her eyes dropped. "It's so sad. Liriel had such pretty wings too, and she was one of the fastest fliers in the clan . . . Hey, where are you going?"

"Nox!" Ellie cried, grabbing a muddy figure, then recoiling when she realized it was a stranger. "Nox!"

"What?"

She turned and saw him forming another mudball. Knocking it out of his hand, she grabbed for Gussie and Twig too.

"This is it!" she said.

"This is *what*?" said Twig.

"It's time to bring out the skystones."

CHAPTER TWENTY-TWO

NOX

"What the—you kids can't be here!"

The Macaw clan chief threw up a hand, blocking Ellie from getting nearer to the bed where the sick woman, Liriel, lay. Nox held back, clutching the satchel of skystones and bracing for trouble. The infirmary was dark, save for a pool of light cast by three oil lamps hung over Liriel's bed. The woman looked to be in her twenties, and lay on her stomach, tears running down her cheeks. Her clothes were still muddy from the ceremony, but the skin around her wings had been wiped clean. Even from across the room, Nox could see the gray scales of wingrot there. A doctor stood over her, laying out several nasty-looking instruments.

"It's all right," Ellie said. "We're here to help."

"Someone get these kids out of my surgery!" commanded the Macaw doctor.

"Nox!" Ellie turned and held out a hand, still muddy despite her hastily wiping it on her shirt. "Hurry!"

He stuck a hand into the satchel, careful not to open it lest the skystones inside float out. Taking out a large, diamond-shaped stone, he pressed it into Ellie's palm.

"Just give us a chance," he said to the chief. "We really can help her."

But the chief was furious. She grabbed Ellie and Nox by their arms and began to drag them out, just as Granna and a band of other Macaws gathered outside, watching curiously.

"Stop!" Ellie cried. "We have the cure! We brought it back from Tirelas!"

The chief stopped at last, her eyes narrowing. "What did you say?"

"Tirelas," Ellie gasped out. She held up the skystone for all to see. "Just like in your clan's legend. We've been there. We've seen it for ourselves. We know what's causing wingrot—and how to cure it!"

Whispers rose among the Macaws outside. Gussie stepped forward, taking another skystone from the second satchel.

"It's true," she said. "I didn't believe it at first either, but it's all true."

"If it's true," said the chief, "why is your friend wingless?"

Nox flinched, automatically moving in front of Twig, but the boy shook his head and stepped forward.

"They're telling the truth," he said softly. "Please. Just let them try."

"If we're wrong," said Ellie, "you can do whatever you like. Throw us out of the Clay altogether if you want."

The chief looked at each of them, as if searching for the lie. It was Tariel who spoke next, stepping forward from her position by the door.

"I think they're telling the truth," she said. "And as the newest adult in Clan Macaw, I vote we let them show us whatever it is they can do."

The chief sniffed. "Just because you've completed your ceremony doesn't make you an *adult*, Tariel. But all right. I'll give you one minute to prove your point."

"Thank you!" Ellie said. She turned to Nox, holding out the stone. "You do it."

"Me? Why?"

He knew why, of course. She was up to her tricks again, trying to push him in the direction *she* wanted him to go. Trying to make him share in her delusions of grandeur.

But with everyone watching, waiting for them to prove they weren't raving lunatics, he caved.

"Fine." Grumbling, he wiped his hand clean and took the stone. His stomach knotted up as he realized there were now Macaw clanners crowding every window and doorway, watching him.

"Um. Hi." He gave Liriel an awkward wave, his cheeks red.

"Wh-what are you gonna do?" she asked. Her eyes were still wet with tears.

"Don't worry. It's pretty boring actually. You just gotta hold this. Carefully. If you let go . . ." He opened his fingers, and at once the skystone floated off his palm, bobbing gently toward the ceiling.

Gasps sounded from all the Macaws, followed by a tide of whispers.

Grabbing the stone again, Nox held it toward Liriel. "It's okay. It . . ." He looked down at the stone again.

It's all right, Ma, I can fix you.

His own words wrapped around his throat like a noose, tightening.

"Go on, Nox," Ellie urged.

They were all staring at him, waiting. But he couldn't move. The stone filled his vision, and in its eerie blue depths he saw his own reflection swirling, distorting, his eyes shifting to his mother's eyes.

You failed her, a voice hissed in his mind. *You let her die.*

What if he gave the stone to Liriel and it didn't work? What if he failed her too, the way he'd been letting down everyone else in his life? Who was he to save anyone?

"Nox?" Ellie put a hand on his arm.

Abruptly, he turned and thrust the stone into her hand. "You do it. I can't."

Before she could object, he joined Twig and Gussie at the far end of the room, slumping against the wall to catch his breath. His chest still felt tight.

"It's fine," said Ellie, giving the watching Macaws a nervous smile. "I'll do it."

She put the skystone into Liriel's hand. The very room seemed to hold its breath.

C'mon, c'mon, Nox thought, watching the stone. He couldn't stop seeing his mother, her frail hands, and the skystone flickering out like a candle that'd run out of wick.

But then the stone began to flare in Liriel's fingers.

Nox stepped back, breathing out in relief.

It was just like how it had happened the first time, with little Mally of the Doves in Bluebriar Forest. Liriel's eyes grew heavy, then shut, as the stone's glow grew brighter. Light flowed over her skin and gathered, pulsing, around her wings.

"Skies above," breathed the Macaw chief.

Everyone was perfectly silent as the spectators outside began slipping in through the doors for a closer look. The doctor didn't turn them away; she looked as entranced as the rest of them. Soon, it seemed half the clan was packed into the infirmary, most of them still muddy from toe to wingtip. They all watched the sleeping Liriel in her corona of blue light.

"C'mon," Ellie said, pulling at Nox's shirt. "Let's give them space."

He was more than happy to follow her, Gussie, and Twig outside, where they settled on a bench by one of the kapoks.

"Did you feel it?" Ellie whispered. "Spreading through that room, filling up their eyes?"

"Feel what?"

She looked up at him, smiling. *"Change."*

Nox grunted and looked away. All he'd felt had been the past, coiling like a snake around his chest.

CHAPTER TWENTY-THREE
· ELLIE ·

"We want to help," said the Macaw clan chief.

It was afternoon of the following day, and a clan meet had been called. Every Macaw had gathered at the clearing where Tariel had undergone her Seed Ceremony, with Ellie, Nox, Gussie, and Twig seated in the front row. Liriel stood nearby, glowing with pride as she showed her healed wings to anyone who asked.

The skystone that had restored her was now in the chief's grasp.

"For generations we have told the legend of Tirelas," she said. "But for me, and I think for many of us, it had become just that—a legend, true and yet untrue. This proves otherwise." She held up the stone. "Tirelas is real. And I believe we must return there or lose our wings for good."

"What did I tell you?" Ellie whispered to Nox. "Once they know the truth, they'll do the right thing."

He only grunted, clearly not wanting to give her the satisfaction of saying she was right.

"I think we were led to the Macaw clan on purpose," Ellie sad to the crowd. "I think destiny brought us to you, one of the only clans that still remembers Tirelas." She stood up, spreading her hands. "With this many of us, we could probably even retake one of the islands!"

"Whoa, now," said the chief. "I said nothing about retaking anything."

"But—you just said you want to help."

"We understand the dire need for action," said the chief. "But we are only one clan—and a small clan at that. We're potters, not warriors. We won't be attacking the gargols head-on."

Ellie sat down with a short exhale, her excitement wilting.

Nox cleared his throat and glanced at her sidelong. At the look in his eyes—a clear *I told you so*—she scowled, crossing her arms.

"However," continued the chief, "we Macaws have a part to play. You've told us there is one doctor in Khadreen who possesses a skystone now, and the truth that goes with it. But there are many cities in the south, and many clans hidden beneath the jungle canopy. My people will take half your skystones and spread them throughout the south, along with the story of Tirelas."

Ellie brightened. "That makes sense."

The chief nodded. "The other half of the skystones I leave to you for the Clandoms."

Ellie frowned; the chief was talking as if the skystones were hers to distribute. Ellie would have reminded her *they* were the ones who'd risked their necks to find them in the first place, but the woman kept speaking.

"We will provide you with everything you need to continue your journey, and to carry these stones as far as the wind blows. When the time comes for the Skyborn to rise against the gargols, the south will be ready."

The Skyborn.

A chill ran down Ellie's back. It was the first time she'd heard someone else say the word aloud, and the truth of it struck her heart like a drum.

We are the Skyborn.

It was a word that transcended clan, and even the Clandoms and the southern cities. It was a word that encompassed them all, every fledgling testing her new wings, every farmer and warrior and craftsman and sailor. It was a word to which everyone belonged . . . even Ellie.

"We will take the skystones back to the Clandoms," Ellie announced, rising to her feet again. "We'll make sure everyone hears the truth." Then, wincing as her leg throbbed with pain, she sat slowly down again. "At least . . . after my leg's a bit better, anyway."

The meet continued as the chief called for volunteers among the Macaws to take one skystone each and carry it to the neighboring cities. Ellie watched with awe as young men and women leaped up eagerly, offering themselves for the job. She felt a ripple of purpose through her soul. The dream that had been buried in her heart began to grow into something bigger and stronger—something carried by many wings, not just her own.

"We could tell them the rest," she said softly to her friends.

"The rest?" echoed Nox.

She just looked at him, until his eyes flared wide.

"No! Ellie! Don't you dare."

"Oh," said Twig. "You mean the bit about Nox being the prince of the sky islands?"

Nox choked. "The prince of the— *Twig!*" He whirled on Ellie. "You told them your stupid theory?"

"Actually," said Gussie, "it is plausible, given the Eagle clan's obsession with your family, Nox. And there is the matter of your family crest clearly matching that of the . . . *you know what* clan."

"Oh, not you too," he groaned.

"I'm not saying it's true, only that it's possible. There's enough evidence to merit further investigation."

"I'm not even going to talk about this anymore. It's completely nuts." He stood and turned away.

Ellie sighed, shoulders slumping a little. "If only there was a way to prove it, so even he couldn't deny the truth."

"You *are* kind of pushing him," said Twig. "It's a lot to dump on someone."

"I'm not dumping anything. I just . . ."

“This is about Elder Rue’s vision, isn’t it?” asked Gussie. “You think that prophecy has something to do with Nox.”

“Well, it did mention the sky falling if I fail at . . . whatever it is I’m supposed to do!” She heard the exasperation in her own voice. “Look, I just want to do the right thing, whatever it means.”

“So we’re really going home?” Twig asked, his eyes lowering.

Going home. The words felt strange to Ellie. He meant the Clandoms, of course, but she couldn’t help but think of Linden, and the Sparrow clan. How would her own clan react if she showed up with a skystone, and wild tales of islands in the clouds? It was hard to imagine the peaceful Sparrows taking up weapons to fight gargols.

“We need the high clans,” Ellie said. She looked at Gussie. “Someone has to travel to the Hawks, Falcons, and all the others. Someone . . . who speaks their language, and who they’ll listen to.”

Gussie stared at her, her mouth pressing into a thin line. “You want me to go to Vestra.”

Ellie nodded. “And . . . I think we need to split up. We’ll cover more ground that way, and if one of us gets caught . . .”

“The others will still be out there, spreading skystones,” sighed Gussie. “It *is* the more logical option.”

“Nox?”

His back was to them, but Ellie knew he was still listening. Eventually, he turned and shrugged.

“For once I agree with you. There’s no point in you three risking your necks just because Garion’s after *mine*.”

“Whoa, whoa.” Ellie raised a finger. “What I meant was, we go in groups of two.”

She waited for someone to argue, but there was only silence.

Until Twig said, “But I don’t want to split up. We’re a crew. We’re . . . like family.”

Nox put an arm around Twig, giving him a lopsided grin. “Yeah, and we argue like one too. But Ellie's right. Our chances are better this way. How about we agree to meet up after a month and no more splitting up after that?"

Twig nodded sullenly. "Promise?"

"Promise."

Ellie smiled, though her insides twisted. She didn't like it any more than Twig, but it was the right choice.

"Promise," she said.

Three weeks later, they were ready.

Ellie's leg wasn't strong enough to walk on, and she still wore splints, but she had learned how to take off on one leg, using the lockstave for balance, and then to fly without jarring her broken bones too much.

They'd split the remaining sack of skystones between them. The Macaws had crafted heavy clay pendants to hold each one, so they were no longer in danger of floating away—though they were still far lighter than they looked.

As Ellie packed her satchel for yet another long journey, she realized it had been over four months since she'd left Linden. When they returned to the Clandoms, it would be late autumn, her favorite season. In the south, there was only wet and dry season. Ellie had almost forgotten how much time had passed here.

A large group of Macaws gathered to watch them go. Their own ambassadors had already departed with their precious skystones, to every corner of the south. Ellie, Nox, Gussie, and Twig would be the last to leave.

Ellie's nerves jittered as she limped outside on her lockstave. When she'd left Linden, it had been to pursue her dream of being a Goldwing knight. She'd been naive and wide-eyed, jumping at every new sight and sound. Then, when she'd fled the Clandoms, it had been under the cover of night, with no idea what would become of her. Now she had a purpose, a plan, and a healthy respect for the dangers that awaited but still felt as nervous as she had the morning of the Race of Ascension.

"Hey," she said to Nox, who stood with his satchel and traveling cloak, looking as apprehensive as she felt.

"Hey."

"So we're really doing this, huh?"

"Don't get cold wings on me now, Sparrow. This was your idea."

"Meaning it's my fault if it all goes wrong?" She raised an eyebrow.

"Absolutely."

She looked around for Twig and Gussie, and saw them by a row of elephants. Twig was tearfully saying goodbye to each beast, and Ellie could have sworn they looked just as mournful to see him go. They wrapped their trunks around him and gave sad little trumpets. Gussie looked on in resignation, her satchel of skystones hanging from her belt, along with an assortment of new inventions and parts she'd collected over the weeks.

Saying goodbye to them would be the hardest. She would save it till last.

Instead, she went to find Tariel and Granna, who'd decided to stay in the Clay until after Ellie and her friends had left on their journey. Ellie suspected Tariel would have asked to come along with them, if she weren't more anxious about Gade back in Brightbay.

"Ellie!" Tariel caught sight of her and waved.

She hugged them both and took the coconut cake Granna had made for her, wrapped in banana leaves and tied with string. Tariel gave her a folded piece of cloth, her cheeks turning pink.

"It's my first cloak," she said, looking so shy Ellie almost didn't recognize her. "I . . . sort of messed up a few times but—"

"I *love* it!" Ellie said, unfolding the cloak. It was made of kapok fibers and dyed dark green, with clumsy, meandering embroidery along the hems. The cut was a bit asymmetrical and the wing holes were crooked, but Ellie had meant it. She was touched that Tariel's first piece was for her. "Help me put it on?"

The cloak fastened with a clay pin shaped like a sun. Ellie twirled, and Tariel brightened, clearly pleased.

She hugged Granna, and then another Macaw called her attention, wanting to say goodbye. She'd come to know quite a few of them over the weeks, particularly the doctor and her assistants, whose expertise and care had quickened her leg's healing.

When all the goodbyes were said, there were only Gussie and Twig left. They'd be heading northeast, where the many coastal towns and cities were close together, and easier for Twig to get to on foot. Nox and Ellie were headed northwest, to the more rural roads and spread-out towns—farther from any searching Goldwings, they hoped.

"Well." Ellie drew a deep breath. "I guess this is it. Thank you all, for doing this."

"We're not just doing it for you," said Gussie. "Sure, it was your idea, but we wouldn't do it if we didn't agree it's important."

Twig nodded, his eyes puffy from crying. "I don't want anyone else to get wingrot, or to go through . . ." He swallowed, his shoulders flexing the way they did whenever he seemed to be particularly aware of his missing wings.

Ellie hugged them both tight, then stepped back so Nox could do the same.

"You're the best crew a thief could ask for," he said. "We'll meet you in one month. Be smart out there. Remember our old motto: If you sense danger, *run*. No matter what."

"And watch the skies," Ellie added softly.

"Watch the skies," Gussie and Twig murmured back.

CHAPTER TWENTY-FOUR
· NOX ·

Nox hovered on a thermal, his wings ruffling in the rising warm air, and studied the town below.

"Looks quiet enough," he commented.

"It's so small," said Ellie, flitting just above him. "What if there isn't anyone there with wingrot? No one's going to listen to us if we can't show them the skystone's power first."

"I guess we'll find out."

They spiraled downward, gliding out of the warm thermal and into the cooler air. Nox kept an eye on Ellie the whole way; they'd been flying for nearly a week since they'd left the Clay, and he knew her leg hurt more than she let on.

But her wings seemed steady enough as they landed a short distance outside the town. The day was hot; he'd already sweated through his clothes. Though they'd left the jungle behind days ago, the heat seemed to only be getting worse. The land here flowed in endless plains of golden grass. They'd gone two full days without seeing a single tree or river. How anyone lived out here, he couldn't imagine.

Ellie leaned on her lockstave while Nox took out the Clandoms map the Macaws had given them. He had no idea how it had ended up in the Clay, but according to the notation in the corner, it had been drawn by a cartographer in Thelantis.

"This place isn't even labeled," he said. "We don't know its name."

"Then I *guess*," Ellie said, prodding him with her staff, "we'll just have to ask!"

"All right, all right. Don't break your leg all over again."

"If I do, it'll be from kicking your butt into motion. Honestly, why are you so jittery?"

"Excuse me, but I happen to have an entire army after my head and here I am prancing back into their territory. I think I've earned the right to be *jittery*."

"Got the skystones?"

He patted the satchel on his belt for the hundredth time since they'd set out, and sighed.

"Okay, then." Ellie breathed in. "Let's do this."

"Remember our fake names?"

"I'm Tabby and you're Cor . . . Um."

"Cornelian."

"Right. Cornelian." She pronounced the name with a stuffy aristocratic accent, rolling her eyes. "Really, Nox? Sounds like some dopey high clanner with feathers for brains."

"It does not!" He sulked. "It sounds . . . daring. Like some noble outlaw."

"It's so long and flowery. I'm going to forget it. Just you watch."

"Let's get on with it, please? My wings are tired."

A farmhouse sat outside the town, surrounded by fields of potato plants. It looked like a normal home, and he supposed it likely wasn't a Goldwing trap. Still, Nox insisted on circling the entire stead before finally approaching the door.

Ellie knocked and was answered by a middle-aged man with short brown wings flecked with white. His face was leathery and dry, his beard full. He peered at them suspiciously, not opening the door more than a crack.

"Who are you?" he demanded.

"Hello!" Ellie put on a winning smile. "I'm Tabby and this is, uh, Corn . . . cob."

"Corncob?" echoed the farmer.

Nox barely refrained from smacking his face. Ellie gave him a defiant *I told you I'd forget it* look.

The potato farmer looked them up and down, his expression not changing. "What do you want?"

"Well, sir, I'm glad you asked. Y'see, the thing is, we're doctors—I mean, we're *assistants* to doctors, doing research."

Nox rolled his eyes. He could *see* the nervous sweat running down the Sparrow girl's neck. The speech had been written by Gussie, but it seemed no amount of practice would erase Ellie's inability to tell even the weakest lie. If the world depended on this Sparrow convincing people she'd eaten oats for breakfast instead of seedbread, they'd all be doomed.

Resigned, he stepped forward to take over.

"We're apprenticed to doctors in Thelantis who are studying the spread of wingrot, trying to determine its cause. We're going town to town to document cases and report back."

The farmer peered at him more closely, as if trying to see through his words to their real intentions. But he didn't seem to have Twig's gift because finally his demeanor shifted as he smiled warmly.

"Why don't you two come inside? You must have been flying for some time to reach Quail clan country. I'll pour cold water for you."

"Thanks!" chirped Ellie.

The interior of the house was dim and dusty. It looked like no one had cleaned in months. Mud was tracked all over the floors, and the table he had them sit at was covered in stains and dirty dishes.

"So you're tracking wingrot, eh?" The farmer set down two cups of water.

"That's right," said Nox, taking out the ledger and pencil Gussie had said would make them look more official. "So, is there anyone in your town who might have it?"

"Hmm." The farmer moved around the kitchen, rummaging in drawers. "Can't say as there is, Corncob."

"Oh." Ellie's face fell. "I mean—good! That's good. Of course we don't *want* people to be sick. That would be completely messed up, right?"

Great, now she was babbling.

Nox intervened again, while inwardly wondering if every town they came to would be as awkward as this. "If you could point us to the next town, then, we'll be off. Research must go on and all that."

"What's this?" The farmer finally turned around, holding a long butcher knife. "But it'd be a shame for you to run off so soon, *Nox Hatcher*."

Nox jolted to his feet, but not before the farmer put his knife against Ellie's neck.

"How—" Nox gasped. "Don't hurt her!"

"I know who you are, boy," the farmer growled. "Just as I know what you've done."

"What I've done?" Nox echoed. His head was reeling. How did this farmer in the back of nowhere know his real name? And what he looked like?

"Brenn!" called the farmer. "Quint! Get out here!"

Nox heard the tramping of heavy boots above, and then two burly boys about five years older than him came downstairs. They were identical, each with a shaggy thatch of blond hair and a round, stubbled chin.

"What's going on, Pop?" said one, ogling.

"Get that poster the knight left!" ordered the farmer. "Quick!"

One of the boys went to a drawer and pulled out a grease-stained paper while the other gaped with his mouth open, his small eyes darting from Nox to Ellie to the knife in his father's hand.

"Give it here, boy." The farmer grabbed the paper and held it up. "Aye, that's him, all right. The scum that killed your mother."

Nox choked. "I didn't kill anyone!"

The farmer turned the paper, and there Nox saw a sketch of himself, rendered in blocky woodcut print. His name was emblazoned across the top, along with the words WANTED FOR INSTIGATING GARGOL ATTACKS!

"My wife was taken in broad daylight," said the farmer, his voice hoarse with rage. "No clouds, not even a strong wind. Because *you* stirred them up. Now they strike out of blue skies, tear open houses, maiming and destroying and slaughtering!"

Not wanting to startle the man into doing something rash with that knife, Nox slowly raised his hands. "Look, I'm sorry about your wife. But I didn't do that. I'm just a kid!"

"A kid who led a host of gargols to attack the king's own men!"

Nox's eyes met Ellie's; she winced.

So that was what this was about. The Crag. He *had* caused a horde of gargols to attack the prison, but he didn't see how . . .

He sucked in a breath.

Clearly, the abnormal gargol attacks were happening across the Clandoms as well, and King Garion must have been circulating posters that blamed *Nox* for it. But was it just a wild lie to turn the people against Nox and induce them to turn him over to the Eagles?

Or . . . was the king, wittingly or unwittingly, telling the truth?

Until now, it hadn't occurred to Nox that the reason the gargols might be ramping up attacks could be connected to his crew's trips to the islands in the sky. But what if they were? What if setting foot in Tirelas had violated some ancient treaty or law, and now the increase in gargol raids was the consequence?

Horror curdled his stomach.

Still, he wasn't just going to let some potato farmer turn him over to the Goldwings.

"Tie him up, Brenn!" the farmer ordered. "We'll see justice for your mother yet."

One of the twins lumbered toward Nox, who darted another glance at Ellie.

She nodded once, her eyes hard.

Just as Brenn reached out to grab Nox, he ducked and rolled, and Ellie's wings shot open, knocking aside the farmer's hand long enough for her to scramble away.

"Stop them!" the farmer roared. "Boys! Grab the little rats!"

Ellie snatched her lockstave and jabbed one of the twins in the eye. He fell back, howling. But she couldn't run on her broken leg. Nox searched his pockets for a distraction.

Inwardly thanking Gussie for her forethought, he took out a clay ball she'd crafted in the Macaw clan pottery and hurled it to the floor. It shattered, releasing a cloud of dark smoke that quickly filled the house, blinding them all.

"Ellie!" He reached for her, and her arm came stretching out of the smoke. Pulling her behind him, he made for the door while the farmer and his sons coughed and cursed behind them.

Spilling outside, Nox immediately took to his wings. Ellie was just behind him. They tore for open sky, searching for a swift wind to carry them.

"They're following," Ellie called out.

Nox looked back but saw the Quails were struggling to give chase. Their wings were too short to keep up, and Nox and Ellie's were as strong as they'd ever been after weeks of flying. Even with his clipped flight feathers, Nox easily outpaced them. It wasn't long before the Quails and their town faded into the landscape.

Finally, they felt safe enough to glide, letting their muscles rest.

Ellie sighed. "Nox, this is a problem."

"I know."

"If those goons could recognize you that fast, no town in the Clandoms will be safe for you."

Nox let out a wordless growl of anger. If everyone believed he was responsible for colluding with the gargols, they wouldn't hesitate to do whatever it took to bring him in.

He wasn't just hunted by the Goldwings now.

He was hunted by every person in the Clandoms.

CHAPTER TWENTY-FIVE
· ELLIE ·

"Maybe we can use this to our advantage," Ellie said.

They'd camped in a cluster of boulders in the open prairie. A panel of sturdy brown kapok silk, framed with collapsible wooden rods, created a canopy for them to sit under—one of the Macaw clan's gifts. It was patterned in shades of brown and green and yellow, with the hope that it might camouflage their camp from any curious gargol eyes.

They sat with a small oil lamp between them, the only light they dared risk. They ate dried plantains, kapok seeds, and hard coconut biscuits, washed down with water they'd bottled from a stream. It was the last of their food supplies from the Clay; they'd have no choice but to stop in a town tomorrow to buy more.

Nox traced a potential flight path on the map. "Use what?"

Ellie was massaging sunflower oil into her wings. Her supply was running low; it had been months since her shopping spree in Porton, and the diminishing supply of wing oil served to remind her just how far she was from home. If she closed her eyes, the smell still took her right back to Linden and its endless fields of sunflowers.

"Your new reputation. I know it's dangerous, but . . . if we met it head-on, and told people who you were right away, maybe we could convince them of the *real* reason why King Garion's hunting you."

He looked up from the map, scowling. "So *that's* what this is about. Your stupid Phoenix theory."

She'd known he'd be opposed to the idea, but still her wings bristled. "It's not stupid, Nox, and you know it. Gussie and Twig agreed with me."

"Your plan to deliver skystones to every town in the Clandoms sounded like a good idea too, at first. Yet here we are—barely getting through the first day alive."

"So, what? You think just because things are going to be a little harder now, we should just give up?"

"I didn't say that."

"Nox, you've been against all this from the start. Not just the Phoenix thing, but *all* of it. This might be easier if you actually started to believe it was important!"

"I just don't get why it has to be us!" he said, planting a fist on the map so the paper wrinkled. "The Macaw clanners are spreading word through the south. Why couldn't they have gone to the Clandoms too? Why couldn't we have found some adults to do it? We're just kids, Ellie. Kids with targets on our backs. How long until someone plants an arrow in one?"

She stared at him, her jaw tightening. "I thought you'd changed after we left Thelantis. All that stuff you used to believe about only taking care of yourself, and avoiding taking responsibility for anything other than survival—I thought you left that behind."

"For what? *Your* obsession with playing the hero and saving the world?"

"I'm not *playing* at anything. What we're doing here, with *these*"—she rattled the bag of skystones—"that matters. That matters a lot, Nox. We've already seen it change the mind of that doctor in Khadreen, and the entire Macaw clan."

"I know it matters, which is why I'm saying maybe we're not the best people for the job. Why does it have to be *us*?"

"Because it's our destiny."

"Is it? Or is it just you needing to be a hero again? You say I haven't changed, but what about you? Why do you always have to be Ellie the knight, Ellie the savior of the world—what's wrong with being *just* Ellie?"

"That's not— Oh, I'm done trying to talk to you!"

The lamp flickered, its oil running low. To distract herself from the angry buzz in her ears, Ellie took out the extra bottle and refilled the lamp. Nox had turned away, arms wrapped around his knees, to stare across the dark prairie. Night breezes caressed the long grass, filling the air with a constant sound like flowing water. Above, the sky was all stars and moonlight.

They didn't speak again. Nox fell asleep first, leaving Ellie with first watch. She shifted so her back leaned on a rock and her bad leg could stretch out, and sorted idly through the contents of her satchel.

After a minute's pause, she took out the letter Nox's grandfather had given her. The old envelope was yellow and creased from countless foldings. She rubbed it between her fingers for several minutes, wrestling with her conscience.

Give it to him when the time is right.

Well, how would she know when the time was right if she didn't even know what the letter was about? He hadn't specifically told her *not* to read it.

Glancing at Nox, curled in the warmth of his wings, she finally shoved aside any moral reservations and unfolded the letter in the envelope. She had to bend over the oil lamp to read it.

As she read, her grip tightened on the page until a tiny rip formed on one side.

My Beloved Jaff,

I am so sorry to be leaving you without much explanation, but I knew if I told you this before I left, you'd never consent to remaining behind. As it is, I cannot risk you falling afoul of my bad Corvain luck—or should I say, my family's habit of vanishing at the Eagle clan's hands. I am not departing on a mere candle-making research trip, as I told you. But I owe you the truth, so here it is. In case of the worst, I want you to know why I left, and what I considered to be worth the risk.

As you know, our clan was shattered long ago by order of King Dremmond of the Eagles. What is not as well known is that we Corvains were at the center of this shattering, and that we are the reason the Eagles' wrath fell upon all the Crows.

I have long sought the truth of that dreadful day, when the Eagles and their knights laid waste to our clan seat of Thraille. My mother once told me what her mother told her—that the answer was still there in the ruins of our lost home. And so I'm returning there, though it means crossing the dangerous Thornmoors, to search for the truth in hopes that we can better understand why *the Eagles despise us so, and perhaps even to finally set things right. Until we know who we are and what we did, we Corvains will never be free.*

All my love,
Tanra

Ellie's heart pounded as she reread the letter. Then she read it a third time. Then she sat for several long minutes, staring at the flame on the oil lamp.

Finally, she folded the paper carefully and put it into her satchel pocket.

Nox's map peeked out of his bag; she slipped it free and unfolded it as quietly as she could.

The Thornmoors were easy enough to locate—a wilderness to the northwest. She'd heard stories about it being a death trap, due to the fact it rained almost every day. The cloud cover made travel nearly impossible because gargol attacks were a constant risk.

But then, the world was changing. Apparently attacks were now a constant risk no matter where they were.

The ruins of Thraille had to be there, between the Thornmoors and the west mountains.

Along with the buried secret about the Corvains and the shattering of the Crows.

Ellie had a good idea what that secret might be.

If there was something hidden in Thraille that might prove Nox was a Phoenix, it was worth finding. It could be the evidence that finally persuaded him to accept the truth—and become who he was meant to be.

Ellie refolded the map and put it into her own satchel, pausing to peer at the crown tucked inside. Nox didn't know she still had it, though she was sure he wouldn't be surprised to find out.

A sudden, distant screech startled her, and she dropped the satchel. Nox's eyes shot open. He sat up silently, face tight with apprehension.

Ellie leaned forward and blew out the lamp. Nox's face shifted from gold to silver blue. The only light now reaching them was the moon's.

The screech sounded again, still far off, but undoubtedly that of a gargol.

Hunting in clear skies.

There were enough stars and moonlight to have shown any cloud, especially with no trees or hills around to block the sky. This gargol was hunting outside the rules, and there was no telling whether they were hidden well enough, or if it could see through their flimsy tent or smell them on the wind.

They could do nothing but huddle in the dark, waiting.

The rules of the sky were changing. And if the clans didn't change with them, they'd be hunted as helplessly as mice in a cattery.

A few minutes later, they heard another screech. This was farther off, but Ellie didn't relax a bit. There was no reason to believe the gargol wouldn't circle back, or that there might not be more of them up there, invisible against the night.

She finally lay down, her lockstave in her hand, trying to let her body rest even if her mind could not. Tariel's cloak, for all its crooked seams, made for a soft and warm blanket. Nox lay awake beside her, his breathing tense.

Tomorrow, Ellie would take over navigating. Nox hadn't wanted to do it anyway. She'd plot their course, town by town, and they'd figure out a way to deliver the skystones without getting caught.

All she had to do was keep Nox distracted, thinking that was *all* they were doing. He couldn't catch on that her real plan—and the course she plotted—would be taking them closer and closer to Thraille.

And to the truth about Nox's ancestry.

Nox couldn't help but feel numb as he watched the blue glow of the skystone fill the small house. Ellie knelt by the bedside of a sleeping young mother, her baby in the arms of his father nearby. She grinned as the healing powers of the stone began clearing the woman's skin and straightening the bones of her wings. The Finch clanners peering through the windows looked on in amazement, many with tears running down their cheeks.

This was the seventh town they'd stopped in, and the fifth healing they'd witnessed since leaving the jungle. And every time, with each life saved, he found himself bitterly thinking of his mother.

The one life the stones had chosen *not* to save.

It was unfair and selfish, he knew. He was glad that they'd been able to help the people they'd met, and the relief was clear on their families' faces. Despite his argument with Ellie, he knew what they were doing was important. That it was making a difference.

But still.

He didn't think the sting would ever go away.

"It's magic," whispered a Finch girl standing beside Nox. He always hung back during these things, glad to let Ellie be the center of attention.

"I guess so," he replied.

"Where did you find such a thing, Cob?" she asked.

As usual, the alias made him wince. Once *Corncob* had gotten stuck in Ellie's head, there had been no changing it, but at least he usually got people to shorten it. "Just wait. My friend will explain soon."

The Finch girl edged closer, till their arms touched. "I like your hair," she whispered coyly.

He grimaced, resisting the urge to run his hand over the shaved sides of his head. He was *not* a fan of the hairstyle, but Ellie had been right—they had to do something to disguise him. He just wished that something hadn't involved Ellie's knife coming in *dangerously* close contact with his skull. His remaining hair—he'd flat-out refused to go totally shaven—was brushed in a crest over the top of his head. And he had to admit, it made him look pretty cool, even if it was a style more suited to the flashy Jay clanners he'd known back in Thelantis.

That wasn't the only change they'd wrought. Ellie had procured white chalk and used it to paint temporary stripes on Nox's wings, making him look less Crow and more ambiguously mixed-clan. He could have been part Warbler, part Woodpecker, with perhaps a touch of Magpie blood. At least, that was what he told people when they, rather rudely, asked. It had worked so far, though he hated the inconvenience of having to recolor his feathers every morning. The slightest dampness washed it out completely.

Still, he couldn't let down his guard. They'd seen more posters with his face on them plastered in each town they came to. The Goldwings had been thorough in their distribution. And more than once he'd caught someone staring at him a bit too curiously.

He and Ellie had made a habit of swooping in, delivering their skystone and their tale of Tirelas, then flying away as fast as possible, before anyone started asking questions about Nox's identity. Even now, Ellie was rising to begin the speech.

"We were given this stone by a brave adventurer," she began. They'd agreed it cast less suspicion on Nox if they told the story as if it had been told to them. "He told us he'd been blown into a storm and there discovered an island borne up by skystones much bigger than this one. This land, which the Macaws call *Tirelas*, is our true home."

She went on to describe the ruined city and palaces, and the connection between wingrot and the clans' exile from the sky. Nox watched the faces of the listeners, careful to note any trouble that might be brewing in their eyes. As usual, many of them looked skeptical, but at least half followed Ellie's words with wide-eyed intensity, and a few nodded.

"I think the dream of Tirelas has lived in all our hearts," Ellie had said to Nox after their second successful stop. "Did you see how some of them lit up when I told them the story? It was like I was telling them something they already knew but hadn't been able to remember."

Even Nox couldn't deny the power of the tale. When Ellie finished speaking, a hush fell over the Finch clan, one that was soon followed by a flurry of questions. Nox moved toward the door, giving Ellie a nod. She followed, answering what questions she could before they managed to slip outside.

"Thank you for listening!" Ellie called out. "But we must go—there are other clans who haven't yet heard, and other sick in need of skystones. Please, tell everyone you know what you heard and saw today! The time will come soon when we must return to our true home!"

She shouted the last words as she shot into the sky alongside Nox. Finch clanners rose after them, shouting, demanding more information, but they'd already stayed too long. Nox uneasily watched a trio of older men who were looking at him suspiciously. When one pointed toward the town board where his sketch hung, he gave Ellie their sign for *big trouble*: crossed wrists in the air.

She nodded and put on a burst of speed. In minutes they'd left the Finch town behind.

"That went great!" Ellie said breathlessly. She swooped to and fro, held aloft by a warm breeze. They saw more trees now, their foliage red and gold, growing in copses between farmland ripe with wheat, pumpkins, and corn. Ellie was in charge of plotting their course now, which Nox didn't mind. She seemed very determined to reach each town as quickly as possible, probably wanting to pack as many stops as they could into the ten days they had left before they were to meet up with Gussie and Twig.

"You're getting better at the whole speech part," Nox commented.

"You could do it better," she said. "I still feel like I'm going to melt through the floor every time I start talking. Public speaking is scarier than a horde of gargols."

He laughed. "At least if they're looking at you, they're not looking at me."

"Yeah, yeah, *Corncob*." She did a playful barrel roll, tucking her wings and then spreading them wide again. "I wonder how Gussie and Twig are getting on. Which one's making the speeches, d'you reckon?"

He tried to picture Gussie standing on a chair, droning on about skystones, and failed. Then he imagined Twig doing it—even worse.

"I'm sure they're doing great."

"We should have made it a contest! See who can give out the most skystones before— Oh!"

"What? What's wrong?"

Then he saw it: a cart overturned on the road below them, its donkey galloping away across the wheat fields.

And hunched over the cart—a gargol the size of a bear.

Ellie and Nox dove to the ground, taking cover in the tall wheat. They were close enough that Nox could hear the gargol's body grinding and creaking.

"Not a cloud in sight," whispered Ellie.

He nodded, carefully parting the wheat so he could peer out.

The gargol was smashing apart the cart, along with the pumpkins inside. The driver—a Finch clanner—lay motionless in the road.

Finally, with a screech that nearly flattened the wheat, the gargol took off, hauling its heavy body into the sky with slow, onerous wing beats.

"Have you ever seen one that size?" Ellie asked.

"Not even close."

The gargol was *enormous*. It looked almost ridiculous up in the sky—no thing that size should be able to fly. But fly it did, gaining altitude quickly and then speeding away in the direction of the Finch town.

"We have to warn them!" Ellie said.

Nox grabbed her arm, stopping her from taking off. "It'll reach the town long before we could. There's nothing we can do if it decides to attack."

She brushed a hand over her eyes, which glittered with angry tears. "What if it *is* our fault, Nox? What if us going to Tirelas is the reason for . . ." She sniffed, then burst out of the wheat.

"Ellie! Wait! It could still turn back!"

She ignored him and ran into the road, dropping to her knees by the Finch man lying there. But Nox knew even before he reached them that it was too late.

Ellie pulled a gingham blanket out of the smashed cart's remains and drew it over the man, tears running down her cheeks.

"It's getting worse," she whispered. "Every town we visit, there are more and more stories of strange gargol attacks, and bigger and bigger monsters."

He nodded woodenly, and thought of her question: *What if it's our fault?*

His fault, really. He was the one who'd brainlessly charged into that storm over the Crag. He was the reason they'd reached Tirelas at all.

How many people had died since then by gargols' claws?

The next week passed in a blur; as they traveled through more settled land, and the weather held clear, they were able to visit a new town each day. Some were only a cluster of houses; others were home to as many as three different clans. The larger ones made Nox doubly nervous, with thrice as many eyes to see through his changed hair and chalked wings.

Even Ellie was showing signs of exhaustion, but she pushed them at a rapid pace, flying as if the world depended on it.

Of course, she thought just that. And he had to admit that maybe she was right.

Eight days after they'd seen the massive gargol in the road, they landed outside a large town built on the banks of a wide, peaceful river.

"Gruston," Ellie read, pointing to a painted sign beside the road. "Clan seat of the Cranes."

"Even I've heard of this place," Nox said. "It's more city than town."

They hadn't been anywhere nearly this size yet. He eyed the buildings ahead nervously.

"Maybe I should wait out here," he said.

"And let all that time I spent chalking your wings this morning go to waste? C'mon, it'll be fine. Just blend in like you always do."

"Just," he snorted. There was nothing *just* about it. Blending in had been getting harder and harder.

They walked into Gruston. Ellie managed to put a little weight on her leg now but still needed her lockstave for support. She made Nox check and double-check the sack of skystones; they were down to just six.

"When we're out, we're out," Nox said. "It's too risky going back up there for more."

Ellie nodded reluctantly, but he half worried he'd wake up one morning to find she'd gone flapping off to find another sky island. It was just the sort of lunatic thing she'd do.

They headed for the first person they saw, a milliner closing up her hat shop at the town's outskirts. She looked to be in a hurry, frantically jamming her key in the door.

"Excuse me!" Ellie called, waving.

"Not now!" snapped the woman, shoving her key in her pocket and spreading her wide, white Crane wings. "There's a commotion in the square, and I don't want to miss it!"

She took off, gliding away toward the center of Gruston. Nox noticed she wasn't the only one. Cranes and a various scattering of other clanners were swooping through the sky, settling somewhere in the buildings ahead.

"I don't like this," Nox said. "Maybe we should skip this town."

"Don't be silly. Place this size? You *know* there's gotta be someone with wingrot. Maybe even several! If we help them, every person who comes through here will leave hearing the story. It's too good a chance to pass up."

He sighed; as usual, Ellie got her way.

They flew after the Crane woman and landed on the roof of a bakery overlooking the town square. It was paved in cobblestones, with a covered stage at the center where musicians or performers might usually set up shows. But today it held only one person, a young man with dusty blond hair and the brown wings of a Robin clanner.

"Nice crowd," Nox said. "It'd be a perfect time to pick some pockets."

Ellie elbowed him so hard he choked.

"Joking," he gasped out.

"Wait a minute . . ." Ellie squinted, trying to get a better look at him. "Is he holding . . . *a skystone*?"

Nox stared, struck speechless.

"I bring you news of a world above ours!" called out the Robin man. "Islands, floating on the clouds—full of ruins of ancient cities. *Our* ancient cities. And I can prove it! Bring me anyone suffering from wingrot, and I'll use this stone, stolen from these very islands, to heal them!"

Ellie and Nox slowly looked at each other.

"That's *our* speech," Nox whispered.

A smile began to spread across Ellie's face. "Skies, Nox. Do you know what this *means*?"

He did but let her say it anyway.

"It's working. It's working! The story is spreading on its own! That must be the skystone we left in the Robin village four days ago!"

"He must've flown hard to reach this place before us," Nox said. He grinned. "Guess we get to skip Gruston after all."

"Hold on, I want to see what happens." She frowned. "He's going about it all wrong. Should've done the healing, *then* the story. See? They don't believe him."

The spectators had begun pelting the man with insults and outright laughter. He looked confused, then angry, holding up the stone even higher, so the light glinted off it. "I can prove it! This stone, from the land of Tirsela above, will heal wingrot!"

"Tirsela," Ellie groaned, rubbing her face.

"Young man!" shouted a voice, louder than the others. "Step down from there at once! You are under arrest for inciting riots and spreading treason!"

Wait, *what*?

Nox gripped the edge of the roof, leaning forward to see who was speaking.

Ellie spotted them first. Squeezing Nox's arm, she pointed and gasped out, "Goldwings!"

Three knights pushed through the crowd and stormed the stage, surrounding the Robin clanner, who looked terrified. One grabbed the skystone while the others bound the man's hands behind his back. The crowd shouted and pressed forward, but Nox couldn't tell if it was in support of the Robin clanner or the Goldwings.

The knight who'd confiscated the skystone turned to address the spectators. "These rumors spreading about islands in the sky are false and dangerous! Clearly they are meant to lead gullible fools to their deaths. These stones are charlatans' tricks and nothing more. By His Majesty King Garion's decree, anyone in possession of one must turn it over to the Goldwings immediately—or face extreme consequences!" Turning back to the Robin clanner, he said, "As for those who willfully spread these lies, there can be only one punishment: execution."

The Robin clanner cried out, and Ellie jumped to her feet.

"Get down!" Nox hissed.

"They're going to kill him!" she said. "Nox, we can't let them—"

"We can't *stop* them." If anyone knew that, it was him. He turned away, sick to his stomach. The roar of the crowd became the sound of his past, of the people of Thelantis calling out while the Goldwings murdered his father.

"Let's go, Ellie. Before we're next in the noose."

She let him pull her away, her eyes blazing. "It's not fair, Nox."

"I know. Believe me, I know."

"He knows. Garion knows what we're doing and he's trying to stop us. Why? *Why?* Why does he hate his own people so much that he's willing to let them lose their wings? It's like he's breaking us on purpose!"

Nox paused, thinking.

Then he said softly, "I suppose it's easier to control people with broken wings."

CHAPTER TWENTY-SEVEN
· ELLIE ·

They camped that night near the eastern edge of the Thornmoors, in a copse of gnarled oak trees. With thunder rumbling to the west, they'd searched until they found a hollow tree to shelter in.

Ellie used her charcoal stick to draw an ashmark on the tree trunk. After she finished, she stared at it a moment, wondering how, long after Tirelas and its ruling Phoenix clan had been forgotten, this one little mark had remained, passed down through generations. Did it actually ward off gargols? She didn't know, but some habits were too ingrained to break.

Later, by the light of the oil lamp, Ellie stared at the map, tracing the path they'd have to take to reach the ruins of the Crow clan seat, but the prospect of closing in on their destination did nothing to lift her spirits.

She couldn't shut out the memory of the Robin clanner being dragged away by the Goldwings. She couldn't wash away the guilt that sat like acid on her tongue. *They* were the reason that young man was dead. Their story, *their* words, had been his death sentence.

No.

No, she couldn't think that way. That was how Garion wanted them to think. He wanted them to destroy themselves, saving him the trouble.

He was the one responsible for the Robin clanner's execution. He was the one trying to stamp out what little hope she and Nox, and Gussie and Twig on the coast, had been able to spread.

It's easier to control people with broken wings.

“So where are we going next?” asked Nox, kicking off his shoes.

“West,” Ellie said, refolding the map. “Across the Thornmoors.”

His eyebrows drew together. “Wait a second. I never properly went to school, and let’s face it—I know as much about geography as a gargol knows about ballroom dancing—but even I’ve heard of the Thornmoors. Aren’t they trapped under constant storms?”

Ellie swiped her hand toward the sky. “Does that matter anymore? Gargols attack no matter what now, rain or shine.”

“Yeah, but I’d still say the chances of them attacking from a storm are higher. Let me see that map. There’s gotta be a better direction we can go.”

“No!” Ellie said, too sharply. She cleared her throat and added more calmly, “I mean, I checked already. And this is the best route.”

He frowned, and for a moment she worried he’d push the issue, but then he shrugged. “Whatever.”

Ellie leaned back against the trunk. “You’ve got first watch, right?”

“Yep.”

“Okay. Wake me when—” She paused and cocked an ear. “Did you hear something?”

“Thunder, critters, wind, general unexplained spookiness . . .” Nox spread his hands. “We’re sitting in a creepy tree in a creepy forest. Take your pick.”

“No . . . it sounded like . . .” She frowned, then crawled to the opening in the trunk. *“Laughter.”*

At that moment, a hand clamped around the back of Ellie’s neck and dragged her out of the tree. She screamed and kicked, but the grip was too strong to break.

“Well, well, *well*,” a low voice chuckled above her.

Ellie froze. If it was talking, it wasn’t a gargol, at least.

“I admit,” said the man, “you gave me a merrier hunt than I had foreseen. Impressive, yes. You have been worthy prey.”

The Hunter.

He was alive.

Ellie reached very slowly toward her belt, where her knife was sheathed.

"Let go of her!" Nox said.

Ellie made a grab for the knife's hilt—only to feel it slide out of reach as the Hunter drew it instead. He twisted her around, so she was pinned against him, her own knife laid against her ribs.

She was getting *really* tired of people doing that.

Nox stood in the hollow of the tree, hands raised. "All right. Look, it's me you came for, not her. Let her go and I'll—"

"Ah, but the rules have changed," hissed the Hunter. "Oh yes. *You* brats upped the ante. Don't you see what you made of the Hunter?"

Ellie looked up, finally seeing the man's face for the first time, and gasped.

The whole left side of his face was an ugly mass of twisting scars, as if his face had been caved in.

"Aren't I beauteous?" he snarled, noting Ellie's look of horror. "Aren't I a masterpiece? Well? Do you like your handiwork?"

His face must have been crushed in the rockslide. And now, Ellie realized, he was hunting them not just for the king—but for revenge.

"Nox, *fly*!" she shouted.

Then the Hunter clubbed her with the hilt of her knife, and she dropped.

When Ellie woke, it was to a headache so painful she imagined her skill had split. Groaning, she blinked and looked around.

It was morning, the sky dim gray and cloudy, and she was tied up on the ground below an outcrop of dirt and roots. They were still in the woods, then, and alive. She saw Nox lying beside her, conscious but also bound.

"I tried to fight him off," he whispered. "But he moves like one of those jungle snakes Twig found."

"Boa constrictor," Ellie rasped, her voice dry and sticky.

He nodded.

Ellie pushed herself up to sit. Her arms, tied behind her back, had gone numb, and her bad leg burned with agony. She wondered if she'd been dragged on it.

The Hunter lounged against a log nearby, watching them through hooded eyes, his lips smirking. In the light, his face was even more horrendous. The wounds seem to extend down the side of his body, out of sight beneath his clothes.

Then she caught her breath.

In his hand was the Phoenix crown. He twirled it curiously.

"So." His hand stopped, locking around the crown. "Where are the other two? The Falcon and the piebald? Tell me, and I'll make your ends quick and . . . relatively painless."

Ellie and Nox both tightened their jaws.

The Hunter chuckled. "Oh, good. I did hope you'd choose the slow, agonizing route. Much more fun for the Hunter." He waggled the crown. "And isn't *this* fascinating? What would two mice like you be doing with such a relic?" He set it on his own head. "How do I look?"

"Handsome!" said Ellie. "Oh, *so* very handsome."

Nox looked at her like she was nuts, but she kept her gaze on the Hunter.

"It's just a shame you don't have a scepter to match it, or a whole *chest* of jewels. Because we know where to find all of that. We can take you there. There are whole troves of treasure to be found—and only Nox and I know where."

"Oh, yes!" said Nox, thankfully catching on. "Whole treasuries of . . . um, treasure. Just pick your flavor. Emeralds, rubies, gold."

"And skystones," added Ellie. "You know about skystones, right? How they heal wingrot? How they're the key to saving us all from losing our wings?"

Looking unamused, the Hunter leaned back and crossed his arms, the crown still resting at an angle across his brow. "Ugh. *We can lead you to treasure if you only spare us!* Boo-hoo. How *boring*. How *predictable*. As if I had any interest in such trinkets anyway." He removed the crown and let it fall into the dirt, then gave them a nasty grin. "There is only one thing in this world that brings the Hunter pleasure, pets, and that is *pain*. Exquisite, pure, symphonic pain! Pain like music, an orchestra of hurt and fear and terror, composed by a master—*me*." He rose and began walking toward them. "Pain with all its rhythms and harmonies. Pain with its hills, valleys, and at last, *crescendo*! And then, of course, the end. The final note. The darkness . . ."

Ellie began shivering, her feathers ruffling. She tried to twist out of her bonds, to no avail.

The Hunter bent over her and traced his finger down her nose, and Ellie felt a tear squeeze from her eye. He laughed, then turned to Nox.

"The Crow first? Hmm. Yes. So angry, so determined. Such fire in this mouse's eyes! I'll break you slowly."

"No!" Ellie cried.

The Hunter grabbed Nox and dragged him into the open. Nox thrashed and cursed, but the Hunter had tied them in such a way that struggling only made the ropes squeeze tighter.

"You can't hurt him!" Ellie wailed. "You don't understand! He's important. He's the key!"

If you drop the flame, Elder Rue's voice warned, *the sky will fall.*

"We need him!" Ellie pleaded. "The *world* needs him! He's—he's the Phoenix!"

The Hunter looked at her, curious. *"Phoenix,"* he muttered, as if he recognized the word but was trying to recall its meaning.

"Yes!" Ellie scooted forward as best she could, trying to ignore the pain that shot through her leg. "He's the one who will lead us home!"

Nox groaned.

"And he could be the *last*," she continued. "If we lose him, we'll lose our wings, or the gargols will wipe us out. But with Nox, we have a chance, don't you see? He's descended from the Phoenix clan, the kings and queens of the islands in the sky! And I can prove it!"

The Hunter watched her, while Nox sighed and let his head drop. But Ellie ignored him; she was desperate now. There had to be some part of the Hunter that was still sane enough to understand the bigger picture.

"Trust me," she said, putting every ounce of persuasion in her body into her voice. "Nox is worth more to you alive. Just come with us west, to the ruins of Thraille, and I can prove it."

"Thraille." Nox's head lifted, and he looked at Ellie with bewilderment. "You were leading us to Thraille?"

"The old clan seat of the Crows," she said, nodding. "It's where your grandmother was headed, Nox, when she disappeared. There's a secret buried there about your family, and I believe it's proof that you're actually a Phoenix, and a prince."

"You were leading me to this place without telling me? You were . . . *luring* me there?"

"Enough!" said the Hunter. "Phoenixes, Thrailles, princes, I don't care. Pah! What does the world need with more princes and kings? They bleed the same as the rest."

He flipped Ellie's knife and caught it, then knelt over Nox. He looked at the Crow boy as if he were a feast he was about to devour, and was only deciding upon which course to begin.

Ellie cried out and tried to crawl toward them, but her leg seized and she fell hard, getting a mouthful of dirt.

"Stop!" she spluttered. "Please!"

The Hunter laughed, then began humming gleefully to himself as he dragged the knife down the side of Nox's face.

"An eye, I think," he concluded. "Then an ear. Then a finger. Then a toe." He turned it into a ghoulish song as his blade tapped across Nox's skin to his left eye.

Ellie sobbed, utterly helpless.

Then, out of nowhere, came a wild cry.

A figure dove from the sky on wide, powerful dark wings, colliding with the Hunter and knocking him to the ground.

CHAPTER TWENTY-EIGHT

· ELLIE ·

The Hunter and the mysterious attacker rolled over each other, yelling and clawing, wings thrashing.

Ellie pushed herself up, gasping with pain as the movement wrenched her leg.

The stranger was bigger and stronger, but the Hunter had his preternatural flexibility, and he managed to twist away and pop up with a pair of knives. But the stranger was ready. He drew a sword from his belt and sliced the Hunter's arm.

Howling, the Hunter dropped one of the knives and danced backward. Ellie figured he didn't enjoy pain quite so much when it was his own.

Ellie spotted her knife lying in the dirt where the Hunter had dropped it. Grabbing it in her bound hands, she turned and held it out so Nox could lift his ankles and saw away the rope binding them. Then he turned and did the same with his wrists.

Once he was free, he cut Ellie loose as well.

"Thraille," he whispered angrily as he cut her hands loose. "Really, Ellie?"

"This is not the time to argue about it! Help him!"

The stranger was keeping the Hunter at bay, but Ellie saw he'd already been cut a few times on his arm and chest, and was bleeding through his clothes. He was dressed in all black, with a dark mask tied over his face so only his eyes showed. His wings, which he kept tightly folded, were clearly Hawk clan.

Ellie frowned, peering closer as the stranger and Hunter circled each other. Then, when the stranger whirled and slashed with his sword, she gasped, recognizing the moves—because she'd blocked them a thousand times.

"Zain?"

Her former best friend, whom she'd known since she was a fledgling—and whom she'd last seen in King Garion's dungeons, where she'd left him unconscious in his new Goldwing uniform.

But this was no time for reunions. He needed help.

Ellie spotted their satchels nearby, the contents strewn across the ground where the Hunter had rifled through them. She pointed them out to Nox, who found his slingshot amid the mess.

He fired a few stones, each one thwacking the Hunter's head and chest. The Hunter snarled, lunging toward Nox, but Zain intercepted him and managed to slice his thigh.

The Hunter's enraged scream ripped through the trees.

He suddenly changed tactics, opening his dark Vulture wings and flapping clumsily over the ground—toward Ellie.

She gasped and ducked, but she wasn't his target. Instead, he scooped up the Phoenix crown and then shot for open sky.

"We'll see how the *king* likes this!" he cackled. "A new shiny for his collection, yes, yes!"

"Follow him!" Ellie cried, opening her wings. "We need that crown!"

"No!" Nox said, grabbing her before she could take off. "Ellie, stop! He's dangerous, you're still hurt, and this guy needs help."

She blinked, then shook herself. Of course Nox was right. Chasing the Hunter through clouded skies would be madness, and what would she do if she caught up to him? Probably get her neck broken.

So she folded her wings again and tried not to think about the fact they'd lost the one piece of evidence she'd had of Nox's identity.

Instead, she focused on the Hawk boy. Zain was leaning against a tree, hand clasped to a wound in his side.

"Hello, Zain."

He gave a hoarse laugh, then pulled down his mask. "Hey, Ellie."

"You know each other?" asked Nox, looking bewildered.

"Zain is . . . an old friend," said Ellie uncertainly. They hadn't parted in the best circumstances. She wasn't honestly sure where they stood anymore.

She shook her head as she walked toward him. "Zain, what are you doing here? How in the skies did you find us?"

"Long story." He winced, his hand tightening on his side.

"How bad is it?" She lifted his bloody shirt and saw the cut from his hip to navel. "Not deep. But it'll keep bleeding unless I stitch it."

"You can do that?"

She rolled her eyes. "Did you completely forget the summer I apprenticed to Healer Vera?"

"Oh. Right." He grimaced and lay back.

"Nox, get me that thread and needle Granna packed for me. And we'll need fire, water, and the kettle."

The Crow, who'd been watching them both with an expression of exasperated confusion, nodded and leaped to work. Ellie knelt over Zain and checked his other wounds, but the rest were shallow enough to only need a bit of bandaging. As she eased his shirt off, she asked, "Want to tell me that long story now?"

"Right. Well . . . it's been a few months, hasn't it? You know, when I came to on that dungeon floor and found you gone, I was—"

"Furious?" Ellie winced. "Betrayed?"

"Glad."

Her eyebrows shot up.

"Yeah, I know. You pulled one over on me, and I got reamed by my captain and stuck on manure-shoveling duty for a month. It hasn't been *all* bad. I've gotten to know the crown prince a bit, actually, and he's not a bad sort. Full of surprises, actually . . . But anyway, I felt better, knowing you were free. Even if it meant you were running around with criminals." He tossed a dark look toward Nox, who was returning with a kettle of water from the nearby stream.

"Hey!" Nox protested.

But Zain's expression soon softened. "Thanks for distracting that creep. I don't think I'd have hit him otherwise. He was freakishly fast."

Nox returned the cautious stare, then gave a curt nod. "Thanks for swooping in when you did."

Ellie's stomach tumbled with nerves, as her past and present lives collided in that moment. Zain, her best friend since childhood and now a Goldwing knight, talking to Nox, the thief with whom she'd escaped death and crossed the world. It was enough to make her head spin.

"Get that water boiling," she told Nox. "I'll need to wash the needle and thread before I use them."

"I see she's just as bossy as ever," said Zain.

Nox barked a laugh. "Yeah, makes me want to stick my head in a bucket and scream."

"Right?" Zain nodded emphatically. "Like, *hello*, Ellie Meadows, but I actually have a brain too."

"Only if you *tell* her that, she gives you a face like . . ." Nox pressed his lips together, screwing them to one side, and flattened his eyebrows.

"*Yes!*" agreed Zain. "Just like that! *The face!*"

Ellie had worried they might end up arguing.

This was much worse.

"OKAY!" Ellie crossed her arms. "If that's how this is going to go, why don't I just flit off and let Nox sew you up, Zain? Oh, I'd love to see how that goes."

"She's making the face," said Zain.

Nox nodded solemnly. "She's making the face."

With a growl, Ellie snatched the kettle from Nox. "I'll do it myself!"

While she built the fire, Zain told his story.

"After a month of chucking horse poo around, I got assigned to a search squad. I guess normally new recruits aren't sent into the field, but this was a special circumstance. The king wants . . . well, um." He darted a sheepish look at Nox. "He wants this guy's head on a pike. I don't know what you did, Crow, but he acts like you're the incarnation of evil."

Nox sighed.

"Anyway. My unit was sent south, to the midlands. We didn't have much to go on, so we generally mucked about, staying in inns, asking questions, getting nowhere. Then, about two weeks ago, we find out there's weird rumors starting to spread through the southern farmlands. People talking about floating islands, skystones. And I thought, huh! Doesn't that sound like something Ellie went on about before she brained me and stole my knife?"

"Sorry about that," Ellie said. "I . . . still have it, by the way." She took the knife from her belt.

"Keep it," he said. "I got a new one. Anyway, there we were, suddenly with new orders: Crush these rumors, whatever it took. And, uh, execute anyone spreading them. Skystones were to be destroyed on the spot. And *then* there are the reports of weird gargol attacks. All while our primary objective is still to chop off this Crow's head." His brow furrowed. "It's getting strange out there, Ellie. The king . . . he's acting odd. Paranoid. Other Goldwings told me he hasn't left his palace in weeks, and rages about *that Crow scum* night and day."

Zain gave Nox a curious look. "What *did* you do to tick him off like that?"

"I was born," Nox said flatly.

"Well, whatever's going on, it's got everyone worried. Most of the

Goldwings go along with it. He's the king, he gets to act weird—and we don't get to ask questions. But some of us don't like it. I've avoided the executions mostly, like yesterday, when they did in this Robin guy over in Gruston."

"We saw it," Ellie whispered.

"Yeah, I know. Because later, I heard someone say they spotted two strangers flying out of the city—a Sparrow and an unknown clanner. I didn't think much of it, till I saw that Hunter guy sneaking around town. And I remembered the Goldwings gossiping about how King Garion had sent some sort of assassin to track down the Crow kid."

"So you guessed we were nearby?"

"Yeah. I put on this awesome disguise and followed the creep, then lost him in the dark." He blew out a breath. "You're lucky I found him again."

"You have no idea." Ellie saw the water begin to boil and dropped in the thread and needle. "Zain . . . why *did* you stop the Hunter? After all, you're supposed to be bringing Nox in too, right?"

"I was just wondering that myself," said Nox, narrowing his eyes.

"Oh! Yeah, don't worry about that. I won't tell anyone I saw you two. I mean, I know I'm a Goldwing and I'm supposed to obey the king's orders no matter what, but . . . This doesn't feel right. He's like a madman these days. And you're my friend, Ellie. I don't know what you're up to or why, but I don't want to see you get hurt."

Ellie's heart softened. After everything she'd done to Zain, he still thought of her as a friend. She didn't know if she even deserved that. Honestly, she had fully expected Zain would have turned into the same careless brute so many of the Goldwings were.

But maybe there was more to him than she'd known.

Once the water was cooled enough, she poured it over her hands to clean them, then threaded the needle. "I hope you still think of us as friends after this, then. Because, well, it's gonna hurt."

While Zain bit down on a stick to keep from yelling, and Ellie stitched him up as quickly as she could, Nox flew to the treetops to keep an eye out for the Hunter. None of them felt safe enough to let down their guard, knowing he was out there with vengeance burning in his belly.

"Ellie," Zain said around the stick. His face creased with pain, but he was holding up admirably. "What *are* you doing out here?"

"You already know," she said. "Those rumors? We started them, Nox and me and our friends. But they're true, Zain. I've been there, to the islands in the sky. I've seen the skystones heal so many people from wingrot. But things are only going to get worse." She glanced at his face. "Bite down. This is the last stitch, and I've got to tie it off."

When it was done, she let out a long breath and dabbed the excess blood that had leaked from his wound.

"The king is hunting Nox because he's part of it all," she added. "He . . . has a link to the islands that threatens King Garion's reign, and I don't think he's going to give up until Nox is dead, and probably me too. I know too much now."

"About *what*? Ellie, it's all so wild and impossible. I wouldn't even begin to believe it's true if it weren't obviously so important to the king."

Ellie went to her satchel and found, to her relief, the six remaining skystones were still there. The Hunter had scattered them around, but their clay settings had kept them from floating away. Taking three, she returned to Zain.

"Do you know what these are?" she asked.

He grimaced. "Trouble, that's what."

"Yes, but they're also what can save us. Wingrot is spreading, Zain, and it will keep spreading until either we've all lost our wings, or we've returned home."

"Home?"

She pointed up, wordlessly.

Zain sighed. "I was afraid you'd say that."

"Will you take these stones back to Thelantis?" she asked. "Don't destroy them. Don't tell anyone you have them. But when you get there . . . make sure they go to Rottown. You know, the slums where all the wingrot sufferers are sent? Do it in secret, so you don't get in trouble."

"Ellie . . ."

"Zain, *please*. I know I don't have the right to ask anything of you, but this is bigger than you and me. And . . . you'll be a hero, even if no one knows who you are. These stones will save so many lives."

He took them reluctantly and eyed them as if they were venomous. "I can't promise I will, or that I'd even succeed if I tried."

"I know. And the last thing I want is you getting in trouble for it. If it comes down to it, dump them. But if there's any way . . . promise you'll try."

He looked up at her, a rueful smile on his lips. "Some things never change, huh? Like Ellie Meadows talking me into things I'll definitely regret."

She smiled, then hugged him—carefully, so as not to pull on his fresh stitches.

"You don't know how happy I am knowing I can still count on you," she whispered.

"Yeah, yeah. Well, I'm just glad you're not dead. Even if you are friends with the most wanted criminal in the Clandoms."

"He's not a criminal. Well, not really. Not anymore. He's . . ." She looked up at the treetops, where she could just make out Nox atop a tall pine. "He's more than meets the eye. Even if I'm the only one who realizes it yet."

"Ugh." Zain made a face. "Are you in *love* with him?"

Ellie squealed. "No!"

He laughed and pushed to his feet, pressing a hand to his side. "I have to get back. They'll be looking for me already. I need to make up some story to explain this."

Impulsively, Ellie hugged him one last time. "We'll see each other again, Zain. And I hope when we do, everything's better."

"Yeah, me too."

She watched him fly away, anxious that his wound would send him tumbling back down, but he managed well enough. Of all the people . . . Zain, in the middle of nowhere, her knight in shining . . . well, disguise. Ellie shook her head at the strangeness of the world.

Then she turned and found Nox had landed behind her, his face hard and his arms crossed.

"So," he said. "Let's talk about Thraille."

CHAPTER TWENTY-NINE
· NOX ·

"One of the first things you ever said to me was *I never lie*." Nox was boiling. He'd been holding the words back all through the time it had taken her to stitch up her Hawk friend, but he couldn't wait any longer. "But you lied to me, Sparrow."

Ellie winced, her hand knotting on the bloodied cloth. "I . . . didn't exactly lie. I just never told you *where* we were heading."

"*Thraille.*" He gave an empty laugh. "So you could prove to me that I'm a Phoenix. So you could tell *everyone* that I'm some kind of long-lost princeling come down from the sky to save them."

"I just wanted to know the truth, and for you to know it too! But, Nox, now the Hunter knows there's some Corvain family secret in Thraille. He could be on his way there right now to get it first. If we lose that evidence, we may never get another chance to prove your lineage. And our future, everyone's future—it all depends on returning to Tirelas. Who will lead them if—"

"Let them lead themselves," said Nox. "Let the world save itself!"

"If there's really some secret buried in Thraille—"

"Maybe I don't want to know it!" he shouted. "Maybe I'm sick of you pushing, pushing, *pushing* me no matter how many times I tell you to stop! You're worse than a liar, Ellie. You're manipulative and you can't for one minute *leave me alone*! At some point, you've got to let go."

"Nox!" Her face reddened. "I'm sorry I didn't tell you. It's just that I knew this is how you'd react. And I don't understand why you can't, for even one minute, *consider* that I might be right? That there might be more to you than . . ."

"Than this?" Nox asked, gesturing at himself. "I'm not enough for you, Ellie, just like you're not enough for yourself."

"What's *that* supposed to mean?"

"Why do you have to save the world? Why do you have to be the hero?"

"I don't—it's not about being a hero."

"Then what is it about?"

Ellie looked ready to club him with her lockstave. She dropped the rag and picked up her satchel. "Fine. If you don't want to go to Thraille, stay here. I'll go myself."

"Huh? Wait—Ellie!"

She launched into the air, not looking to see if Nox followed. In moments, she'd risen above the treetops and was winging toward the vast gray expanse of the Thornmoors.

Nox swore and took off after her.

It soon became clear how the place had gotten its name. The ground was covered in thick tangles of briars, as far as he could see. The sky above hung low and heavy with clouds, and what little light filtered through them was dull gray. With terrain that impenetrable, there'd be no walking across the Thornmoors, no sneaking through the foliage in an attempt to evade watching gargols.

No wonder people told horror stories about this place.

Nox struggled to keep up with Ellie, who flew low and fast, following the rise and fall of the gray hills. It was infuriating how those few inches of feather missing from his wing could so slow him down.

Then he saw Ellie pitch suddenly, as if hit by a strong wind. He tilted as the gust swept over him moments later, but Ellie hadn't had enough warning to adjust her angle. The wind bowled her over and slammed her into a thorn-covered bank.

"Ellie!"

He dove toward her, seeing her struggling in the briar patch. But it seemed the more she fought to get free, the more tightly the thorny vines ensnared her.

"Just be still!" he shouted. He slowed to hover over her, and watched in exasperation as she only struggled harder. Her arms were covered in scratches, and every time she twisted, she left a few more feathers stuck to the thorns.

"Need a hand?" he asked.

Blowing hair out of her eyes, she growled, "No."

He lifted an eyebrow.

"I'm fine!" She wrenched a shoulder forward, and gasped as thorns tore her arm and ripped a hole in the cloak Tariel had gifted her.

"You don't look fine."

"I can do this!"

"Just stop struggling!" Nox said. He carefully landed next to her, bracing his feet on two thick, barbed vines. "You're making it worse."

"No, *you* are!" She tried to peel her left wing free, only to have the thorns rip away a few more feathers.

"Why can't you just admit this isn't working?"

"I can do it! I just need—to fight—*harder*!" With each word she tugged her limbs but ended up more snarled than ever. Exhausted and panting, Ellie sagged in the thorns, her eyes shut. Nox shook his head at her stubbornness.

"This is just one more stupid thing to overcome," she said.

"Like a test?"

Ellie opened her eyes and glared at him.

"Remember that old book you used to carry around?" Nox asked.

"*The King's Ladder*." Her book of knightly virtues, with all its lessons and stories about heroes of old. "Of course I remember."

"You treated that thing like it was made of gold. Like it was the only thing that mattered, and everything else in the world was just designed to test your commitment to it."

Ellie winced. "So?"

"*So*, ever since you talked to Elder Rue back in Cloudstone, you've been carrying around her vision like it was your new *King's Ladder*."

"I . . . never said I believed it was true."

"But you do, don't you? You think it has something to do with me, which is why you're pushing us both on this insane quest. Because it's your *destiny*, right? Just like becoming a Goldwing was your destiny."

Ellie looked away. Above them, the sky grumbled. A few raindrops fell onto Nox's wings.

"It has to mean something," she murmured.

"What does?"

"*This.* All of it. Finding the skystone, then Tirelas, then that crown. Don't you understand that? Everything that's happened to us since the day we met. It was all leading somewhere."

"To this?" He looked pointedly at the thorns. "Seems to be working out well."

"Nox! Just—stop it! Stop telling me I'm wrong! I'm not wrong. I'm not. I *can't* be . . ."

"Why? What if you *are* wrong, Ellie? What if I'm not the person you want me to be? What if all of this isn't your problem to solve? What if there is no such thing as destiny?"

"You're only saying that because you're scared it might be true."

He scoffed.

With a grunt, Ellie pushed her feet into the ground and then thrust herself upward. Nox felt his own feathers crawl at the way the thorns scraped her arms and wings. But she finally managed to stand, her skin red from a thousand tiny cuts.

"You're scared," she said again. "That's the real reason you don't want to go to Thraille. It's why you won't admit it might be true that you're a Phoenix."

Nox bristled. "Have you ever thought that even if I *am* this Phoenix you want me to be—that maybe I don't *want* to be him? What if you did trick me into visiting Thraille and finding this so-called proof, but it didn't change my mind at all?"

"How could it not?" she whispered. "If you're really a Phoenix, and your ancestors ruled Tirelas—how could you turn your back on that? How could you ignore the responsibility, the—the *destiny* of it?"

Destiny.

Oh, how he'd come to hate that word.

"Because I don't need it," he said simply. "I am who I am, and my blood doesn't change that. I'm not *you*, Ellie, no matter how much you try to change me. I'm not a hero, not a prince, certainly not some kind of revolutionary."

"Then what *are* you?" she demanded.

"Huh?"

She took a step forward, and he took one back. "Who *are* you, Nox Hatcher? Tannox Corvain? Whatever you want to call yourself?"

"I'm a thief."

"You *were* a thief. Then you left that behind. Will you go back to it? Picking pockets for the rest of your life? Is that your future?"

"Well . . . no, I don't want to go back to that. It was only ever to survive."

"So you're a candle maker, like your grandfather?"

"Ugh, no. Takes way too much patience."

"So what are you?"

"I'm just a kid!" he shouted. "I'm just a Crow kid on the run with the bossiest, nosiest girl in the Clandoms, stuck in this thorn-covered wasteland!"

Skies, what was happening? He was the one who'd picked this fight. So how had he lost control of it so quickly?

"On the run," she echoed. "On the run to *what*, Nox? Will you just keep skittering across the countryside until the king finally catches up with you? Until the Hunter stabs out your eyes or some Goldwing lops off your head?"

"I—I don't know. Maybe if you weren't always shoving me into some new plan of yours, I'd have time to figure it out!"

"You know what I think?" She stepped back, hands finding her hips. "I think you're still just that thief I found half dead in the sunflowers, saying the only thing that matters is looking out for yourself. *Listen to your wings, not your heart.* Isn't that what you used to say? But you know what *looking out for yourself* really means? It means you're so scared of getting hurt that all you do is run and hide and turn your back on the people who need you. It means you're a coward."

Nox reeled as if she'd punched him.

"A coward?" He spat the word. "You think I'm a coward?"

"Well, what else could you be?"

His teeth ground together until pain coursed through his jaw. "I'm not a coward and I'm not scared. I'm—I'm—"

"What? *What are you?*"

"I'm a failure!" he shouted, his throat burning. "There! There's your truth! There's your destiny! What is Nox Hatcher? Well, turns out he's nothing but a rotten, lousy failure who breaks everything he touches! Don't you see what I leave behind me? The death, the destruction? How many people's lives have I ruined? They burned down all of Knock Street because of me! My grandfather's shop!"

Ellie stared at him, shocked into silence.

"You want me to be a hero?" he continued. "You want me to save people, to fix everything? Ha! I don't save people, Ellie, I break them. People *die* because of me. My father. Those guards at the Crag who got shredded by gargols. *Everyone* who's been killed since I flew into that storm—the chief in Brightbay. That Finch man on the road. That potato farmer's wife. Twig . . . skies, I was too late to save *Twig*. I started all that, just like the king says."

"Nox, no—"

"And *you*! You could be home right now with your clan, safe, if not for me. Instead, they'll hang you right alongside me. And that's my fault too. I'm a failure, Ellie, and a killer. I—my mother—I *killed my mother*."

He jumped into the air and took flight, winging back toward the forest. He wouldn't let her see his tears.

Curse Ellie Meadows!

Curse her for opening the door he'd so carefully locked.

Curse her for cracking him open and revealing how rotten he was.

He flew between the trees, heedless of direction, just trying to get away from the pain and guilt eating through his belly.

I killed her.

He'd shut it out for so long, pretending he'd moved on, that it didn't matter.

But I killed her.

The rain was falling faster now. His eyes blurry with tears, he flew clumsily, then finally slammed right into a pine tree. He gasped and tumbled down, barely finding his wings before he hit the ground. Struggling onward, he pushed through the low branches, their sharp ends scraping his skin and pulling his feathers. Still Nox barreled through, shoving branches in rage, trying to gain altitude but being buffeted by the wind. His chest felt like it was full of rocks, making him too heavy to fly.

Then, out of nowhere, Ellie came swooping from his left. She smashed into him and they rolled through the air, then hit the ground hard, tumbling over each other.

Nox landed with a gasp on his back, Ellie pinning him down.

"Get off me!" he yelled. "Skies curse you, Ellie Meadows!"

She had him by his shoulders and refused to budge. "Look at me, Nox."

"I hate you! You push and push until you break people!"

"Look at me."

"I killed her." He stared blankly at the clouded sky over her shoulder. A raindrop fell and he watched it, all the way down to where it broke on her hair. "I killed my ma. I was too late. I was too stupid. I promised her I would save her but I didn't. I broke her because something's broken in me. She died . . . and I let her."

Ellie finally slid off him, but he was too shattered to fly away again. He couldn't even sit up. So she pulled him up, pressed his face into her shoulder, and wrapped her arms around him. His wings lay limp in the dirt.

"It's not your fault," she whispered in his ear.

"Stop it, Ellie."

"It's not," she said again.

He tried to push her away, but she held him tighter.

"You didn't kill her, Nox."

"You saw it!" he snarled. "You were there!"

"Garion did that. Garion did all of it."

"*Because* of me!"

"It's not your fault."

His chest grew tighter and tighter. He hated Ellie for following him, for forcing these words into his head. She didn't get it. She didn't see how rotten he was. The curse that he was. Why didn't she see it? Everyone else did. Every person he'd passed on the streets of Thelantis who'd spit on him, shoved him, called him *garbage*, *scum*, *dirty*, *thieving Crow*, ever since he was little. If perfect strangers could see it, why couldn't she?

"It's not your fault."

"Ellie—" His heart squeezed into a fist. He was having trouble breathing.

"You're not a killer. You're not a failure. And you're not broken, Nox Hatcher."

Raindrops fell, sliding down his face, his wings. Everything in Nox pulled back, like water receding from the shoreline into a massive wave, building, rising, black as night.

"It's not your fault."

The wave broke.

He began to sob, his arms tightening around her, her feathers crushed under his forearms. Ellie held still, though he was surely squeezing the air from her small frame. But he couldn't help it. He clung to her as the wave crashed through him and threatened to pull him apart. She was the only thing holding him together. The rain fell harder, drenching them both, but Nox couldn't seem to stop weeping.

He didn't know how long they sat like that in the downpour. His face was buried in her shoulder, his body heaving with tears and pent-up pain and guilt.

But as the minutes passed, the obliterating sweep of the wave turned into something gentler, a steady, cool current that flowed through him. The guilt he'd carried for so long was uprooted and swept away. He was left empty. Clean.

Forgiven.

"It's not your fault," Ellie whispered one last time.

And at last, Nox believed her.

CHAPTER THIRTY
· ELLIE ·

With the rain showing no sign of stopping, they had little choice but to wait it out. Ellie, worried the Hunter might return, scouted the woods for a place to hole up.

They were quiet as they walked, moving in the pattern they'd established over weeks of finding and setting up camp. But something had changed between them. Ellie sensed it in the set of Nox's wings and shoulders. He was looser, lighter.

He carries his troubles deep, his grandfather had told Ellie. But she'd never imagined just *how* deep. She felt like a terrible friend; all this time he'd been carrying such heavy guilt, and she'd been too wrapped up in visions of *destiny* to notice.

"Find anything?" Nox called out from a short distance away.

"No. You?"

They regrouped and stood for a moment in the scant shelter of a cedar's branches, shivering.

"Here. We haven't eaten in hours." Nox handed her a wrapped loaf of bread from his pack. She took it and tore it in half, sharing it between them.

They chewed in silence for a few minutes, watching the rain.

"I'll go with you," Nox said at last.

Ellie looked at him.

"To Thraille," he added. "I'll go. That doesn't mean I believe your theory, or that I'm going along with your plans, but I'll go and see what's there. If there even *is* anything to find."

She nodded, looking down at her bread. "What if there isn't?"

He flicked the raindrops from his wings. "Then we keep going. We spread the skystones, and the story of Tirelas. You're right. All of this is Garion's fault. He wants to keep everyone crushed against the ground, where he can control them. *He* killed my mother. And if us spreading the truth ruffles his feathers, then I say let's shout it into every ear in the Clandoms!"

Ellie grinned. "Right. After Thraille, we'll go to—"

She cut herself short, her eyes fixing on a shadow that dropped suddenly from the clouds above.

"Nox!"

"Gargol," he muttered, drawing his slingshot. "And I'm out of rocks." He fitted one of Gussie's smoke tubes into the weapon instead, then drew it back. "It's moving fast!"

"We could split up."

"I'm not leaving you. No more splitting up."

"Nox—!"

He fired.

The tube exploded in front of the gargol, spreading a cloud of blue smoke. But it would do little good except to blind the creature for a moment.

"C'mon, Ellie!" Nox grabbed her hand and pulled her into the trees.

"It's still coming!" she shouted.

They both looked back as the shadow sped through the smoke and descended upon them, covered in blue chalk powder and . . . coughing.

Coughing?

"It's . . . not a gargol," Ellie concluded, slowing to a stop.

"Gargol?" shouted the now-blue shadow. It swooped lower and hovered over them, shedding chalk dust from its wings. "Seriously? Using my own weapons against me? Which, by the way, wouldn't do any harm against a *real* gargol."

Nox and Ellie exchanged looks.

"Gussie?" they chorused.

The Falcon girl wiped powder from her face and glared at them. "Honestly! I know it's been a few weeks, but did you completely forget what I look like?"

"What are you *doing* here?" Ellie asked.

"And where's Twig?" added Nox.

Gussie's expression turned grim. "That's why I'm here. In . . . the Thornmoors, apparently. What are you two doing out here, anyway? There's nothing—"

"Gussie!" Nox's wings curled. *"Where. Is. Twig?"*

She shut her eyes. "He's been captured by Goldwings. And . . . taken to Thelantis."

Ellie and Nox stared in horror.

"It's bad," Gussie said. "Really bad. They're going to execute him."

"How did you find us?" Ellie asked.

They were sheltered in an old burrow large enough it might once have housed a bear. Whatever trouble Twig was in, there was nothing they could do until morning, when it would be safe to fly again. While Ellie swept out the leaves and sticks that had gathered inside, Nox piled brush over the opening, until they were as hidden as could be. Gussie, who'd apparently run out of her own supplies, had torn into theirs with ravenous hunger.

"Oh. Right." Gussie took something out of her pocket—a small brass box made to hold a ring or trinket. When she opened it, though, Ellie saw she'd fashioned some kind of contraption inside. A clear glass ball rested in the middle, supported by small metal rods that held it suspended in the air. Inside the ball were a bunch of small blue crystals, none larger than a sunflower seed.

"Wait a minute . . ." Ellie peered closer. "Are those . . . ?"

"Skystones," Gussie confirmed. "Well, pieces of one. I sort of maybe smashed a few . . . for scientific purposes . . ."

"Gussie!" Ellie groaned.

"Hey, look what came of it!" Gussie rattled the contraption. "I call it a skycompass. You see, it turns out that skystones don't float for no reason—they're attracted to one another. Once I figured that out, I of course saw the navigational implications. That is, I realized we could use them to locate more skystones. So I invented this compass. On clear days when there are no sky islands floating overhead, the bits instead point toward the nearest stones—*yours*. See?"

She turned the box, and the skystone shards in the glass globe shifted, so no matter which way she held it, they pressed toward Ellie's satchel—where her and Nox's three remaining skystones were stored.

"That's . . . incredible," said Ellie.

"I know. It's pretty ingenious." Gussie took the compliment with her usual grace. "I did get a little off track chasing down dead ends. Stopped in a Finch town before this; guess you two were already there and left a stone behind. Anyway, the compass finally led me to you. So it wasn't all for—"

"How do you know Twig's in Thelantis?" interrupted Nox. "And how long have they had him?"

"They ambushed us five days ago, outside Vestra. I got away, but Twig . . ."

Couldn't fly. Of course. Ellie pressed a hand to her churning stomach, thinking of how terrified Twig must have been.

"Anyway," said Gussie, "before I got away, I heard them talking about how they wanted to bring us back to Garion for questioning before they executed us. They knew who we were, and . . . well, I guess they wanted us to help them find Nox."

Ellie nodded, wishing there was room to pace. Her body buzzed with restless energy. "So he's safe for a little while. I mean, as long as they think he has information they need . . . They might even try to use him as bait to lure us in."

"Then it's working," said Nox. "Because we're going to Thelantis."

"What are you *doing* all the way out here, anyway?" asked Gussie. "There aren't any towns nearby, just those awful Thornmoors."

"Ah . . ." Ellie exchanged a look with Nox. "Long story. But obviously we're changing course now. We go to Thelantis in the morning. For Twig."

Nox gave her a surprised look. "Even if it means giving up on Thraille? Like you said, the Hunter could be on his way there now."

"Wait, wait, wait." Gussie raised her hands. "The Hunter? He's *alive*?" She glanced between them as if wondering what she'd missed, but then she shrugged it off. "Right, well, it can wait till tomorrow. Because I'm exhausted. You have no idea how hard I had to fly to find you two." Yawning, she curled up right where she sat, her wings folding around herself. "Wake me for third watch. Or better yet, not at all."

After Gussie had fallen asleep, Ellie sheepishly gave Nox the letter his grandmother had written.

"I should have given it to you the night I opened it," she admitted. "I'm sorry."

He read it a few times by the light of their dwindling oil lamp. Then he sat in silence for a long while. Though Ellie ached to discuss the letter with him—and the secret that might be hiding in Thraille—for once, she held her tongue. She busied herself with her satchel instead, reorganizing its contents and taking stock of their remaining supplies.

After several minutes, Nox put the letter in his pocket and looked up. "Well, I guess I should tell you that Granna gave *me* something for *you*."

"What?"

He pulled out a small leather bag from his own satchel and handed it to her. "I . . . probably should have given it to you days ago too. I guess I was sort of, um, not in the mood."

She raised an eyebrow at that and took the bag. Its contents clinked enticingly. When she opened it, her confusion only grew.

"Seeds of destiny?" Ellie whispered. "Like from Tariel's Seed Ceremony?"

Nox nodded. "Granna said you seemed pretty interested in them, and that there might come a time when you needed a little . . . guidance. I guess these were the ones left over from Tariel's ceremony. I hope you didn't have your heart set on being a dressmaker because that one's already taken."

Ellie tilted a few of the clay balls into her hand. There were dozens in the bag, each the size of a large blackberry.

"Did she say anything else?" she asked.

"Uh . . . yeah. *Choose wisely.* That was all."

"Huh." She ran her hand through the bag, wondering how many different destinies were hidden inside.

"Well? You gonna open one?"

Her stomach flooded with butterflies. What if she opened one and it was something completely different than she wanted? Like a fishmonger or a traveling minstrel? Did anyone ever get a destiny they were totally unsuited for?

But then, that wasn't how destiny worked, was it? It wasn't random. It had meaning and purpose. That's *why* it was destiny.

"What if Thelantis is a trap?" she said, rolling one of the shells between her fingers.

"It almost certainly is. They're using Twig to lure us in."

"And by abandoning our quest now, everything we've worked for these past few weeks will be lost. The Goldwings are destroying the skystones we gave away, and the truth about Tirelas with them." She closed her fist around the shells. "Things will go on as they always have. Or worse."

The gargol attacks would increase. Wingrot would spread faster.

And there'd be no one to stop it from happening.

"Maybe," Nox conceded.

"What if this is it?" she whispered. "What if choosing to save Twig means turning our backs on destiny? What if this is the moment when I *drop the flame* and the sky falls as a result?"

Nox shrugged. "You know what I think? Destiny or no destiny, that's not what matters. What matters is that *you* make the choice. *You* decide which way to fly."

She looked down at her hands, her brow furrowed.

"Ellie, you asked me why I was so scared that destiny might be real. Well, what about you? Why are you so scared it might *not* be?"

"Because . . . I can't be wrong again," Ellie said quietly. "I spent my whole life believing in the King's Ladder, in the Goldwings, in honor and law. I truly believed that if I worked hard and followed the rules, I'd find a place where I could . . . belong. But then it turned out none of those things were true, were they? I was wrong about everything, and I *lost* everything. My home, my clan, my dream."

Nox watched her quietly, and this time, he made no snarky interruptions.

"After that," whispered Ellie, "it was like *I* was lost. I didn't know who I was, or where I fit in, or what I was meant to do. I was just one more . . ."

"Outcast?" Nox asked, with a sad smile.

Ellie lowered her eyes. "I'm not like you, Nox. I'm not cut out to be on my own, looking out for just myself. It's not that I want to save everyone so I can be a hero. It's that . . . I want . . . to figure out where *I* belong. If it's not with Sparrow clan, or with the Goldwings . . . then where? I want a *home*, Nox. And maybe Tirelas is supposed to be that home. Not just for everyone else, but for me too. Isn't that what this destiny thing is about? And Elder Rue's vision?"

"Ellie." He sank into a crouch, his elbows resting on his knees. "Do you really not see it? That place where you belong? It's with *us*—with me and Gussie and Twig. You don't have to prove anything to us. Skies, Ellie. You flew into a storm after me. You faced gargols to try and save Twig. You . . . you didn't give up on me, even when I'd given up on myself. If that doesn't prove you're one of us, what does?"

Her lip quivered. She looked down at the shells clenched in her hands.

"When you protected us from the king back in Thelantis, you didn't lose everything. Because you still had me, Gussie, and Twig. *We're* your clan now. Not because destiny told you so. But because you *chose* us and we chose you. Home's not always a place, you know. Sometimes . . . it's people."

Deep in Ellie's heart, it was like a knot had come loose. She let out a long, shaky breath, and finally the tear she was holding back slipped free to run down her cheek. "Even if I'm too bossy and manipulative?"

"Well, I'm not saying those are my *favorite* things about you."

"You have a favorite thing about me?"

He laughed. "Nice try."

She studied the shells thoughtfully. "Well. Can't hurt to ask. If destiny wants to weigh in, let's give it one last chance."

She cleared a space in front of her and used her knife to carve a shallow basin in the dirt floor. Then she poured the seeds of destiny into it, watching them roll and clack together until at last, they all settled.

Right.

Choose wisely.

She pulled the oil lamp closer and drew a deep breath. Then she held her hand over the shells, trying to let destiny guide her. One of them was the right one, but which? Her fingers roamed, brushing each seed, until at last she felt it—a *tug*, right in her belly.

This one.

She lifted the clay shell between her thumb and forefinger, holding it level with her eyes. It looked like all the others, insignificant and plain, but the swelling pressure in her chest and the goose bumps prickling her arms told her this was the right one.

Before she could start second-guessing herself, Ellie set the ball down and split it with the hilt of her knife.

Then, heart, hammering, she lifted the two halves and stared inside. She felt Nox leaning closer, trying to get a look at . . .

Nothing.

No slip of paper or carving or trinket. Just two empty half-moons of clay.

"Uh . . ." Nox frowned. "Maybe a dud? Like with Gussie's smoke bombs? One in every four doesn't work, you know."

"Right. Like the smoke bombs." She just had to choose another.

Ellie's fingers grazed over the seeds until she felt another tug. This time, she didn't wait. She split it open right away.

Empty.

For a long minute, Ellie stared at the remaining clay seeds. Then she began choosing them at random and cracking them open as fast as she could.

Empty.

Empty.

Empty.

Finally, she sat over a floor littered with clay shards and nothing else.

Then she began to laugh.

"Uh . . . Ellie? You okay?"

"Of *course* they're empty," she said.

That was the point, wasn't it? It was just like Nox had said. He might have known they were empty and planned the whole thing for all she knew.

"Destiny or no destiny," she murmured. "That's not what matters, is it?"

Life wasn't as simple as reading your future in clay, or smoke, or even the crystals in Elder Rue's cavern. If there was such a thing as destiny, it didn't go around revealing itself to anyone. She thought of Tariel in her ceremony, cracking open her seed and announcing her future to the world.

Tariel hadn't received her destiny. She'd *chosen* it. She'd chosen where she belonged.

As Granna was trying to tell Ellie to do. As Nox had.

Choose wisely.

Her destiny could come from nowhere but inside her own heart. Only she could decide which path to take now. And whatever the flame was, and whatever Elder Rue's vision had meant, Ellie had already sacrificed too much trying to fulfill it. She'd almost lost Nox. She'd split up their group. She'd manipulated and pushed and prodded everyone around her.

All for a destiny that may or may not be real.

But she knew what *was* real—her love for Nox, Gussie, and Twig, and the knowledge that no matter what, they'd be there for her.

And she'd be there for them.

Ellie brushed dirt back over the basin she'd dug, burying the pieces of the clay shells.

"Forget Thraille, then," she said. "I'm done trying to force things to happen. If there is such a thing as destiny . . . it'll have to take care of itself."

"So we're going for Twig?"

"We're going for Twig." She met Nox's eyes. "And skies help Garion if he gets in our way. Because *nobody* messes with my clan."

CHAPTER THIRTY-ONE
· NOX ·

Three months after he'd fled Thelantis, Nox found himself looking down on his city with dread.

The question wasn't whether there would be a trap so much as what form it would take. But they had no choice.

The only advantage Nox had was that he knew Thelantis as well as his own feathers. And he was less recognizable now. He was taller, his hair was different, and he knew he'd put on muscle—not that he'd spent time admiring himself in any ponds lately.

Well. Not *much* time, anyway.

Still, this was going to be very difficult. And if Twig was being held in the Eagles' dungeons, it would be next to impossible.

"Breathe," said Ellie, nudging him. "If I got out of there, Twig can too."

They sat on a broad limb atop an oak outside the city walls, just far enough away to avoid being spotted by the high clan sentries. Gussie was using one of her inventions to scan the city, a tube of clay with a glass panel inserted in one end she called a *farscope*.

"What do you see?" Nox asked.

"It's . . . weird. I can see Knock Street—still burned up, by the way. Doesn't look like they've even tried rebuilding. The rest is quiet. Nobody hanging out in the streets, no performers in Center Square, no skyball matches or kids racing above the market. It's like the city's asleep."

"Look over there." Ellie pointed, her expression pained, toward the slums piling outside the city walls. From a distance, it looked like a heap of garbage, but Nox knew it was Rottown, the wretched place where anyone with wingrot was sent to suffer alone.

He blinked, realizing at once what Ellie meant.

Since they'd been gone, Rottown had more than doubled in size. It rivaled any of the districts of Thelantis now.

"It's spreading faster than ever," murmured Gussie, turning her farscope to the slums. "There must be a couple thousand people in there."

Nox had a bad feeling as he took the farscope and had a look.

Hadn't Ellie's Goldwing friend said the king was going over the edge with paranoia? Thelantis followed the king's moods and it certainly bent to his will. If the state of its streets was any indication, Garion was losing it. Nox had never seen it so quiet, the windows all shuttered and its people slinking from door to door as if afraid of being spotted.

"We better get moving," he said. "It'll be dark soon."

"Wonderful," sighed Gussie. "I love a good sewer crawl."

"Sewer crawl?" echoed Ellie.

A few hours later, as he pushed open the grate below Knock Street for them to stumble out, Nox held back a laugh.

Ellie was *boiling* mad. She glared at him, shaking unidentifiable refuse from her shoes.

"Sewer crawl," he explained.

"Never, ever, *ever* again, Nox—"

"Shh!" He popped a hand over her mouth. "You wanna skip over the whole rescue mission and go straight to the part where we get killed?"

Shoving his hand away, Ellie hissed, "Fine, *Corncob*."

"Corncob?" Gussie snorted.

"Okay, shut it," Nox said. "Let's keep going."

"What's the plan?" asked Ellie. "Got any old friends around we could recruit?"

"None I'd trust now," he sighed. His old boss, the Talon, was dead, and his thieving crew had likely split up to join the other crime rings still active in the city. But even if they hadn't, Nox wouldn't trust a single one of them beyond Gussie and Twig. There was a reward on his head large enough that it was almost worth turning *himself* in.

"We're on our own," he said. "Twig is almost certainly in the dungeons, which means we'll have to infiltrate the palace first."

"I can steal a Goldwing uniform," said Gussie. "I'm tall enough to pass for one."

And she had the right wings. Her Falcon feathers were the perfect disguise.

"If you go in first," he said, "Ellie and I can cause a distraction in the city. Got any more smoke bombs?"

Gussie nodded and handed over a leather satchel. "Give me an hour, then smoke up the whole city. Start in the high clan district—they'll turn out the whole guard if they think their precious nobles are in danger."

"Good idea."

They worked out the last few remaining wrinkles in the plan, then Gussie gave a farewell salute. She looked more nervous than Nox had ever seen her, and he hoped she'd be able to pull it off. Subterfuge had never been Gussie's strength.

"If anything goes wrong . . ." she began.

"When do my plans ever go off less than perfectly?" asked Nox.

Gussie only frowned deeper. "Just be smart. I . . . care about you guys. You know that, right?"

Ellie and Nox exchanged surprised looks. This was not the Gussie they knew. Twig's capture must have really rattled her.

"Sure," said Nox. "We care about you too, Gus."

When she'd flown off, he and Ellie slunk through the streets, walking rather than flying to avoid notice. In the time it had taken them to navigate the sewers and work out their plan, darkness had fallen, filling the streets with inky shadows. Even in Thelantis, people kept indoors at night in case of gargol attacks. They happened here much more rarely than outside the walls, but he wondered if that had changed, given the gargols' new behavior patterns.

Minutes later, he saw he'd guessed right.

"Skies above," breathed Ellie. "They took out the whole block."

Nox counted six buildings torn open at the roofs. The debris still littered the street; the attack must have only been a day or two old.

"C'mon," he whispered. "It's a long walk to the upper districts."

Nox made use of every secret alley, unlocked gate, and shadowed street he knew to get them through the various districts of Thelantis. It was easier than usual, with everyone locked in their houses. Even at this hour—halfway between midnight and dawn—there should have been folk about, setting up stalls, getting a start on baking the day's bread, sweeping the streets. But the only people they spotted were guards, most of whom occupied the rooftops.

"Curfew, I bet," he whispered as they flittered up and over the wall separating the middle district from the upper. "The way those guards are scanning the streets—it's people they're watching for, not gargols."

"Why?"

He shrugged. "Something's going on here. I don't like it one bit."

The streets in the upper district were wider and more difficult to navigate unseen. They had to go through gardens instead, making use of the ample green space the nobility kept to show off their fortunes. Up here, a square wingspan of grass cost more than a whole building in the lower districts.

After they'd traveled a few streets, Nox stopped in a walled garden. Beyond it, on a quiet dead end, several enormous houses sat in silence. A few oil lamps burned in their windows and along the street, and no one stirred.

"Good a place as any," Nox said. He checked the tiny sandglass

Gussie had left them to keep time. "It's almost been an hour. Let's make some smoke."

Ellie froze. "Did you hear something?"

Nox looked up—just as a dozen shapes dropped out of the sky and landed all around them on a flurry of wings.

"Ellie! Fly!" He bolted, but three Goldwing knights converged on him at once. He only made it two steps before their hands clamped on his arms. He tried to see if Ellie had gotten away, and heard the telltale *thwack* of her lockstave hitting flesh.

"Yow!" yelled a knight. "Little brat! Give me that thing!"

"Ellie!" Nox shouted. "Get out of—*mmf*!"

One of the knights drove a knee into Nox's stomach. He doubled over, gasping, as they wrenched his hands behind his back and bound them. He finally glimpsed Ellie, saw her thrashing as she too was tied up, her knife and lockstave pulled away.

"H-how . . ." he groaned.

It shouldn't have happened this quickly. A trap would have been set nearer to the palace—not this random street. The Goldwings couldn't have known . . .

His heart fell.

Gussie.

"What did you do to our friend?" he wheezed.

"What, the Falcon girl?" asked the knight now binding Nox's wings. "We gave her a nice cup of tea and cinnamon cake. She's resting easy in the palace kitchens, last I heard."

"Liar!"

"He's telling the truth," said a solemn voice. Nox looked up into the face of Sir Aglassine, the Goldwing commander. Every criminal in the city knew the Hawk woman by sight and reputation; her ruthlessness had condemned many a good thief to the gallows. "Agustina Berel has been working for us for weeks."

"Wh-what?"

Ignoring him, the captain flicked a hand through the air. "Take them both to the dungeons. The king has already ordered their execution. It will be held at dawn."

When she looked at Nox, he thought there might be a tiny trace of pity in her stern eyes. "You have only a few hours left, boy. Use them to dwell on happier memories. In other words . . . don't waste them trying to escape."

CHAPTER THIRTY-TWO
·NOX·

Well, he'd found Twig.

They were only two cells apart, with Ellie between them. Their reunion had been a grim one.

Nox had no way to tell the passage of time. But he knew it was moving far too quickly. Dawn—and his death—were closing in with the inevitability of the changing tide.

He sat for a long while, listening to Ellie pry at the bars of her cell, then the walls themselves, to no avail. She cursed and shouted for the guards, pretended to choke, anything to induce them to open the door. They didn't fall for it.

"Can't you call an army of rats or something to free us?" she asked Twig.

"No rats down here," he said mournfully. "They keep dungeon cats. And cats are the only creatures that *never* listen to me."

"Where's Lirri?"

"I . . . I sent her away when the knights captured me."

Nox winced; he knew the little marten was more important to Twig than anyone else in the world.

"What happened with Gussie?" he asked.

Twig was silent a long time before answering. "It's not her fault. Don't be angry at her. They have her little sister, you know. They were going to hurt her if Gussie didn't turn on us."

With a sinking stomach, Nox remembered how worried Gussie had been for her sister. She might have been the only person in the world the Falcon girl truly cared for. Of *course* Garion would use that against her.

But Nox didn't want to feel sorry for Gussie. He wanted to rage at her. It made him angry that Twig was so ready to forgive her betrayal, no matter her reasons.

"I can't believe after all we've done," Ellie sighed, "I ended up right back here. You know, I think this is actually the same cell they put me in last time."

"How did you escape again?" asked Twig.

"Zain. My Goldwing friend. I . . . don't think that will work twice. But maybe he knows we're here! He could—"

"Just give it up," groaned Nox.

"Someone's coming," said Twig.

"Zain?" whispered Ellie.

Nox didn't even lift his head. It was probably just the guards changing shifts. Or—and this sent a spike of terror through him—time had gone by even faster than he'd feared, and they were coming to lead them away. One last walk. One last dawn.

Three nooses.

He would go out just like his father. Just the way his mother had feared he would. Just the way hundreds of people all his life had told him he would.

Fit for nothing but the noose, that Crow scum.

Nox hung his head between his knees, his heart empty.

Then he heard a soft, "Hello?"

That didn't sound like a Goldwing or one of the guards.

Nox looked up.

There was a boy his own age standing outside Nox's cell, staring at him curiously from beneath a dark hood that hid most of his face and his wings.

Nox's gaze darted down the corridor, where the guard should have been standing. No one was there. Nor was the second guard at his post on the stairs.

They'd all been dismissed.

The boy tilted his head. "So you're the one my father's been turning the world over for."

"Your father . . . ?" Nox's eyes widened. "You're Prince Corion."

"What's *he* doing here?" asked Ellie.

It was the prince, all right. Nox recognized him now—those brown eyes, that golden hair. He couldn't hide the proudness of his chin beneath that hood. Here was a kid who had spent his entire life looking down at people.

Nox's feathers bristled. "Come to gloat, have you? Well, here I am!" He spread his hands and wings. "Am I as terrible and frightening as you'd heard?"

"Well, you are a bit shorter," said the prince.

Nox refolded his wings, scowling. "Tell your father I said he can—"

"Oh, no, I can't do that. He doesn't know I'm here. I prefer to keep it that way."

Well, now, *that* was interesting.

Nox cocked his head, studying the prince. "So, what? You're just morbidly curious? Will you be watching when they hang the three of us?"

"Yes. I don't have much choice about that, I'm afraid."

"Well, I hope we put on a good show for you."

The prince stepped closer, and Nox's fingers twitched. But Corion was still just out of reach. And even if he did manage to grab the boy, what could he do, really? He had no knife to threaten him with, no leverage to use him as a hostage and demand their release. And anyway, Corion had at least six inches on him and twice the wingspan—not to mention who knew how many hours of training under his feathers. He could probably take Nox down all on his own.

Cursed Eagles and their cursed golden children.

"Who are you?" Corion asked.

"Seriously? Check the nearest bounty board—I bet it's plastered with my face."

"No, I mean . . . who are you, that you could drive my father to madness just by existing?"

Nox shrugged. "Unlucky, I guess."

"Undoubtedly. And here I thought the only boy who could ruffle his feathers was me, every time I lose a sparring match to my cousin Freylon." He took another step, put one hand on the bars. Now he was within reach, but only if Nox sprinted across the cell faster than Corion could pull back. Not likely.

"You're just a kid," said the prince. "What's so special about you?"

"Well, I'm fireproof, for one thing." Nox laughed hollowly.

"Nox!" Ellie exclaimed in alarm.

He shrugged. What did it matter now that people knew? What would they do—execute him twice?

"Fireproof . . ." murmured the prince. Curiously, Corion didn't laugh or ask for more explanation. He echoed the word as if it confirmed something in his own mind.

"Yeah, I'm a real freak. What about you, Corion of the Eagles? What's so special about you that *we* should all bow down before you and kiss your toes and worship your every word?"

Corion frowned. "Nothing, I suppose. I'm not particularly good at anything. Just . . . lucky, I guess you'd say."

"Lucky." Maybe that really was all it came down to—good luck and bad luck. Random chance.

Ellie piped up again. "Your Highness, isn't there anything you can say to your father to change his mind about us? Like you said, we're just kids. We're not traitors or spies. We're not even all that dangerous."

Corion gave her a thoughtful look. "I remember you, Sparrow. After the Race of Ascension, you stood before my father and defied him in front of everyone."

"Going to tell me how stupid I was?" she asked.

"It was pretty stupid. But also . . . I thought it was the bravest thing I'd ever seen."

Ellie seemed shocked at that. She gave a small "Oh."

"Now, my father says you're undoing the world as we know it."

Nox scoffed. "C'mon, you believe that?"

"I don't know what to believe. That's why I'm down here." He looked back at Nox. "What is Tirelas?"

Blowing out a breath, Nox sat down again. "Ask Ellie. She does the speeches."

"I'm asking *you*."

"And I'm telling you *no*." Nox grinned savagely. "How d'you like that, princey? No no no no *no*. Listen close. It's probably the first and last time anyone will ever say it to your face."

"Have you been there? To Tirelas?"

"We have," said Ellie. "The islands in the sky. They're terrifying and magnificent all at once. The city we saw . . . it could have held ten Thelantises. And, Your Highness, if we don't return there—"

"I know, I know," he said. "I've heard the rumors. We'll all lose our wings, they say."

"Did you hear they're executing anyone who speaks those rumors?" asked Nox. "Have you watched any of *those* hangings? Did you bring along a few friends, make a party of it?"

Corion scowled, the first real emotion he'd shown. Nox was glad. He tended to respect people whose skin he couldn't get under, and he did *not* want to respect this kid.

"You know your people are dying of wingrot, don't you?" Ellie, as usual, did not seem to know when to give up. "We know how to save them. Tirelas is the answer!"

"My father says it's a lie. That those words are treason, and you're trying to lure people into the sky so the gargols can slaughter them. He says you're in league with the gargols."

"Maybe we are," Nox said sepulchrally. "Maybe if you hang us, our deaths will bring down a horde of gargols seeking vengeance."

"Now, that would be something to see," said Corion coolly. Skies! Was the boy made of the same marble as his palace?

"Why are you here?" sighed Nox. "I have, what, two hours left to live? I don't want to waste them on your raggedy feathers."

"I'm here because I have questions."

"Go ask your father. Sounds like he says quite a lot."

"Are you a Phoenix?"

That stopped Nox cold. He stared at Corion, all snark evaporating from his lips.

Ellie leaped on his words. "Where did you hear that? Did the Hunter tell you?"

Corion winced; the mention of the Hunter seemed to strike a nerve in him. "You don't *look* like a Phoenix. Not like I've heard them described, anyway. Wings of fire, born out of an inferno, and all that."

"Yes, well," Nox said. "I'm fresh out of flames today. Try again tomorrow."

"So you don't deny it?"

Nox rolled his eyes. "Does it matter what I do or don't deny? You'll hang me just the same."

"Yes. But then I'll never know the truth."

"He might be a Phoenix," said Ellie. "If you kill us, we'll never find out. But if you *help* us . . ."

Corion looked at her a moment, then back at Nox. "I have to go. The guards only agreed to a short break. But it was . . . interesting meeting you, Nox. And your friends." He tipped his head toward Ellie and Twig as if they were at a fancy dinner, not trapped in a cold dungeon hours away from execution. "Sorry about . . . you know. My father killing you and all."

"Hey!" Nox shouted, standing and going to the cell doors. Corion had turned and was walking quickly away. "Come back here, you fancy-feathered, pompous creep! You want the truth? The truth is, Ellie and Twig did nothing wrong! Hang me, fine! I always knew I was headed to the gallows anyway. But they don't deserve this. Hey. *Hey!*"

Corion swept up the stairs without a backward glance, and Nox slumped to the floor.

This was truly the end.

There was nothing he could do.

CHAPTER THIRTY-THREE
ELLIE

It was a dreary morning to meet her fate.

Ellie shuffled as best she could in the shackles around her ankles. Her hands hung in front of her, also chained, but worse was the heavy manacle around her wings. She couldn't even open them one last time, much less bolt for the open sky. It arched so tantalizingly close, high on the hill where the gallows were built. They were in the central district of the city, in a great square where, according to Twig, musicians and minstrels once performed every day.

No music this morning, though. The air was still and cold, carrying the first bite of winter. She still wore Tariel's cloak, now torn and dirty, but even it couldn't stop her from shivering.

She'd wondered if it would be a quick, private affair, given how yesterday everyone had seemed too frightened to leave their houses. Instead, when she, Nox, and Twig stepped out of the barred cart they'd been transported inside, they found a crowd waiting. Hundreds of Thelantians shivered in the dawn chill, silent under the watch of two dozen Goldwing knights and twice as many city guards.

She shuddered suddenly, her knees nearly buckling.

"Nox . . ."

"I'm here," he whispered from over her shoulder.

"So many people."

"Don't think about them."

Ellie felt as if she were floating through a dream. Her mind couldn't seem to fix on any one thought. She was aware of the platform the guards were pushing them toward, but she couldn't look at it.

"Papa," said a small voice nearby. "It's her. It's the Sparrow who won the Race of Ascension!"

Ellie's head jerked up. She looked around until she spotted a little Dove girl clinging to her father. For a moment, she thought it was Mally, whom she'd seen healed by a skystone months ago. But this girl was younger, her wings still puffy and dark with their fledgling feathers. Why was she here? Why would anyone let a child watch such a horrible thing?

Then Ellie noticed the guards pushing more spectators into the square—most of them low clanners—and she realized many, if not all of them, were not here voluntarily.

The king *wanted* them to watch.

These were not the cheering, happy people who'd watched the Race of Ascension. These were a people with shadows in their eyes and a heaviness to their wings.

Concentrating on their problems was the only distraction she had from her own. Looking back at the Dove girl, she called out, "Watch the skies!"

For that, a guard gave her a cuff on the ear.

"Hey!" someone shouted. "They're just kids!"

"Yeah!" another spectator threw in. "This isn't right!"

"Quiet!" a guard ordered.

But more shouts followed the first, as Ellie suddenly found herself stumbling up rickety wooden steps. Her heart began to pound harder. She heard the ropes creaking as they swung, but couldn't bring herself to look at them.

"It's Knock Street all over again!" yelled a Magpie, flaring her black-and-white wings. "It's senseless and cruel!"

"Silence!" ordered a Goldwing, landing on the gallows in front of

Ellie. He was a broadly built Eagle clanner, his wings spreading a staggering sixteen feet or more. "The *king* approaches!"

At that, the crowd settled, eyes turning skyward as the shadows of wings flickered over them. Moments later, King Garion landed atop the high wall behind the gallows, with Prince Corion at his side. The prince's eyes were cool and his face expressionless; he didn't look at Ellie or the others. Instead he stared down at the crowd. Ellie gave up any hope that he might be sympathetic toward them, even after his strange visit to their cells just hours ago.

Garion, on the other wing, was far from impassive. It had been months since she'd stood before the king, accused of an entirely different set of crimes, and the memory still made her shudder. But that Garion might have been an entirely different man compared to the one standing over her now.

His hair was disheveled, his eyes sunken. He looked ten years older, his skin sagging at the jowls and neck, where only months ago he'd been as shining and beautiful as his many portraits. A savage gleam burned in his eyes. He looked down at her so suddenly that Ellie flinched. But she didn't look away. She didn't want to give him the satisfaction.

And to think, there'd been a time not too long ago when she'd have done absolutely anything this man ordered without question, all to win his approval.

Now she looked at him and felt nothing but contempt.

More high clanners landed beside the royals, all dressed in the fancy clothing of nobility. One of these, another Eagle, stepped forward with a flagpole in hand. From it flicked the royal banner.

He cleared his throat. "These three stand convicted of treason against the crown, collusion with gargols, and the dissemination of illegal and inciting material!"

"You mean *skystones*!" someone shouted from the crowd.

The Eagle spokesman nodded, and at once, three knights converged on the crowd and grabbed the Goldfinch man who'd shouted. They yanked him right off his feet, pinning his yellow-and-black wings with some kind of wooden clamp so he couldn't struggle. Gasps rose as they hauled the man away, vanishing into the city with him still kicking in their grasp.

"Let that remind you that any talk of skystones or their origin will result in swift punishment—even execution!" shouted the Eagle. "There are *no* islands in the sky, only gargols and death. To speak otherwise is to commit treason! This boy is your enemy—this *Tannox Corvain*—and his companions. They are the ones who first flew into a storm and made bargains with monsters! *They* are the reason you cower in your homes for fear of attack!"

"A skystone healed my brother in Rottown!" yelled a woman. "I don't care what you do to me—you can't crush the truth forever!"

Ellie's eyes widened.

Zain.

He'd done it! He must have delivered the skystones to Rottown, as she'd asked him to. He couldn't have arrived more than a few days before them, but apparently he'd wasted no time.

She looked around then, her wings tightening. Where *was* Zain?

Had he been caught with the skystones?

"My mother was healed!" called another person.

"And my daughter!"

"My friend!"

"My cousin!"

"*I* was healed by a skystone!" This last shout drew attention, as a bespectacled Owl clanner raised his hand into the air. His wings were ragged but straight, a sure sign of recent recovery from wingrot. "I am alive because of those brave kids!"

More knights dove toward the crowd, trying to haul away the ones who spoke up. But the others pressed close around them. Some raised broomsticks or canes to fend the knights off, or raised their wings to block their view. The Goldwings began grabbing people at random, but the crowd grabbed back, seizing ankles and legs and refusing to let their neighbors be taken.

Ellie stared in shock.

Chaos was breaking out.

"Enough!" snarled Garion. "Fire on them!"

The guards and knights still standing at attention looked at one another queasily. A few lifted crossbows but stood blinking, as if unsure they'd heard right.

"Cowards!" snapped the king. "Idiots! I said *fire*!"

A few bolts snapped from their bows, but as far as Ellie could tell, they all clattered harmlessly off walls and the ground. Were they missing on purpose?

Garion seemed to think so. He launched into the air and grabbed a crossbow from the nearest guard, then turned it on the crowd.

"Father!" Corion yelled. "Wait—please!"

The crossbow snapped, and Ellie heard a scream of pain below.

For a moment, time seemed to stop, as the people of Thelantis registered what their king had done.

Then, as one, they responded.

The rush of wings exploded like an avalanche breaking. The sky filled with people, some rushing the guards, others bolting into the city.

Ellie lost sight of Garion then, as the sky went dark with bodies and wings. She felt a nudge on her back, then someone grabbed her and dragged her toward the edge of the platform.

She struggled until she heard Nox say, "They're friends, Ellie!"

Strong arms wrapped around her and lifted her down to the street. She saw Nox already there, his hands freed. A man bent over his wings, picking the lock on the manacle around them.

"Thanks, Borge," Nox said.

"You never could get your fill of trouble, Crow," the man chuckled.

"Don't think I forgot you're the reason my tavern burned down."

"Got another pair?" Nox took the set of picks the man handed him and nodded to Ellie. She turned and let him pry the lock on her chains, and in seconds they fell away.

Twig hopped over, pale but grinning. "Borge! Winster!"

The man who'd freed them, along with a one-eyed companion, clapped Twig on the back before loosening his chains. "Ah, it's the feral one! You always did compliment me on my stew."

"Well, the vegetable-only version," said Twig.

The man laughed. "You three split, quick-like. The guards will have this lot whipped into shape in no time, and then they'll come looking for you."

Nox nodded. "Ellie, Twig. You ready to get out of here?"

Ellie nodded. "Skies, yes."

"You two should fly," said Twig. "I can meet you outside the walls."

"No way," said Nox. "We're not splitting—"

They were interrupted by a roar from above.

"Corvain!"

Ellie looked up to see Garion hovering there, his wings obscuring the sun so he'd turned to a silhouette. But there was no mistaking his crazed voice.

"Run!" Nox shouted, pushing Ellie and Twig away. "I'll lead him off!"

He launched into the air before Ellie could stop him.

"NOX!"

She gasped as she saw the sudden glint of a crossbolt tip in Garion's hands. Everything moved slowly.

She shot into the air after Nox.

The king's crossbow snapped.

And Nox exploded backward as the bolt ripped through him.

With a scream, Ellie plunged after Nox. Her hand closed on his shirtfront, slowing him just before he hit the ground. She landed atop him and rolled hard.

"Nox!" Ellie screamed. She lifted him and saw the bolt was still stuck in his chest, just below his heart. Blood flowed over her hands.

His eyes were wide, his gaze disoriented. He blinked hard, his lips moving as if he were trying to speak but couldn't.

"Twig!" Ellie whirled. "We have to get him out of here!"

She lifted Nox's shoulders while Twig took his ankles. Together they shuffled down the street, barely able to carry him. Above their heads, screams and shouts filled the air, and bodies thumped as they hit the ground. The guards seemed to have abandoned their earlier reluctance for weapons.

The effort of carrying Nox sent spikes of hot pain down Ellie's bad leg. With a cry, she felt her strength give out and she fell hard, dropping him.

"No!" She pulled his head into her lap, patting his cheek. "Stay awake, Nox! Stay awake!"

"Let us help."

She stiffened, then turned to the two tall figures standing over her, faces and wings concealed under black cloaks. Before she could stop them, they scooped Nox up between them.

"Zain," she whispered. "And . . . Prince Corion?"

Then her vision went red with rage.

"Get away from him!" she snarled. She tried to lunge for the prince, but her leg gave out again, and she buckled.

Twig caught her, awkwardly. "It's all right, Ellie!"

"He's the enemy! He was going to let us die!"

"We can trust him."

Her eyes blurring with tears, she looked at Twig. He had the distant gaze in his eyes that told her he was using his inner ear, listening to the hidden voices she could not hear.

"Corion's trustworthy," he said. "I promise."

"It's true," Zain said. "The prince is different from his father. He's the one who helped me take the skystones to Rottown, Ellie."

Swallowing, Ellie nodded. Her head was spinning with pain and panic, but if Twig said he trusted someone—she knew she could believe it. And if Corion really had helped Zain . . . maybe he *was* different.

They followed the prince and Zain, Ellie limping and leaning on Twig, through a maze of streets. The Eagle prince seemed to know his way through the city well. He was even able to dodge the guards and knights on patrol above.

The sounds of the riot had died down behind them; perhaps the people had finally been subdued. But by then, she and the others were nearly to the city walls.

"We can fly him up and over," said Corion. "You'll be on your own from there."

Ellie nodded dumbly, still unable to believe this was the prince of the Eagles helping them escape.

They flew over the walls, taking advantage of the guards being gone from their posts to quell the riot. Zain carried Nox and Corion carried Twig. They landed at the forest's edge, not far from the main gates.

"There'll probably be a cart you can put him on that way," said Zain, nodding toward the main road. "Lots of people have been abandoning them there after . . . Well, it's been a hard few weeks."

Corion sighed. "My father's arresting anyone who's even *seen* a skystone. They question everyone at the gates."

Ellie nodded again. "Your Highness . . . why are you helping us?"

As he set Nox gently on the ground, he gave her a quizzical look. "Like I said, I want to know the truth. I think . . . without you three, it would be much harder to find."

"So you believe us, about the skystones and Tirelas?"

"I saw the skystones healing people in Rottown. Zain told me about the rest of it. As for how much I believe . . ." He was quiet a moment, then said, "I hope the Crow will be all right."

"I'll make sure of it."

He nodded. "I meant it, you know, when I said you were the bravest person I'd ever seen."

"Helping us escape was pretty brave."

Corion shrugged. "If you'd been caught, you'd have been killed. If I'm caught . . . well, it wouldn't be pleasant, but I'd survive."

"Don't get caught," Ellie said.

"All right, all right," moaned Nox. "If you're done swooning over each other, can we please proceed with our epic escape?"

"Nox!" Ellie had never been so glad to hear him snark. "How do you feel?"

"Like there's an arrow through me." Nox coughed, and blood trickled from his lip. "Now about that escape . . . ?"

"Right. Twig, get a cart. I'll see if I can get the arrow out."

"Good luck, Ellie of the Sparrows," said Corion.

She nodded. "Thank you. And you too, Zain." Then, on an impulse, she grabbed her old friend's hand.

"Be careful out there," said the Hawk. "I'd join you, but . . ." He glanced at Corion, his cheeks turning curiously pink. "Someone's gotta look out for His Highness, with things getting as bad as they are around here."

"Oh," said Ellie. Then, when she saw Corion return Zain's look with a blush of his own, she gave his hand a quick squeeze. "*Oh.* Right. Well. You two look out for each other. And, uh, you be careful too. The king seems . . . seriously unhinged."

"You have no idea," murmured Corion.

Zain smiled in farewell, then he and Corion took flight, soaring up and over the wall.

"Well," Ellie commented, her mind reeling a bit. "Today has certainly been full of surprises."

On the ground, Nox groaned and passed out again.

CHAPTER THIRTY-FOUR

· NOX ·

Nox gained consciousness long before he found the strength to open his eyes. For what seemed like hours, he floated on a fog of alternating pain and numbness. Sometimes it felt as if he were drifting down a peaceful river; at other times every jolt of the cart brought searing agony.

His mind struggled to grasp the most basic information. Where was he? What had happened? Where were they going?

He couldn't remember.

Occasionally, a vision would break through his mind—a crowd in chaos, a rope swinging in the breeze, Ellie Meadows leaning over him to brush the hair from his feverish face. But just as quickly, the image would slip away again, back beneath the churning muck that was his memory.

When at last he opened his eyes, it was to a sky gray with clouds.

Gargols, he thought vaguely. They should be indoors or at least under some kind of rock or tree.

The cart was still rolling, and it gave a sudden lurch, enough to elicit a whimper from Nox's lips.

"He's awake," said Twig.

"Hang in there, Nox!" Ellie called out. "We're almost there."

Where?

He'd been shot through the shoulder, he suddenly recalled.

No.

Not the shoulder—that injury was months old. This time was different. He'd been shot . . .

His hand shifted, heavy as lead, to his left side. He felt a tight bandage—Ellie's work, no doubt. It was soaked with blood. He was lying under the cloak Tariel had made for Ellie and vaguely fretted that he'd got blood on it.

His hand fell again. He didn't have the strength left to lift a finger. Skies, he felt so heavy . . . and yet light, light as a feather. His head felt like it had come unattached from his body and was floating away.

He started to slip under again, darkness reaching for him with a thick, heavy blanket in its hands. But then a touch roused him, and he managed to lift his eyelids again. It took a mighty effort.

"Easy, Nox," Ellie said, sliding a hand under his head. "We're here."

She and Twig lifted him up and out of the cart. He caught a glance of the horse that had pulled it, and mumbled something unintelligible.

"The horse?" Ellie asked. "I don't really know. Ask Twig. He came running up with it, cart and all."

"She's a pony, technically," said Twig.

Their words flowed through him and passed on, water through a sieve, forgotten as soon as he heard them.

A few moments later, he realized he was lying on the ground. Soft ground. Sand. And there was a sound . . .

"River?" he groaned.

"No, the ocean," said Ellie. "We came straight here from Thelantis. Remember? That was this morning. We haven't stopped once all day. We're lucky the clouds moved in, or the sky'd be crawling with Goldwings right now."

"Yeah, just gargols to worry about," grumbled Twig.

"Gather some driftwood, Twig," Ellie said. "I'll start a fire. He needs to get warm. His skin's so cold. But he's sweating so much . . ."

Nox faded out and in again.

When he looked around next, he saw Ellie had lit a small fire nearby, but he couldn't feel its heat.

Perhaps it was the sea air, but Nox felt a little surge of strength. Enough, in fact, that he managed to open his eyes all the way and unstick his tongue from the roof of his mouth.

Ellie dabbed his face. "How do you feel?"

"I . . . can't."

"Can't what?"

"Feel. Can't feel anything."

Ellie's eyes widened slightly. She checked his bandages, swore, and told Twig to hurry.

"I've already changed them four times today," she muttered. "It just won't stop."

He shut his eyes and listened to the waves. They came and went like breaths.

"Here we are again," he whispered. "Me with an arrow . . . stuck in my bones. You trying . . . to save me."

"To be fair, I got that crossbolt out ages ago. And I *will* save you, just like I did last time."

"Yes, it's a bad habit of yours."

"Like yours is getting into trouble in the first place. Look, you'll be fine. I have a plan."

"Of course you do."

"At first light, I'll fly up and watch for southbound ships. First one we see, we stow aboard. Somehow. Twig and I can make a sling to carry you. Once on board, you heal up, and soon enough we'll be back in the south. We'll go to Brightbay, to Granna and Tariel."

He wanted to laugh but couldn't find the strength, so he only sighed.

Always plotting, Ellie was. Always three steps ahead, never knocked down for long. Never knew when to give up. It was what frustrated him most about her.

It was what he admired most.

"Ellie."

"I'm here."

With great effort, he opened his eyes and looked at her. The sea wind pulled at her hair and ruffled her tawny feathers. She had no lockstave, no satchel, and she was covered in dirt and sweat and scrapes, but the light of determination in her eyes was eternal.

"This time . . ." he whispered. "It feels different."

"Of course it does. Last time, we had supplies. We could all fly. We had . . . Gussie." She winced, her mouth wrenching into a hard line. "But we'll make it."

"Not the ship . . . *me*. I feel different . . . this time."

"Don't say that." She looked at him as if she would drag him back from the edge herself, if he dared take a step further toward the darkness that called his name. He wouldn't put it past her to try.

But he knew there was a line even Ellie, with all her stubbornness and strength, couldn't cross. A path he could only walk alone.

"I have to ask . . . something."

"Is it your bandage? Too tight? I worried it might be—"

"No." He had to pause for a few breaths before he could speak again. Eyes shut, he whispered, "If I . . . My family has a tradition."

Her voice took on a cold edge. "What are you talking about?"

"We're buried . . . at sea."

"Nox, stop."

"Please. Ellie. Promise me."

"I don't need to. Because you're going to be fine."

"Promise me." He looked at her and saw she was starting to cry.

She shook her head, pulling her knees under her chin and hugging them. Twig stood behind her, his eyes round and his face as pale as the sand.

"Ellie, *please*."

"Fine!" she shouted. "When you're old and crumbling and finally kick it, I'll chuck you off a dock, Nox. I promise. Happy?"

He managed one small nod.

"Good. Now you just—get better, all right? So I can smack you without feeling guilty about it."

The darkness was pressing against him now. It swirled across his vision, tugged at the corners of his mind. Where was the light? He'd heard there would be a light.

"Thank you . . ." he whispered. "For believing in me. Even when I gave you . . . every reason not to. Even when no one else did."

"I still believe in you. You hear me? *I still believe*, Nox."

"Yeah." The corner of his mouth curled into the slightest of grins. "You are one . . . nutty . . . Sparrow."

He gave in at last, shutting his eyes and letting the darkness pull him under. High above, he heard Ellie say his name, and then . . . silence.

CHAPTER THIRTY-FIVE
· ELLIE ·

"Ellie, stop." Twig put a hand on her arm, and she pushed it away. "Nox, open your eyes. *Nox!*"

The tide was rising fast; a wave broke over the black rocks, sending up a spray that Ellie felt on her skin. She shook Nox, her heart splintering. "NOX!"

Twig put his hand on hers. "I can't hear him anymore."

She shook her head. Nox was fine. He'd been passing out all day. He just needed rest and clean bandages and . . .

"I can't *hear* him," Twig said, more emphatically. He pressed a hand to his chest, where he'd once told her he could hear the feelings and desires of other people.

She leaned back, eyes wide and unblinking. "I don't understand."

"There's a point where . . . there's nothing *to* hear."

She shot to her feet, backing away from Nox. Staring at his face—skies, he was so still—she felt heat gathering behind her eyes and in her belly.

"You did everything you could," Twig said. He hugged himself, heavy tears rolling down his cheeks as he stared at Nox's pale, pale face.

"He can't be gone," Ellie whispered.

Twig only looked at her silently.

"He *can't*!" She fell to her knees again and pressed her fingertips to his neck, his wrists, his chest. She leaned down and put her ear to his lips.

No pulse.

No breath.

No Nox.

Ellie wailed. She bent over him, her hands clutching her chest, and she felt the burning heat inside her suddenly burst, shooting through every vein. It was too much, too much for her body to contain. Finally she turned and grabbed hold of Twig, and he hugged her back. They rocked and cried, and the waves rolled endlessly over the sand.

"Will it float?" asked Twig, eyeing the raft doubtfully.

Ellie only shrugged. She was bone weary, empty of words.

It had taken them all night to build the raft, assembling driftwood that had taken hours to gather, hours more to lash with the harness they took off the pony. They had no tools, no knives, nothing to work with but rocks and sticks and a few sharp seashells. But they'd pulled it together at last, and Ellie didn't even care that their small fire might draw every gargol in the sky down on them. She couldn't find it in herself to care about much at all.

"It'll be dawn soon," Twig said, looking out at the sea. He shook his head. "Feels like a year since yesterday morning."

On that they could agree. Ellie had never felt more exhausted in her life.

"Well." Twig slipped his hand into hers. "Ready?"

"No." She sighed. "All right."

They carried Nox down to the edge of the water and laid him on the raft, and Ellie spread Tariel's cloak over him. It was an odd thing to do, she knew; it wasn't as if he would be cold. But still, it felt right to cover him. The tide was going out, and it would take the Crow with it. Ellie hadn't known what else to do. If they simply released him to the waves, he'd just wash ashore somewhere along the beach, and she couldn't stand the thought. The raft had been a lot of work, but at least this way, he might make it far out to sea. Perhaps all the way to his mother. They weren't far from the Crag, by her reckoning. And she had a good idea what the guards there did with dead prisoners.

"Should we say something?" Twig asked.

"Okay." Ellie cleared her throat. "Nox. You were a pain from the moment I met you till the moment you . . . but I'd do it all over again. And again. Because we're clan. You are . . . were . . . my friend, Nox Hatcher. The kind worth sticking with."

She looked at Twig and shrugged.

He gave her a sad smile, then added his own words. "Nox, when everyone else looked at me and saw bad luck, you just saw a kid. You didn't listen to what anyone said; you did what you thought was right. And even if you pretended not to care, you still brought me an orange whenever you could steal one, just because you knew I liked them."

With a sniffle, Twig nodded.

"That was nice," Ellie said, hugging him. "You ready?"

They pushed the raft into the waves. The horizon ahead had begun to glow faintly rose with the approaching dawn. It took some effort to get the raft past the surf, and they got thoroughly soaked, but finally the tide took hold of the little craft and pulled it away. Ellie held on just long enough to pull herself up and kiss Nox's cheek.

"Goodbye," she whispered, her chest knotting.

She and Twig waded ashore, holding on to each other. Her leg ached, and all she could think of was lying down and doing nothing for the next three days. A sourness had set on her tongue, a feeling of something left undone. Words left unsaid.

Should she have given a different speech over Nox? Had there been something she should have told him before he'd died?

Halfway up the beach, she stopped.

The fire still burned by the cart; the pony grazed in the dune grass beyond it, swishing its tail.

"Ellie?" Twig stopped and looked back at her.

Her feathers fluttered in a sudden gust of salty wind. The flames danced but did not go out.

I believe in you, Nox. Her last words for him.

Had she meant them? Were they just empty air? Was that what was bothering her—the feeling she'd wasted her last moment with him on hollow, pretty words that meant nothing?

Or do you still believe, Ellie Meadows?

"I don't understand," she whispered.

"What?" Twig tilted his head. "What's wrong?"

"All of it." She looked at him. "This isn't how it was supposed to go. He was supposed to be—I thought—Elder Rue's vision, the crown, all of it was supposed to add up to *something*! Instead, there's just . . ."

Twig frowned. "Why? Because you thought he was part of your destiny?"

"Yes. Yes, exactly." Ellie's heart began to pound. "I believed that. I pushed him too hard on it, I know, but I never stopped believing it."

"So?" Twig's frown deepened; he was getting angry with her. "It's over now, Ellie, isn't it? He's gone. Whatever he was or could have been, it's over."

"I still believe," she whispered.

Twig stared at her, his expression souring. "Nox was right. You don't know when to quit."

"No . . . I really don't."

She began walking again, faster, her bad leg dragging in the sand.

"Ellie! What are you doing?"

She was thinking. Thinking hard and fast and hot, raking through memories.

"Here am I of ashes born." Gussie, reading the inscription on the Phoenix throne in Tirelas, before betrayal was ever planted in her heart.

The murals showing the Phoenix kings and queens, standing in flames, their golden wings spread wide.

Ellie kicked over a seashell, her brow furrowed.

You don't look like a Phoenix . . . Prince Corion, cloaked and curious. *Wings of fire, born in an inferno . . .*

She stopped by the little campfire. It was nearly out of wood, barely more than a bed of coals. Then her gaze shifted to the indentation in the sand where Nox had lain. She and Twig had had to drag him down the beach to the raft, and in the process, he'd left behind a few black feathers.

Ellie picked up the largest of these and twirled it, her heart beating faster.

Then she knelt by the fire and held the feather to the flames. She told herself this was ridiculous, that nothing would happen. Nox was—had been—fireproof. Flames didn't leave a mark on his skin.

But his feathers . . .

All at once the barbs caught fire. She sucked in her breath and dropped the quill, but there was no sharp, acrid odor like the one she'd smelled from the Khadreen burn pits where they'd disposed of amputated wings.

Instead, the feather flared white hot . . . and then the flames went out.

The feather remained whole.

Her fingers trembling, Ellie cautiously lifted it by its quill and found it warm to the touch.

She blinked.

Blinked again.

"Oh," Ellie whispered. "Oh *skies*."

Leaping up, Ellie turned to the cart, and the jars cluttered in it. Of all the carts in all the Clandoms, Twig had brought back one full of sunflower oil made by the Sparrow clan.

Almost as if he'd been guided by destiny.

She turned and limped toward the waves, past a bewildered Twig, ignoring the lancing pain in her leg.

"Ellie! What—"

Wordlessly, she handed him the feather she'd set fire to.

His eyes were wide. "What . . . what is this?"

"It's Nox's."

"But . . ." Twig raised it between them.

Where it had once been iridescent black, now the feather glowed orange. It was not the dark, golden-brown hue of the Eagle clan—but as bright and shining as a living flame.

As if it had been this color all along, and the fire had only revealed it, burning away an outer layer.

"I have to get him back," said Ellie.

The raft was well beyond the breakers now, but she didn't hesitate. Ellie spread her wings and launched into the air, diving into the headwind blowing off the sea. It tried to push her back; she fought against it.

When she reached the raft, she dove, piercing the water and coming up with a splutter. Gripping the driftwood, she began kicking with her good leg. The caps of the waves had turned golden pink, hinting at the coming sun.

Twig swam out to her. "What are you *doing*?"

"I know it sounds stupid!" she gasped. "But those murals we saw in the palace, of the Phoenixes standing in fire . . . I don't think they were funerals."

"Huh?"

"I think—oh, just *help me*!"

"Nox was right—you're one nutty Sparrow." But he took hold of the raft and helped her push.

Once they got the raft into the breakers, the waves did most of the work washing it ashore. Ellie grabbed Nox by his shoulders and dragged him onto the hard wet sand.

"Wait with him," she panted. "Don't let the water take him again."

Of course the Corvains buried their dead at sea, even though nearly every other clan in the world burned theirs on pyres.

Of course they did.

They had secrets to keep, secrets only fire would reveal.

But what if she was too late?

Only one way to find out.

She stumbled up the shore again, too exhausted to fly. First she went to the cart and took a jar of sunflower oil.

"Twig!" she shouted, tossing the jar.

It spun through the air, hit the sand, and rolled toward the waves. Twig scooped it up and set to work. His inner ear really was getting stronger, she realized. He knew exactly what she was thinking.

Then she went to the fire.

The wind was harsher now, almost howling. She scowled at the sky and grabbed a stick from the coals; it came up smoldering, tiny flames dancing along its length.

You will carry a flame through the darkness, to light a great fire.

Ellie walked back down the beach, taking her time so she could shield the flame with her hand, saving it from the wind.

But if you drop it, or if the flame goes out . . . the sky will fall.

Her leg pained her so badly now she had to drag it, limping over the sand, every step a small victory. When she finally reached the raft, Twig had finished smearing the sunflower oil over Nox's body and wings. Tariel's cloak lay in a crumpled heap nearby.

"Stand back," she said.

Twig nodded, his eyes huge.

Kneeling, Ellie held the flame over her friend.

"I'm sorry," she whispered. "You'll probably hate me for this, huh? Whether I'm right or wrong."

Skies, she hoped she wasn't wrong.

She shut her eyes for a moment, holding her breath.

Then she touched the flame to Nox's chest.

The fire caught at once. There was a reason no open flames were allowed in the Sparrows' barn. The oil was a magnificent accelerant, and they'd lost buildings to it before. At the last moment, she thought to grab Nox's red scarf from around his neck and yank it free.

Scrambling back, Ellie felt the heat wash over her. Twig took her arm and pulled her farther away.

They sat in the sand and watched the fire spread until Nox was consumed. Even the waves seemed to hang back from him out of respect. Ellie couldn't see anything through those flames; they burned white hot, far more intensely, she thought, than they should.

"What if I was wrong?" she asked Twig.

He gave her a bitter smile. "Then I reckon Nox will haunt you the rest of your life for breaking your last promise to him."

Ellie stared as the flames leaped higher, showing no signs of stopping. Her heart tightened and her eyes smarted from the heat. What if she'd messed up this one last thing Nox had asked of her?

She squeezed his scarf until her knuckles whitened.

Then—

She sucked in a sharp breath and took hold of Twig's hand.

The fire danced and swayed and shuddered, growing no smaller, but from within its blaze, something . . . *shifted*.

A feather. A wing.

Unfurling, bright as the sun. Two wings, left and right. And a shadowy figure between them.

All at once, Nox fell out of the flames, coughing and gasping, his clothes burned away. He landed on his knees, his hands clawing at the sand. Flames danced over his skin and faded. Arching his back, he let out a wordless cry.

Ellie stopped breathing.

From Nox's shoulder blades lifted two wings, laced with flames and trailing ashes.

His feathers shone as golden as the sun rising over the sea.

THE CLANS OF SKYBORN

The Clandoms and surrounding lands are home to many scores of clans, each with its own unique identity and heritage. Here are a few found in Call of the Crow.

SWAN CLAN

Clan Seat: Luwenza

Clan Type: Low

Wing Description: Wide, large, and usually pure white, though pure black is not uncommon. Ideal for soaring and long-distance flight; less maneuverable.

Wingspan: Long

Traditional Occupations: Dancers, artists, and performers

Known For: Peevish temperaments and mistrust toward outsiders

QUETZAL CLAN

Clan Seat: Brightbay

Clan Type: Free clan

Wing Description: Covert feathers are iridescent green with gold highlights. Primary and secondary feathers are black. Not the strongest fliers, Quetzals usually avoid ranging far.

Wingspan: Medium

Traditional Occupations: Weavers and dyers

Known For: Beautifully dyed and patterned cloth woven from plant fibers

MACAW CLAN

Clan Seat: The Clay

Clan Type: Free clan

Wing Description: Covert feathers are typically bright red and yellow, with bright blue primary and secondary feathers. Wings may also present as entirely blue or entirely green with bright-yellow underwings.

Wingspan: Medium

Traditional Occupations: Potters

Known For: Exquisitely crafted pottery made with the help of their tamed elephants

FLAMINGO CLAN

Clan Seat: Falorian

Clan Type: Free clan

Wing Description: Pale- to dark-pink covert feathers with black primaries and secondaries. Wide and powerful, they are suited for acrobatic flight.

Wingspan: Long

Traditional Occupations: Shrimpers

Known For: Elaborate and acrobatic traditional dances often performed with fire

VULTURE CLAN

Clan Seat: Bone Mountain

Clan Type: Low

Wing Description: Dark-brown feathers with pale underwing. Best suited for long periods of soaring, with minimal flapping.

Wingspan: Long

Traditional Occupations: Undertakers and morticians

Known For: Because of Vultures' traditional roles as undertakers and expertise with dead bodies, they're often feared and mistrusted by other clans. In some areas, even seeing or speaking with a Vulture is seen as an omen of impending death.

KINGFISHER CLAN

Clan Seat: Green River

Clan Type: Free clan

Wing Description: Color ranges from blue to green, with teal being most common, with a pattern of white dots. Underwings are orange. Suited for rapid, direct flight.

Wingspan: Short

Traditional Occupations: Fishers

Known For: In-depth knowledge of the jungle rivers, on which Kingfishers live in their flotillas of houseboats

GULL CLAN

Clan Seat: Porton

Clan Type: Low

Wing Description: Long, tapered wings of gray and white with black tip ideal for soaring on ocean breezes.

Wingspan: Medium

Traditional Occupations: Sea traders, fishers, and sea-transport workers

Known For: Being a large, widespread clan that travels in noisy, boisterous groups but rarely strays far from the coast

QUAIL CLAN

Clan Seat: Gambel

Clan Type: Low

Wing Description: Round, short wings of gray and brown with large white flecks. Unsuited for long or agile flight, Quails usually avoid the air altogether.

Wingspan: Short

Traditional Occupations: Potato farmers

Known For: Aversion to flight; some Quail clanners are known to go for months without using their wings

ABOUT THE AUTHOR

Jessica Khoury is the author of many books for young readers, including *Last of Her Name*, *The Mystwick School of Musicraft*, the Corpus Trilogy, and *The Forbidden Wish*. In addition to writing, she is an artistic mapmaker and spends far too much time scribbling tiny mountains and trees for fictional worlds. She lives in Greenville, South Carolina, with her husband, daughters, and sassy husky, Katara. Find her online at jessicakhoury.com.